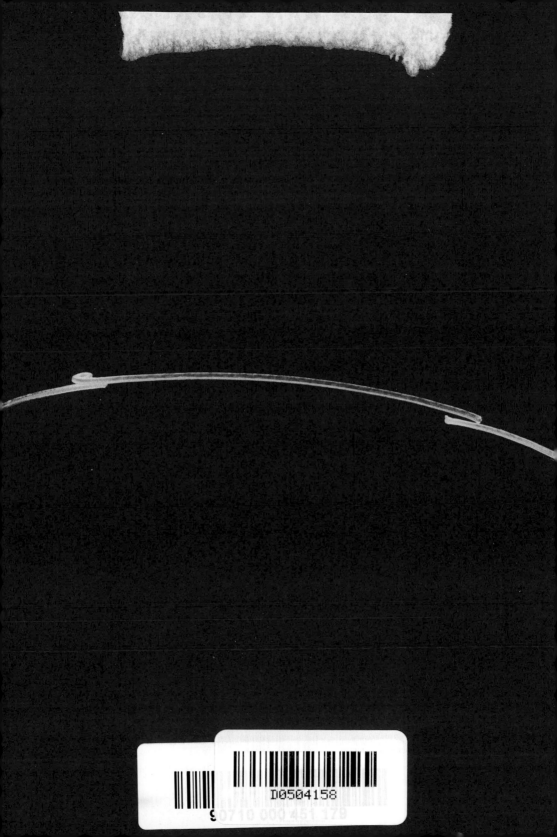

When
the
Music
Stops

Joe Heap was born in 1986 and grew up in Bradford, the son of two teachers. His debut novel *The Rules of Seeing* won Best Debut at the Romantic Novel of the Year Awards in 2019 and was shortlisted for the Books Are My Bag Reader Awards. Joe lives in London with his girlfriend, their two sons and a cat who wishes they would get out of the house more often.

🐦 @Joe_Heap_
📘 joeheap.author
📷 joe_heap_/

Also by Joe Heap

The Rules of Seeing

When
the
Music
Stops

A Novel by Joe Heap
With Music by John Sands

HarperCollins*Publishers*

HarperCollins*Publishers*
1 London Bridge Street
London SE1 9GF

www.harpercollins.co.uk

Published by HarperCollins*Publishers* 2020

1

A catalogue record for this book
is available from the British Library

HB ISBN: 978-0-00-829320-8
TPB ISBN: 978-0-00-829321-5

Typeset in Adobe Caslon by Palimpsest Book Production Ltd, Falkirk, Stirlingshire

Printed and bound by CPI Group (UK) Ltd, Croydon CR0 4YY

MIX
Paper from
responsible sources
FSC
www.fsc.org   FSC™ C007454

To my grandparents, John and Jean,
without whose stories
this story could not have been written.

Greek myth tells of Orpheus, who travelled to the underworld to win back his lost lover, Eurydice. His means of transport was music – music that made the gods weep to hear it, music that stopped the rivers and made nature pause. The Hymns of Orpheus are lost to us now, but their voices are still ours to use, that we may each bring back our own Eurydice.

Musicologists disagree about how many of these voices, called modes, there are. Some say five, or nine, or twelve. For this book, we will cover the seven commonly accepted modes used in antiquity. The number seven was important to the ancients – seven Olympian gods, seven days of the week, seven ages of man. Seven is a mystical number, a magical number, and perhaps this little book yearns to do something magical.

I do not believe in gods, but I believe in music. Music can draw the dead close to us, for a while. If we could meet them, in the sunlit fields of song, surely we would stay forever.

– Jack Shapiro, The Songs of the Dead

1.

The Child

THE STORM WAKES ME. It must have been going for a while. The boat is rocking like a rollercoaster and the sea is loud. I squint at my clock. The red numbers say it's half two in the morning, but this clock hasn't been set since we left . . . where was it we left? Somewhere else. Somewhere not home. I can't guess the time these days. Now that I'm an ancient ruin. I'm not sure how long I slept. I stare at the flashing dots on the clock: : : : : : :

Someone is banging at the door.

'Mum? Are you awake?'

'Abigail?'

The door opens. 'Yes Mum, it's me. Do you mind if I put the light on?'

'Mind? Why?'

The light clicks on and there is Abigail. She looks flustered,

1

and she's hanging onto the doorframe. The bedroom tips to one side.

'Are you okay?' Abigail staggers over and sits on the side of my bed like a nurse. She was a nurse, before this. Her auburn hair is unbrushed and I want to get a comb.

'I just wanted to check you're okay.'

'Why?'

'Because of the storm.'

'Oh . . . Bad?'

Abigail sighs. 'Yes, Mum, it's pretty bad.'

'Don't need helping.' I look up into my daughter's face. She has freckles but no wrinkles. She's still so young.

'I know you don't need helping, you stubborn old goat.'

I make horns with fingers at the sides of my head and bleat. Abigail laughs and kisses my forehead. 'I just need to help David secure the boat, and I don't want you to worry if you can't find me.'

I take a deep breath. 'Don't worry. Go. Take care.'

The older I get, the less I talk. The words are still there in my head, I just can't get them out. Or if I do, they're wrong. I say 'knife' when I mean 'fork' and 'hello' when I mean 'goodbye'. I used to be a musician, and I preferred playing music to talking. Maybe this is nature's punishment – use it or lose it. Meanwhile, the trapped words boil away in my head like the contents of a pressure cooker. Long, rolling sentences bubble up. Presumably in this metaphor my brain is the old piece of meat, liquefying in its juices. I don't like it but there's nothing to be done. I sling one arm around Abigail's neck and half-hug her.

'See you soon, Mum. Sleep tight.'

Abigail clicks the light off and closes the door. I settle back into bed. The storm seems worse, in the dark. I feel it throwing our boat up and down. Out of habit, I count the things I remember.

1) My name is Ella Campbell.

2) I'm on a boat.

3) I'm on the boat because I'm on holiday.

4) I'm on holiday with Abigail, the baby and . . . and . . . him. Abigail just said his name, but it never seems to stick in my head.

5) The boat belongs to 'him'.

I wish I could remember his name. The man who brought us on holiday. He wears a lot of aftershave and thinks that because I am from Glasgow I must be mad for porridge and bagpipes. The only places he's visited in Scotland are golf courses. He bought this boat and he's sailing it back to England. He's a roaster, but I don't tell this to Abigail.

Another wave breaks over us. The boat shudders and I feel sick. Perhaps if it weren't so dark, I'd feel better. At home (*The Home*), I have a light that comes on when I clap. I try this, but it doesn't work. Perhaps the light can't hear me over the storm.

'Abigail?'

There's no reply. Abigail will come to check on me, of course. Over my bunk, on the right-hand side, is a window. Push yourself up with both hands. Careful, you old codger, feel for the porthole. I touch my nose to the cold glass. On other nights there has been a moon or stars. One night, the ocean looked like silver velvet being shaken over a stage. I remember the Palladium . . . or was it the Lyceum? I don't remember the show. There's no light now.

I'm about to get back under the covers when the boat lifts up,

up,

up . . .

It's like a hand is scooping us out of a bathtub. I feel weightless.

Now the boat drops again, smacking the waves. I'm knocked backwards, out of bed and onto the cabin floor. For a moment I forget to breathe. The pain follows. I can hardly hear my own cry. There's not much space between the bed and the door, and I've hit my head on something. It's still dark except for the glow of the clock. This is awful. When I next see Abigail and him, I'm asking to go home. I don't want 'one more adventure', as he calls it. He doesn't know the meaning of the word.

I'm near the door, so if I reach up, somewhere above me . . .

my fingers brush a pom-pom, dancing at the end of a string. I grab hold and pull. The light comes on. My legs are tangled in white sheet. Get up, don't lie on the floor, get yourself sitting. I could try to stand, but the boat is still bucking and I don't want to be thrown again.

I crawl to bed and settle down to sleep. But I can hear something. Very faint. I'm not hearing it through the air but through my pillow. It's coming through the floor, through the walls. High and thin, almost drowned out by the storm.

A baby crying.

My mouth curls up in a smile. My grandson. He is four months old. Or is it five? Too young to be dragged out on this boat, just like I'm too old. Thunder rattles my chest as I think about the baby. If the memory is hazy, that's just what babies are like. Blurry, not-quite-developed. One day he might be a judge or a poet or a landscape gardener. But we can't see that yet; he's keeping it to himself. I hope he's not too miserable. The sea has been making him sick. How long have we been on this boat?

I open my eyes and stare at the light. Abigail could be with the baby. Sometimes he can't be soothed, for all her trying. No wonder, in this storm. But the doubt is there in my mind, getting stronger. Abigail is good at soothing him. There's something reassuring about her that she didn't get from me. She must have been a good nurse, before he made her give it up. She says he didn't *make her*, that she wanted to . . .

The baby is still crying.

The boat is rolling through hills and valleys. But what's to lose, when you're eighty-seven? I get to sitting, holding tight to the bed. The cabin light flickers and dies. I sit in darkness and say several words that an eighty-seven-year-old isn't meant to know.

Deep breath.

I launch myself toward the door. The boat tips and I slam into solid wood. Out of the cabin, into the narrow corridor. That's the one good thing about this cramped boat – never far to fall. In the dark, I feel the walls either side. There's something else, an unfamiliar feeling. My feet are cold. There's water in the corridor.

I edge along, legs threatening to mutiny. Opposite me are two doors, one Abigail's room, the other a spare bedroom which has been the baby's playroom. On my side is the door to the nursery.

'Abigail?'

There's no reply but the storm. I grab the handle to the nursery, but there's more water in the hallway now, pressing against it. Are we sinking? One foot against the wall and both hands on the handle, I pull. The door opens onto the sound of wailing.

'Abigail? Are you in there?'

No reply. My head swims with darkness. If there were light I would feel better. I can't see the baby and there's water in the nursery. That's not right. *I'm* the one who opened the door, *I'm* the one who let the water in. Have I made a mistake? Too late to go back. I edge forward, guided by the crying. Inside there's less to hold onto. Each cabin has a built-in bed, but the baby sleeps in a travel cot on the floor.

A cot which is level with the floor.

Hold onto the crying – he's still there. The boat starts to race downhill like a bobsled. I grip the doorjamb just in time and for a moment all the water around my ankles is gone, washing to the far end of the room. The baby falls silent. Is he drowned? My fall is broken and I almost lose my grip. The baby coughs and screams.

This room is a mirror image of my own. Clothes have started to baffle me in the last year, the landscape of blouses and underwear leaves me frustrated. In the dark, this mirror-room is a cruel puzzle. There is a sudden flash of dazzling blue light. In that moment I can see the cot, can see the baby kicking his legs against the wet mattress. Then the light is gone, replaced by thunder. Before I can lose the image, I step forward.

The baby is frantic, his wails staccato, as though he can't wait to draw breath before the next one. Not the cry of a baby who is tired, hungry or sick. A cry of terror. I feel over the mattress until my hands close around his warm, squirming body. Tiny hands grip the edges of my own as I lift him. He's big for his age – I've never lifted him myself. I'm usually in a chair, propped with cushions. My vertebrae pop-pop-pop. His hot face screams into my ear.

'Sssh, sssh, there now.' He squirms in his soaked sleeping bag and batters me with tiny fists. 'Come on lovey, I'm here now.'

My arms tremble with the strain. I just want to lie down and go to sleep. Maybe it's safest if I stay here. Abigail must be busy, making the boat right. But then I remember the water – the water that I let in. We can't stay here, it isn't safe. How will I get him upstairs, in the dark? I remember his nightlight. It's made of soft plastic, shaped like an egg. If you press on the pointy end, a light comes on.

I put him on the bed. I crouch down and feel in the cold water for the box of toys. My hands turn numb as I run them over rattles and teething rings, fabric books and soft animals. I throw the rejects into the water. Finally, I have it. The cabin is lit by blue light, shifting to green as I look to the baby on the bed, staring at me with his mouth an 'O'. Regaining composure, he resumes his wailing.

'Sssh, hush now, I'm coming.'

My head feels waterlogged. I get the baby as far as the hallway without much trouble. Then the boat tips back, like a rollercoaster climbing to the top of a big drop. I can see the stairs up to the saloon but can't move toward them.

Wait. Wait for it . . .

The boat tilts a little, then we're racing down, faster than before. I launch myself at the stairs like a nightie-clad Olympian. I catch the first stair with my foot, and the next. Though I'm climbing the stairs, it's like running downhill.

We reach the top stair. We're in the lounge, except now I can't stop –I've too much speed and the tilt of the boat means that the wooden floor is a polished slide. My feet go out from under me and I land heavily. We slide across the length of the room and crash into the back wall.

I'm still holding the baby. There's no way of telling whether I've broken any bones. Everything hurts. The deck here is wet, like downstairs, but there's no water sloshing around. The baby squirms against my chest and the room is lit by changing colours. I look around and see the baby's nightlight, rolling on the floor, turning red, then blue, then green. How did that get there? Abigail must have brought it to see by.

The door to the deck is flapping open, letting in rain. Papers skitter and Abigail's novel flaps on the floor like a wounded bird. I shuffle to the door and shut it with one foot. The room is suddenly calm, though the storm still rattles the windows. In one corner of the cabin is the baby's bouncy chair, with straps to stop him falling out. I shuffle over and put him down, then struggle for a minute to get him out of his wet sleeping bag.

I look around the cabin. On each side is a sofa. I can sleep on one of those. It will be comfortable. But the baby is still crying so hard. If I could feed him, he might be happier, but Abigail only gives him breastmilk. If I could just sing one nursery rhyme, maybe he would calm down. But with the sound of the storm and the baby crying, I can't remember. What was that one – 'Old Man Farmer'? 'Clip Clop Horsey'? I try to hum, but the melodies have rusted away.

I look around the room, seeing by the ghostly nightlight. There's a barometer set into a model ship's wheel. There's a picture of a Greek village, with white walls and blue domes and more sea in the background. There's a guitar . . .

A guitar.

I fix on the guitar. It glows in the blue phase of the night-light. I've seen it before. But I feel like I never really *noticed* it. It's mounted upright on the wall by two brackets. One under the body and one higher up, around the neck.

I don't know much about objects these days. The microwave on the boat is just a microwave. I couldn't guess how old it is, whether it was cheap or expensive. A pair of shoes is a pair of shoes. Pens and pencils, rubber balls and jackets – they're like pictures in a children's book.

But . . . I know a lot about this guitar. It's acoustic. It's concert size. It may be here as decoration, but it's not cheap. Inlaid mother-of-pearl on the headstock for the logo: *GUILD*. Yes, an M-20. American made. Nylon strings. There's a plectrum wedged between the strings at the headstock. The bridge and fingerboard are rosewood, satin finish. Bone nut and saddle. Mahogany body with a sunburst finish.

There's a flash of lightning, burning the shape of the guitar onto my eyes. I struggle to stand. Then the deck sinks and I make my run. I grab hold of the guitar, to stop myself falling. I hope whichever idiot decorated this boat didn't bolt it to the wall. After a moment of fiddling with the neck clasp, the guitar tumbles into my arms.

I take my prize back to the baby. I sit, legs complaining at being forced to sit like a four-year-old at nursery. Can I play it? I don't know. Abigail used to like hearing me play. Maybe Abigail's baby will like to hear me play as well.

The guitar is out of tune. I pluck the top string a few times and fiddle with the tuning peg. Without having to think about it, I continue up the strings. I hold down a fret of the last string to match it with the sound of the next. A squall of rain on the windows drowns me out for a moment. The guitar sounds grateful to be tuned. I strum with the plectrum and the guitar raises its voice over the storm.

For that strum, the baby stops crying. He opens bloodshot eyes and looks at me. This feels so familiar, but I can't think of anything to play. My left hand tries to form a chord, but my fingers tangle over one another. Perhaps if I could remember a song, the chords would come. I cast around the room, the rain-streaked windows, the baby, the nightlight. I can't remember songs about these things. I take things out of my dressing gown pockets. An open packet of sherbet lemons, some balled-up tissues, a piece of folded paper. I unfold it and find it's a brochure . . .

IONIAN FISHING TOURS.

That word, *Ionian* . . .

I remember a tune. A song called 'The Child'. I smile at the coincidence. My fingers form the first chord and my hand strums down. Cmaj7. It rings out and again the baby falls silent.

I hum the first note. My voice is thin, but I feel the buzz in my ears as the note from the guitar and the note from my throat rub against each other. I'd forgotten this feeling. How long since I played? How deep is the ocean?

The life behind me is lit through broken cloud. Close to where I stand, everything is in shadow – the nursing home, the last years with my husband, the journey which brought us here. I can see the space but not the detail. Off on the horizon I can see a few acres of golden light, my childhood. Between the light and the shade, there are patches of sun, but most of the land is dark. My life is a mystery to me. Mostly I think about the distance between me and that golden horizon.

But the guitar is in my hands and the sound is in my throat. I'm ready to play again. There's a roll of thunder but I ignore it. Just a show-off percussionist. I strum the first chord and start to sing.

The song tumbles out of me and the boat tumbles over darkened sea. Though my hands are stiff, though my fingertips sting with the pressure of the strings, though my voice is cracked like an unrosined bow, I feel light. It's as if, after hobbling around for so long, I tried running and found I could sprint like a teenager.

The sounds ring in the cabin. If I play hard enough, it's as though I'm driving the storm back. The song is simple. That word, 'Ionian', comes back to me. Ionian is a way of playing music. A 'mode'. A way of spacing the notes apart. And it's old. Before music became Handel and Beethoven and Charlie Parker, there were modes. As old as the hills, as old as the sea. They were played on instruments with one string, clay pipes and ocarinas, instruments made of animal bone and hollowed turtle shells. I can't remember the others yet, but I'll try. I'll try anything to feel this way again, racing downhill.

The song isn't long. It would fit onto a single page. So I play it again and again, strumming the chords and humming the melody. Without pausing, I look at the baby. He's watching me calmly. The storm still beats against our thin shell, the room still races up and down, but his eyes are drooping. I smile at him. He looks at me like he looks at Abigail on her breast. His breaths become long and deep.

Even when he's asleep, I don't stop playing. I want to enjoy this a little longer. The dizzy feeling has become almost nice. My bones ache, I'm sore from my salt-stained nightie, but I don't want to stop. I close my eyes. Perhaps it's the rolling of the sea, perhaps the reeling repetition of the music, but I'm spinning. Not dizzying but slow, like a gigantic whirlpool. Is the boat swirling? Has someone pulled the plug out of the ocean?

As the light starts to fade, I cling to the guitar like a buoyancy aid and keep playing until, swoosh-swoosh-swoosh, I circle the drain and tumble into darkness, the tune echoing in my ears like falling water.

THE CHILD

Jack Shapiro

1936

ELEANOR CAMPBELL HAS NEVER been this angry in her
whole life. Her skirt has rucked up and her knees scrape
the tarmac of the playground. Her tiny fists, balled so tight
that the knuckles shine, are pounding the sides and stomach
of Kevin MacAndrew, who is curled like a hedgehog in self-
defence.

'Give . . . her . . . it . . . back!'

Kevin makes a wordless cry but does not open. If there is
any sense in his bellow, it is lost in the noise of the crowd
which has swallowed them both. Ella and Kevin are just seven,
but the older kids don't step in – there are rules. The grey
Glaswegian sky is starting to spit rain, so she has to finish
this before a teacher calls them in. The thing that Ella wants
from Kevin is tightly clamped in the folded stodge of him,
like a shilling in a Christmas pudding. She punches him again,

in the small of the back. Rene hovers somewhere over Ella's shoulder, hands cupped over her mouth in an expression of suppressed horror, or laughter, or both.

'Give . . . it . . . back, you wee . . . you wee . . .' Ella summons the worst swear word she knows. 'You wee *bugger*!'

She punches him hard in the ribs at the moment of the curse and, like an unvanquishable picture-book dragon whose weak spot has been pierced by an arrow, Kevin's eyes go wide. He uncurls, lying flat on his back, gasping for breath, the object of Ella's battle displayed on his heaving belly – Rene's calf-leather pencil case, with the red ribbon tied on the zip.

'Ha! I win,' Ella pants, and has a moment to savour her victory before she is lifted off the ground, upwards and backwards, by her collar.

'Hey! Geddoff me you bugger!'

The curse, used once, slips out with the intoxication of triumph. The crowd gasps.

'Eleanor Campbell!'

Ella's eyes go wide at the adult voice, fear quenching her anger. She sees Kevin being hauled to his feet by another teacher while the headmistress marches her in the direction of the school, parting the tide of children like Moses. She hears whispers as they pass.

'Man, she's crazy.'

'What's her name?'

'She's a gypsy – they're all like that.'

'She's no a gypsy – gypsies don't go tae school.'

'She is too! She has dark eyes and hair.'

'Ella Knorr?'

'No, Eleanor. Eleanor Campbell.'

'She fights like an animal.'

With a backward glance, Ella spots Rene. She has escaped punishment, picking her pencil case off the floor and holding it tight to her chest. Nobody comes close; Rene is protected. Ella smiles and does not fight as the headmistress steers her with one hand toward the office.

* * *

'Thank you, Ella.'

Rene is skipping, blonde ringlets bobbing. By Ella's count, she has already thanked her eleven times since they left school.

'Stop thankin' me,' she mutters under her breath.

Ella has spent the last three hours in the headmistress' office, writing lines on soft paper with a blunt pencil until her hand cramped. She was spanked first, of course – ten strokes on the bottom being the highest penalty at Peterhead Primary. She would have taken many more to avoid the lines.

Three hours seemed like an eternity packed with eternities, only divided up by the heavy tick of the office clock and a sharp word from the secretary if she stopped. Ella would write some more, then stop, and count by the clock how long it took for the telling-off to come. Her record was forty-seven seconds. Ella finds that the memory of a punishment fades fast after it is over, but this one is taking its time. Like the time she sucked the ink from her father's fountain pen and had to have her tongue scrubbed with soap.

'But you got it back!' Rene chirps happily. 'I would never have got it back!'

Ella enjoyed the praise at first, but since they got out of the school gates it's giving her a funny feeling in her stomach. She's trying to ignore the children in the crowd who are looking or pointing at her, the ones who are whispering to their parents, who turn to look. She hasn't seen Kevin or his parents. Maybe he went home.

Ella feels heavy, like she can barely lift her feet off the ground. Perhaps it's the folded paper sitting in her pocket like a girder. She can't stop thinking of the note, awaiting her father's signature like a pact with the devil. Two weeks of no playtime, eating her lunch in the headmistress' office and reading quietly while the sounds of the playground ring at the window.

'I don't want to go home.'

She says it quietly, and she's not sure if Rene has heard her. She whispers because she doesn't want anyone to hear, but also because it's an admission of weakness. Rene draws a little closer and puts her arm around Ella.

'I'm sorry . . .'

Most kids in their year are met by parents, but she and Rene live so close to the school, in adjacent Bedlay Street, they're allowed to walk home together. They go to one of their houses, and whichever mother it is will give them something to eat. They do this every weekday except Wednesday, when Rene goes for her guitar lesson with Mr Veitch and her mother picks her up later.

Rene comes to school in the morning with the guitar in its case, smaller than a full-sized one, but still huge compared to Rene, painted blue with an apple tree on one side, done by her dad. Of all Rene's possessions, this is the one that Ella envies the most, and the one which first convinced her that the Mauchlen family must be wealthy.

Ella has seen the guitar only once, because Rene is under strict instruction not to open the case until her lesson after school. But Ella has a very good memory. Like a camera, says her dad. (Sometimes, when Eleanor wants to remember something, she makes a little click under her breath like she's taking a picture with her eyes, though she's never held a real camera.) Ella can close her eyes and see the guitar. The body is the colour of caramel, the tuning pegs shine like six pearls in the dark case, which is purple velvet. The guitar even *smells* expensive. She ran her fingers over the strings, just once, and listened to them purr before Rene shut the case nervously.

Ella speaks again, feeling the shape of her plan before she knows what it is.

'If we didn't go home, we could go to the park . . .'

Rene takes her hand silently and keeps walking.

'And if we went to the park . . . we would be late . . . Mam would be worried . . .'

Rene looks around for her older brother, Robert. Ella can't see him in the crowds.

Ella can't remember a time when Robert wasn't around, though it feels like they've said no more than a dozen words to each other in all that time. Robert is like Rene's shadow. He usually walks near to them on the way to and from school, making sure they don't stray. But sometimes he stops to talk to a friend.

When they're at Rene's house, Robert is often sitting in the corner with a book from the library. Books with no pictures. Books with covers the colour of dust. Ella thinks he must be very clever. She's impressed and irritated by the thought. She thinks Robert must look down on them – all of two years younger than him – as simple creatures. Ella wants to prove to him that she's not a baby, but also wants to know what's so interesting in all those books.

'We'd get in trouble,' Rene says.

'I'm already in trouble . . .' Ella lets this point hang in the air, leaves the 'for you' unspoken.

'Yes,' Rene concedes. 'But . . . why do you want to be late? We could play in front of the fire. Mama might make us griddle cakes.'

This is a good point. The house alternates, and today it should be Rene's house. Rene's mother makes them hot cakes with butter, or brings out biscuits and cheese. Sometimes, she will fry them each a sausage, which they eat with slices of bread dipped in the fat. They have to share with Robert, but he doesn't talk much and offers Ella the biscuit tin first. If the food is not as good at Ella's house, Rene never says anything about it.

Her stomach rumbles, and for a moment Ella thinks about ditching her plan. But no – the note weighs heavy in her pocket, tugging one side of her cardigan lower than the other. Her father is a quiet man, which makes his temper all the more frightening. Ella wishes he would just yell at her, but his anger stays bottled up. The sandstone tenements tower either side of them like a canyon, and she can't escape the feeling that this tide of bodies is washing her to her doom.

'No, we should go to the park. Not far, just over the hill.'

Rene's hand loosens on hers for a second, and Ella thinks she will lose her to the tide. But then she grips tight again.

'Okay. We'll go to the park.'

Ella smiles – she feels better right away. She's sure that this plan is a good one. It's so good, it's like she didn't even think of it herself. They will go to the park. They will hide until Ella is sure they're going to be missed. Then they will go home. Her mum will be so relieved to see her that she won't care about the note from the headmistress. She'll just be happy that they're safe.

* * *

'Can we go now?' Rene asks, for the fifth time.

'Just five more minutes,' Ella says, for the fifth time.

The park is empty, or near enough. It's not really a park, just some open land at the top of Bedlay Street which crests into a small hill. Down on the other side are more tenements and Sighthill Church, where they go on a Sunday to hear about God. To the east, separated by a metal fence, is Petershill Football Ground. There aren't any trees here, but everybody knows it as 'Paddy's Park' and nobody knows why.

They aren't far from Springburn Park, with its bandstand, Winter Gardens, and overflowing baskets of flowers. But even Ella wouldn't dream of wandering that far. In Paddy's Park they look like what they are – a couple of kids playing out after school.

Ella isn't sure how much time has passed. It feels like hours, but there's no clock in sight. She's good at reading the time and likes clocks. She likes pressing her ear to her dad's watch, listening to the ticking inside, the invisible mechanism hammering away like a tiny factory, forging the present moment.

Ella looks at her friend, who is sitting on the hill facing north, away from Bedlay Street, playing with the buckles on her satchel. They can see the church from where they are, and it's hard not to feel that it's watching them back. Ella believes in *Him* but is still on the fence about His rules and regulations. She thinks the priest might be exaggerating to stop her having any fun.

Rene coughs.

Rene Mauchlen is everything that Ella isn't – blonde,

rosy-cheeked, and (to Ella's mind at least) rich. In later years, it will seem ridiculous to Ella that she ever thought of Rene's family as wealthy. They live on the same street, in the same kind of two-room tenement flat. But in addition to a radio they have a gramophone, and more than a dozen shiny black records to play. They always have powdered chocolate in the cupboard for cocoa, and biscuits in the tin. The door on their cast iron range has brass hinges, which shine like gold ingots in the gaslight, whereas the hob in Ella's house is dull black.

And there's the guitar, of course.

Every minute or so Rene coughs again, but Ella is used to it. Rene always coughs or wheezes, especially in the winter. She has something called asthma, which is like having a cold except it doesn't really ever go away. She has to take medicine for it every morning – a treacly syrup which is supposed to taste like strawberries, but which Rene says is like licking a penny. Sometimes, when it's bad, she doesn't come to school. Ella thinks this is pretty good, but Rene says it's no fun. When the wind doesn't blow, all the smoke from the houses and factories curls up on the city like a cat on a rug. That's when it's worst. Rene will sit at the edge of the playground with a look of concentration.

'We should play a game,' Ella says, though her mind is elsewhere. She needs to keep Rene here for now.

'Hmm . . .' Rene looks around, at the empty park. 'What sort of game?'

Ella sighs and sits down next to her friend. 'I Spy?'

'Aye, okay. I'll go first.' She thinks for a long moment. 'I spy with my little eye, something beginning with . . . G.'

Ella fixes her gaze on the grey horizon.

* * *

When they finally leave, the light has gone from the sky and the lamps are all lit down Bedlay Street. At regular intervals down the roofs on either side of them, chimney rows smoulder. Rene has gone very quiet with the cold and is breathing quickly. Her arms are hugged around her. Ella is clenching her jaw shut to stop her teeth chattering. They go up the steps to Ella's front door, into the gas-lit close. The light wavers over the bottle-green tiles covering the walls, which are scrubbed clean every Tuesday. They could go to Rene's first, where they're expected, but Eleanor wants Rene there to back up her story if her mum doesn't believe her.

They climb the stairs to the third floor and knock. There are noises inside, and the door opens to reveal Ella's mum, framed in golden light. She's wearing her apron, and her hair is up in curlers and paper.

'Girls? Isn't it your day with Lorna?'

Lorna is Rene's mum. With a sinking feeling, Ella realizes that her plan hasn't worked – they've been gone all this time, and her mum hasn't even missed them. Neither of them says anything, stunned by the warmth coming through the door and their own failure.

'Well, you better come in before you let all the heat out. Come on now. I'll make you some tea.'

Ella and Rene follow dumbly. There are two rooms in Ella's house, unless you count the passage. The first room on their right is Ella's bedroom. The second is the main room, where they cook and eat their meals. Her parents sleep in here on the fold-down bed. They step into the main room and Ella feels shivers of heat running up her spine. The fire is built up, and there's something bubbling in a pan on the hob. The room smells of ironing.

'What do you want, girls? Has Lorna already given you something to eat?'

She turns and speaks directly to Rene, who seems unable to say anything. Ella wants to say something to salvage her plan but can't come up with anything before her mum speaks again.

'Rene? Are you all right, hen? You look pale.'

Ella looks to her friend, whose eyes have gone wide. She thinks it must be because she has been caught in their lie. Rene opens and closes her mouth a few times, like a fish gulping on a riverbank, then takes a step forward.

'Rene?'

Ella's mum steps forward at the same moment, just in time to catch Rene. She holds under her arms, but Rene's head rolls on her shoulders. She's out cold.

Ella just stands there. What can she do? She doesn't understand what's happening. At least her mother seems to understand, scooping Rene's limp body into her arms and, with a grunt, lifting her.

'Come on,' she says, but Ella doesn't move, blocking her mother's way. 'Eleanor, move!'

'Where are you going?'

'To your room.' Her mother pushes past, and Ella sees the scuffed underside of Rene's shoes pass her face.

'My room? Why?'

'Because the fire's not lit in there and the bed's made.'

'What's wrong with her?'

'She's had a funny turn. Probably because it's too hot, and she's frozen through.'

Eleanor follows into the hallway, and her mother gives her a backward glance.

'Where were you, before this?'

Ella looks down and says nothing. Guilt is curdling in her stomach. Her mother pushes the door of the bedroom open with Rene's feet. The lamps aren't lit in here; the fire is built for later. Not much heat comes through from the main room and Ella can see her breath steaming. When Rene is laid on the bed, her mother goes back to the main room to fetch a taper for the lamps and some water.

Ella walks to where her friend is laid out on her bed. They've played games before where one or the other of them was Sleeping Beauty or Snow White, waiting for the Prince's kiss, but Rene was never much good at lying still – she's too much of a fidget, too suspicious that she's about to be tickled. Now she's playing the part perfectly. Ella is stretching out her hand to touch Rene's cheek when her eyelids flicker. Ella pulls her hand back in shock as though burned.

'Rene?'

Her friend makes a noise which is not words before Ella's mum bustles in, holding a lit taper.

'You back with us, hen?'

She looks down at Rene on the bed, her face lit in flickering light like a painting of Florence Nightingale.

'Mm,' Rene hums, which is the closest she's got to speech.

'Good.'

Ella's mum gets up on tiptoes to light the lamps, putting the taper to the soot-blackened filaments until the flame rears up and is tamed by a turn of the tap. Though they've had electricity in the flat for the last two years, the landlord has never replaced the gaslights, until now. Tomorrow a man is coming to take them out and put brand-new electric lights in. Ella can't wait. She thinks it will feel like living in the future.

Her mother comes to the bed and again nudges Eleanor to one side.

'Have a drink of water, hen. You'll feel better for it.'

Rene nods once, tries to lift her head from the pillow and fails. Eleanor's mum lifts her head for her and brings the glass to her lips.

'I wish your dad was home . . .' she mutters, seemingly to Ella but clearly not looking for a reply. Then, more certainly –

'Eleanor, I need you to go and get Lorna. Go and get Mrs Mauchlen.'

'Mam?'

'Just do it, Eleanor.'

*   *   *

By the time Ella gets back to the house with Mrs Mauchlen in tow, Rene is sitting up in bed, sipping tea and eating a piece of toast with butter. She's still pale, and coughs several times so hard that her eyes water, but she tells them all how she's fine. Mrs Mauchlen, who has wrung her hands and fretted all the way to the house, is visibly annoyed with Ella, who wasn't able to explain what was wrong. They both get a telling-off for staying out, but no punishment is mentioned and Rene climbs onto her mother's back to go home, linking her arms around her neck.

As they're leaving, Rene looks over her shoulder to Ella, and there is something in her eyes that she's trying to communicate, but Ella doesn't know whether it's regret, accusation or apology. It will bother her later that, though she can recall the expression exactly, she still doesn't know what it means. Then they are gone.

*   *   *

A new day breaks. Ella swings her legs out of bed, toes sinking into the colourful rug that her mum made with scraps of fabric, pulling them through hessian. When they read the *Arabian*

Nights in school, she imagined the flying carpets looking like this one. The rug is colder than she expected. She pads to the window in her nightie and, rather than pulling the curtain back, steps around it, as though stepping on stage.

It has snowed. Isn't it too early in the year for that? Ella isn't sure. But it has snowed. Not good snow, sure enough. Not snowball snow, or snowman snow, or sledging snow. A dusting as thin as a sheet, pulled over the streets and rooftops as far as Ella can see. It frosts one side of every drainpipe, silvers the acres of roofing slate. Only the warm chimney pots are free of its shroud.

Though she knows it to be false, Ella cannot shake the feeling that today is Christmas. A day for presents, special food and no school. It annoys her that she can't get this out of her head, because she will be disappointed when she has to get her uniform on. School is no fun without Rene, and she has been off all week, since they came home from the park.

Still, Ella doesn't feel like sleeping any more. She may as well find out if her parents are awake in the next room. Often, she will peek around the crack in the door to see if their bed has been folded into its recess. If not, and she sees the forms of her parents, rising and falling out of sync, she will sit and hum tunes in the corridor until they wake up and notice her. Sometimes she will crawl into the bed between them, though her dad doesn't like this. Ella likes those mornings.

Today, there is no doubt. The bed is up, and the door to

the front room is open a little. There is a soft glow – the lamps are lit. And there is a smell, unfamiliar on a school day. Frying bacon. Ella breathes big lungfuls of it in disbelief. She has skipped forward in time to Christmas Day, that's the only explanation that makes sense.

A smile breaking involuntarily over her face, Ella steps forward, puts a hand to the door and pushes into the warmth and light and good smell of the front room. She stands in the space vacated by her parents' bed and looks expectantly at her mother and father, who are surely waiting for her with presents.

They haven't seen her.

Both of them have their backs to her, her mother hunched slightly over the cast iron range, prodding the frying bacon with the wooden spoon that she cooks everything with – clootie dumplings, onion soup, rice puddings with jam. Usually her father will be sitting in his chair at this time, polishing his shoes or trimming his nails. Always quiet, self-contained, as though he has not really woken up yet, and is performing these actions in a trance.

But today he is not in his chair, he is standing next to her mother, one hand on her shoulder. Ella has become fully convinced that today is, if not Christmas Day, a special occasion, and this is the first inkling that something might be amiss. She watches for a moment, tempted (as she always is when she has entered a room undetected) to creep up and startle them.

'Morning.'

Her voice is cheery, but she does not shout. Nevertheless, her parents startle and spin around.

'Eleanor!' her mother says, taking a step forward hesitantly, still holding the wooden spoon. Her father doesn't move, doesn't say good morning. Her mother seems to think better of walking across the small room to get her.

Ella walks around the low sofa where she and her mother sit in the evenings, while her dad sits in his wingback armchair facing them. Without the sofa in her way, she can see that something is lying on the hearth rug. It makes her stop. She was right after all – it's Christmas, or her birthday, or some other special day which doesn't come every year. Her parents have got her a present. A big one.

She looks at the present. How did they know she wanted one? How did they know she wanted a guitar exactly like Rene's?

No.

Not a guitar *like* Rene's, but Rene's guitar. The blue case painted with an apple tree in four colours – light and dark brown for the trunk, green for the leaves and red for the apples. She knows the painting, done by Rene's pa, like a face, with all its asymmetries and wrinkles. Her parents say nothing. Ella says nothing. In the silence, she kneels down.

Ella has never seen a child's coffin. She's only been to the funeral of her great-aunt Lydia. Suddenly she is possessed by the strange notion that if she opens the case, she will find a body inside. Of course, the dimensions do not allow for that

– the legs would be too squashed up in that long neck of the case.

'Mrs Mauchlen came by this morning . . .' her father begins, but her mother puts a hand on him and he stops abruptly.

Ella crouches forward and puts her hands on the case, then feels around the lid, undoing the clasps. She lifts the lid, which crackles as it hinges upwards. Gleaming in the warm light, Rene's guitar is as beautiful as it ever was. Ella's eyes trail over the floral pattern around the sound hole, the gleam of the tuning pegs, the thick velvet lining the case.

For all this, Ella doesn't want it. She feels no desire for the guitar, to own it or even touch it. This absence of desire is the most troubling thing she has ever felt, so keen it is. She thinks this not-wanting must be a mistake and reaches to take out the guitar.

She lifts it slowly by the neck and body and places it on her knees. She does not strum the strings. She does not want to hear them. Both hands are placed over the strings, muting them, like a hand over a mouth. She hopes they stay silent forever.

* * *

Ella supposes it's because she's a child that she keeps waiting to see Rene. She doubts that adults expect to see their dead friends turning a street corner, or sitting on the step outside their close, waiting for them to come and play. She doubts they feel the same missed-step jolt in their belly when they remember. She doubts adults see those person-shaped holes in the world. It is a stupidity unique to childhood, she thinks, and cannot wait to outgrow it.

She goes to the funeral, undistinguished as Rene's best friend among the rest of her class. She sees Robert, through the crowds, but does not speak to him. He's wearing a black jacket and tie, with black shorts and a black cap. The whole outfit must have been bought for the occasion. Ella thinks he looks like a crow with skinny white legs. She watches as he's hugged by a succession of relatives. They look like they're trying to squeeze the breath out of him, and Ella wants to tell them to stop. Robert just stands there, unmoving, until they let him go.

Back at school, Ella sits at the edge of the playground. It's not because she's mourning, but because she can't think of anything else to do. She comes home every afternoon, spends the evenings with her parents, half-listening to the radio until it's time for bed, where she goes without complaint. On Sundays there is church, but Saturdays drag on endlessly, longer than the rest of the week combined.

Ella fades into the background. People stop noticing her. She becomes ghost-like. She doesn't mind. After all, this is all her fault.

* * *

A month after the funeral, Ella is sitting on the low wall at one edge of the playground, her back against the wire fence.

She's examining her own shadow. The December sun is not shining, exactly, but the clouds today are paper-thin. As she watches, another shadow draws near and intersects with her own, creating a patch between them that is darker than either on its own.

'Hello, Eleanor.'

She looks up and sees a halo of auburn curls surrounding a serious face. If Ella were to say that Robert Mauchlen looks angelic it would not be entirely complimentary. He looks like one of those Old Testament angels she's seen in church, who the Almighty has given an especially onerous task – casting out Satan, evicting Adam and Eve, sweeping over Egypt to take the souls of first-born children. More than the average nine-year-old boy, Robert looks like he has something on his mind.

Ella has been expecting this moment. Hoping for it, even. She wants Robert to tell her off. She wants him to shout at her. She wants him to blame her for Rene. Even as fear curdles in her belly, she's anticipating the relief of punishment. Robert just stands there, as though he's about to say something. But the words never come. Then his hand shoots out and he places something in her lap. He sits next to her.

Ella can feel her heart pounding. The object in her lap is wrapped in brown paper. She assumes it's something disgusting. Dog poo, perhaps. Or insects – a collection of earwigs and centipedes. She resists the urge to shrug the parcel onto the ground and pinches the corner between thumb and forefinger. The brown paper opens almost like a flower.

Sitting in the middle is the biggest block of tablet that Ella has ever seen. Of all the sweets that Ella and Rene most treasured – soor plooms, sherbet straws, Berwick cockles – tablet was the most precious. Mrs Mauchlen makes it herself, with a tin of condensed milk and a huge bag of sugar, stirring the pan until her arm aches and the mixture solidifies into something crumbly at the edges, fudgy in the centre. Ella's mum always gets it wrong, overcooking the mix so it sets hard as toffee.

Ella breaks a piece off and pops it in her mouth. The sugar coats the roof of her mouth, makes the back of her throat tickle, and she finally believes it's real. She quickly wraps up the precious stuff and shoves it in her cardigan before anybody notices what she's got. She tries to think of something to say to Robert. He asks a question instead.

'What do you like to do?' Robert asks.

Before, Ella would have said that she likes playing with Rene.

'I like listening to the radio.'

'Oh?' Robert's eyebrows rise. 'What do you like to listen to?'

Ella thinks. Actually, she doesn't like the radio that much any more. She doesn't like the comedians and the storytellers that were always her favourites. They all seem like they're trying to distract her from how she feels, and she doesn't want to be distracted.

'I like the music,' she says, at last. This is true. Music doesn't distract her. Music lets her feel what she's feeling more strongly. To Ella's surprise, Robert is nodding.

'Me too.'

'You do?'

'I'd like to be a musician, when I grow up.'

'Don't you want to do something with books? You could be a librarian. Or, um . . . the man who delivers books to the library.'

'Hm.' Robert sounds sceptical. 'Maybe. But it would be fun to play music.'

'Fun?'

'Aye. Else why would they call it "play"?'

This is the most insightful thing Ella has heard anyone around her age say, by such a large degree, that it strikes her as mystical. She has never thought a job could be like playing before. It seems like a secret hidden in plain sight. For a minute they are silent. Ella feels she shouldn't waste this opportunity.

'D'you think it gets easier?' she asks, very quietly.

Robert runs a hand through his curls, breathes in and out. He looks so adult to Ella, he might as well be one of the teachers.

'People keep saying that . . . But I don't know. Maybe they're just saying it so that we don't give up.'

'Give up what?'

'On being normal, I guess.'

'Oh.' Ella can't say anything more. She couldn't have

expressed the feeling she has had for the last few weeks better than Robert just has.

'You're clever,' she says at last. When she looks over at him, Robert is blushing furiously. He clears his throat.

'I should go.'

'Okay.'

He gets up to leave and walks away without looking back.

'Thank you!' Ella blurts out.

Robert turns. 'What for?'

Ella frowns, realizing she isn't sure. It just seemed like the right thing to say. Her whole being wants to say thank you to Robert for something bigger and more important than she can understand.

'For the tablet, of course,' she says, remembering the little parcel in her cardigan.

Robert hesitates for a second, nods tightly, and disappears into the crowd.

2.

The Maiden

I WAKE FROM THE DREAM.
Or I wake from the memory.

Or I return to the present.

I'm not sure which and it doesn't really matter. For a moment, I feel nothing. Then there's pain, spreading like ink on blotting paper. I remember I'm not seven but eighty-seven years old. My back hurts. My arse hurts. My wrists and ankles *really* hurt. I open my eyes and find that I'm not in my cabin. It must be sometime in the day; I've had a *siesta* in the saloon. Reflections of sunlight ripple over the wooden ceiling. That's strange . . .

I turn my head to look and my eyes widen. I'm lying on the floor. The floor is covered in water, newspapers and novels strewn around. The guitar is a little way away. The storm comes back to me. A little way from me, in the bouncy chair, I see a small, crumpled body.

I jump up.

Well, my mind jumps up. My body doesn't follow. I try again. Like a choked engine, my body stays on the floor. Pain stalls me. I have pills for my back which I could take. But they're all the way downstairs, in my cabin. I fix my eyes on the baby, his bundled body. He has slept there all night, in a wet sleepsuit, in this draughty room. Nobody has come to him.

I try a third time. Slowly, I sit up. I crawl across the room until I reach him. I kneel and put one hand to his chest. The wet fabric is cold. No movement. No breath. His head is slumped into his chest.

'No, no, no . . .'

The baby's head jerks up. He gasps and his eyes flicker. I gasp too, then laugh with relief. My hands fumble with the straps.

'Oh lovie, come on now . . .'

I lift the limp weight of him up to my chest. As I hold him, he shivers and cries once. Legs and back protesting, I carry the baby to the sofa and sit with him. He doesn't cry again, but the shiver returns. I take a blanket and wrap it around us, rubbing his back and kissing his head. The warmth allows his shiver to blossom. It scares me that his tiny body is shaking so hard, as though it might shake apart. At length his blue eyes open, and he picks his head up.

For a minute there is calm in the room. Just me and the baby, looking into each other's eyes. Then he starts to cry. It's small at first, but he soon warms to it. Outside, the storm has passed. The saloon has windows on all sides. The sun is beating down over endless ocean. There are no boats or ships, no islands.

'Abigail?'

It's silly to call for her, my voice no louder than the baby. If Abigail were able, she would have come already. She must be busy. I swaddle him with the blanket. He kicks, trying to be free. I arrange the cushions so he won't roll off the sofa.

I bend to pick up Abigail's novel. It's been soaked and half-dried in a shaft of sun. The pages are warped and stuck together. I try to smooth it into shape and find it's not a novel at all.

TEN STRANGE LESSONS
Dispatches from the Frontier of Physics

I wonder what Abigail makes of it. She was a curious child, a question-asker. Like her father, I think, though I don't remember Abigail's father at all. I do my best to close the book, but it keeps springing open at the page where it landed in the storm.

I read:

The passage of time is perhaps the clearest, most common-sense aspect of our daily lives. We wake in the morning and go to bed at night. The space in between is obvious to us. But the closer we look, the more 'time' seems to disappear. Our newest theories suggest that time itself is an illusion. It is simply not real.

I set the book down. I don't understand any of it. Wrapping my dressing gown around me, I open the doors onto the deck. I've had trouble walking on the boat; my balance isn't good. Now the ocean is so calm I barely notice it. The varnish is hot and tacky under my bare feet.

'Abigail?'

All around me the ocean laps at the hull. I put my hands on the railing, queen of all I survey. I don't like the sea; I never learned to swim. There's something about not being able to see through the waves to what's underneath. It's not just the fear of drowning. It's the size of the sea, the way it seems to go on forever. It makes me feel small, the opposite of sitting in a room surrounded by chairs, lampshades and yesterday's newspapers. Those things are there for me. The sea isn't there for anyone.

I trudge to the back of the boat and look down, trying to remember what's different about the picture. There's no white water . . .

The engine is quiet.

I remember the sound of the engine. Almost musical – a drone-like hum and, under that, a different vibration, a slow *thrum-thrum-thrum* like a pulse, a bass note that changed tempo depending how fast we were going. Now there is silence, but we're not in port. I don't know anything about sailing, but I think the water looks deep.

I turn around to the stairs on the left of the cabin doors and carefully start to climb. I've only been up these stairs once, when Abigail wanted to take photographs of me pretending to drive. I wouldn't be surprised if he was up here, hiding from his responsibilities with the baby, using all those dials and levers and flashing lights as an excuse not to do any real work. I open the door to the cockpit.

'Hello?'

There is nobody. The engine is off, and the lights are off. I flick a couple of switches. Nothing happens. I hobble back down to the deck. The sun is so strong it could pin me to the deck, and the baby is still crying.

'Abigail?'

I walk the strip of deck that runs down the side of the saloon, up to the bow of the ship. There is no one here, nothing to see except the glare off the polished wood.

Except, near the railings are a pair of shoes. The laces are still tied, as though someone kicked them off in a hurry. They're wet, bleeding twin puddles onto the deck. I look at the shoes for a long moment, trying to remember where I've seen them before. They are running shoes, neon yellow, the sort a young woman would wear . . .

But I can't remember.

I look over the side of the boat to see its name, painted blue on the white hull.

MNEMOSYNE

A memory surfaces of the first time we went to see the boat.

'How do you pronounce it?' Abigail had asked, looking at the painted name.

'Nemmo-sign,' he said, with confidence.

'Nem-oss-inny,' I said at the same moment. He ignored me. I don't know where that came from.

'Anyway,' he went on, 'I'll change the name when we get her back to England. Something classic like *Discovery*.'

Eejit.

I shuffle back down the boat and let myself into the cabin. It's hot in here. When the engine was running, you could come in from outside and feel the cool air. I close the door and turn to see Rene sitting on the sofa next to the baby, stroking his head. She looks up at the sound.

'Hello?'

'Rene? What are you doing here?'

'I dunno. I just woke up. Who are you?'

'It's me, Ella.' I stare down at Rene's frown for a long moment. 'Ella Campbell.'

'Ella? Naw.'

'I am, honest.' I walk over and sit on the sofa, with the baby between us. Rene is still wearing her school uniform – pleated skirt and knee-high socks, white cotton blouse. My friend peers at my face, brows knitting together.

'Oh aye, it is you, Ellie. You cut your hair short. You look like your nan.'

'You remember my nan?'

'She lived in that single-end on Gourlay Street. She made us buttery rollies that one time.'

I haven't thought of Gourlay Street, my nan, or buttery rollies for a long time. Rene's reappearance is like looking under a floorboard and finding a biscuit tin of childhood treasures. I have questions, but the baby chooses this moment to make a single, high-pitched cry. It sounds odd, and I realize he must be very hot, wrapped up in that blanket. I unwrap him and hold him in my arms again.

'Whose wean is that?'

Rene's accent is stronger than I remember. I hadn't realized my own had faded in the years since I left Glasgow.

'He's my daughter, Abigail's.'

'You have a daughter? So, this is your grandson . . .' Rene thinks for a moment. 'What's his name?'

'I don't remember.'

'You don't remember your own grandson's name?' Rene chuckles.

'I forget things. That's what being old is like.'

'Aye, I suppose.'

The baby is quiet, but his eyes dart around the room desperately. He's searching for the same person I am.

'What does it feel like, being old?' Rene sticks her chin out at me and squints as though trying to puzzle something out. I think for a minute, then say –

'What does it feel like being young?' I smile, confident that I've said something wise, but Rene isn't impressed.

'No, that's not an answer. I've always been young; I don't know any different. You've been young and old, and all the bits in the middle. So, what does it feel like?' She squints at me. 'Is it crap?'

I see my friend as an equal, but Rene doesn't see me the same. I feel like I'm looking from behind a mask. Something grotesque I've put on for Halloween and can't get off.

'It feels like . . . it feels like . . .' I shake my head in frustration. 'It feels no different! I feel no different. I'm the same person. You never feel grown up. You just feel like your body has gotten old and creaky and stupid. But you're the same, inside.'

'Okay . . .' Rene nods at her shoes for a second, thinking. 'Do you want to play a game?'

* * *

I wake with the baby still in my arms. The sun is on a different side of *Mnemosyne* now. I don't know whether the sun has moved, or we have. We played I Spy until I fell asleep. Rene is on the sofa opposite, on her front, trying to read a newspaper. Already this seems normal. I've spent a lifetime waiting to turn a corner and see my friend, so it doesn't seem strange that it's finally happened.

The baby is still sleeping. What *is* his name? I must find out; it's embarrassing not knowing. Abigail was always saying it. These facts haven't gone anywhere. My doctor explained it like this – all my memories are still there, in my head, but they've become like locked rooms. The corridors between them have caved in.

I forget everything my doctor tells me, but I've remembered this. A big house, with many rooms in many styles. But now the house has gone to seed, damp has rotted the timbers, the windows leak and mould spots the plaster. If I could get to those locked rooms, I could rescue some trinkets, bring them close to the centre of myself. Even now I have a few dry, tidy rooms, like a down-at-heel aristocrat who can't afford to fix the mansion.

I look down at the baby. He's a good boy. I'll put him in his bouncer while I get some pills. I push us off the sofa as the boat tilts.

'Y'all right?' Rene looks up from the paper.

'Just going to put the baby down.'

'Ellie, what's an "internet"?'

I think for a moment, but my understanding of the internet can barely be more than that of a child of 1936.

'It's a fishing thing.'

'Ah, right. Thought so.'

'I'm just going downstairs.'

'Okay. See if you can find any games to play.'

Downstairs, the lights are out. The doors to the cabins, where portholes let daylight in, are closed. I feel my way down the last few stairs and gasp. I'd forgotten the ankle-deep water.

Some floating thing bumps against my leg and makes me jump. I move forward, feeling against the walls.

I open the first door, the baby's room. A little light fills the corridor. I can see the object that bumped against my leg was a half-empty water bottle. There is more – a teething toy, shaped like the head of an elephant with flappy fabric ears; several jars and sticks which have escaped a bag of make-up; a blue plastic razor.

Is the water higher than before? It's hard to judge, when I only felt it in the dark. I move forward until I get to my own room. All the bedsheets are in a sodden mess on the floor. The contents of my bedside table have spilled out, moisturizing creams and incontinence pads cruising around the room like battleships. I wade back into the corridor.

Here I remember – I should let Abigail know about the water. I try the handle of her bedroom and find it unlocked.

'Abigail? Abigail?'

There is no response, but I wonder if she might be in the bathroom. I sit on the edge of the bed. I want to call his name, just in case he's the one in the bathroom. But I can't remember his name, or his face, or where he met Abigail in the first place, and so entered our lives.

The objects on the dresser have been stirred around but haven't fallen. Only the compact mirror has fallen and shattered. Eventually, I get up and knock on the bathroom door.

'Hello?'

There's no reply, so I turn the handle. Empty. I stand there, trying to remember what I know. Where is Abigail? I'm sure I'm being stupid. It doesn't help that I'm thirsty. Maybe Rene will remember what port we sailed from.

I trudge back around the bed. As I pass, I see something tucked under a pillow in a black case. I pull out a camera and sling it around my neck.

Before I go back up to the main cabin, I look into the room next to Abigail's. The one they've been using as the baby's playroom. The door opens easily. Water rushes around my ankles, as though there was more water in this room than in the corridor. A sodden teddy bear slides past me, face down. I notice that the wall – curved like the curve of the hull – is dented inward. The wood panelling is splintered. A little water dribbles down, like blood from a graze. Something floating in the water bumps against my leg.

I close and lock the door, then put the key in my pocket. I go back up to the main cabin.

'You find anything to do?' Rene kicks her legs back and forth.

'Not really.' I almost mention the playroom, but I don't. 'I found this camera. Maybe we can look at some pictures.'

'Y'can't look at pictures on a camera, Ellie. If y'open the back the film is all spoiled.'

'This one's different.'

I sit next to Rene. After some fiddling, the camera turns on and the little screen lights up with a picture of *Mnemosyne* and a man, arms raised in something like triumph. Rene gasps, mouth forming an 'O'. I'm pleased to have something fancier than Rene Mauchlen, even if it's not really mine.

'Wow, that's . . .' Rene searches for the right word. 'Braw.'

'See, you can look through the pictures like this.'

I flick through more pictures of him posing in front of his new boat. I remember now – we came on holiday so that he could buy the boat second-hand. He was going to sail us back to England. What went wrong?

'Is that your daughter?'

I look at the picture. A family at a restaurant table. On the left is Abigail, smiling brightly, hair tied back in a ponytail. On the right stands him, wearing the look of someone who thinks a stranger is about to drop his expensive camera. In the middle, with the baby on her lap, is a crumpled old woman.

Oh.

That's me.

'Here, you play with it.' I hand the camera to Rene, who folds her legs and bends herself close to the screen. I go over to the baby and stroke his head. He doesn't stir.

'Hello, baby.'

I prod him in the ribs. He still doesn't wake, even as I shake him a little. This isn't how a baby should look. I lift him into my arms and he's limp, like a wet rag. I carry him to the sofa and stroke his head, trying to think. There's a dip, running from one side of his head to the other. This means something, but what? God, I wish I weren't so old.

Rene comes over, peering at the baby. 'What's the matter?'

'I don't know . . . he's all floppy.'

'He looks peely-wally. Perhaps he's tired? Mam says I go floppy like that when I fall asleep next to the radio, and Pa has to carry me through to the next room.'

'But he was sleeping already.'

'Perhaps he's hungry?' Rene frowns.

'Yes, maybe. Oh, where's Abigail?'

'His mam?'

I nod. 'She's the only one who can feed him. But she's been gone for a while now.'

'If she's not around, he must be thirsty.'

'You look after him for a minute.'

'Aye, all right.'

I go to the little kitchen at one end of the living room. There's only enough room for me to stand here, surrounded by the surfaces. I look in the food cupboard first, in case there is baby formula. When Abigail was small, they encouraged you to use formula. Better than breastmilk, they said, fortified with vitamins. Abigail won't touch the stuff.

I can't see any here. Tins of beans, a packet of rice – nothing for a little baby to eat. Next, I look in the fridge. The light doesn't come on and there's no gust of cool air. There are the leftovers from a meal we had, an unopened pack of that salty Greek cheese Abigail likes, jars of pickles and olives.

Why is there no milk? We've had cups of tea and coffee. There are dirty cups in the living room. Abigail was always bringing me cups of tea, even though it meant I always needed the loo. I look in the cupboard under the sink. Here there are bottles of bleach, a dustpan and brush, a clear, green liquid in a squirty bottle, and a pallet of white plastic pots.

Yes – this is it. A quarter of the UHT milk pots have been used. One by one I rip the foil lids off the pots. I make a mess of screwing the parts of the bottle together. I take it all apart again and put the teat in the right way around. Finally, it's ready. I rush back through to the living room. The baby is unmoving.

Rene is stroking his head, unconcerned. She leans over him with the interest of one child in another. 'This is where I was' if they are older, 'this is where I will be' if they are younger, looking for clues to the mystery of their existence. My breath is fast; I can't calm myself. I sit down and pick up the unmoving baby, push the teat past his lips. He does not suck. The bottle just sits in his mouth. His eyes flutter for a second but nothing more. He looks dead.

'Come on, baby. Have a drink. You'll feel better.'

I take the bottle out of his mouth, put it back again. I pinch his cheek, bob him up and down. Nothing. I used to know how to get babies to drink. I put the bottle back in and, as I sit in that position, a memory surfaces. The baby is a different baby. Baby Abigail. I remember. I tilt the bottle down, toward his chest, so the teat is pressed against the roof of his mouth. I rub it from side to side. Without opening his eyes, his lips seal around the bottle and he starts to suck.

'Oh good,' Rene says matter-of-factly. She gets up on her

knees so she can stare out of the window at the sea. I don't
dare move as he takes the bottle. At first it's slow, just one
suck every five seconds or so. But it becomes faster, more
urgent. A minute passes.

'I wish I'd had a baby.'

Rene watches the waves. She looks calm, but her jaw is
clenched. I feel sick, but I should be brave in return.

'I'm sorry you're dead.'

Rene shrugs once and flops down on the sofa, fiddling with
the buttons on her blouse.

'S'all right. It's not so bad. I just wish I'd had time to do
more stuff.'

'We can do stuff now.'

She nods sulkily. 'What happened, after I died?'

I'm about to say I don't remember, then realize this would
be rude. I try to remember. 'Everyone was upset. The whole
school. All our year came to sing at the church.'

'And Mam? And Pa?'

'Of course.'

'And Robert?'

It takes me a moment to remember Robert as he was to
Rene. Nine years to our seven, skinny and quiet.

'He was there.'

'Was he all right, without me?'

'I think he was angry.'

'At who?'

'At everyone. At me.'

'Why you?' Rene looks at me, puzzled.

'Because . . . because I kept you out in the cold. In Paddy's Park all those hours while you coughed.'

'Nah.' Rene shrugs. 'It would still have happened. My lungs were bad. Springburn has all those smoky factories.'

'Well, I felt bad.'

'Y'shouldn't have. Did Robert forgive you?'

'I think so . . .' I change the subject. 'Are you hungry?'

Rene shakes her head.

'Not any more.'

There's a sucking sound – the bottle is empty. Rene comes to the kitchen with me and puzzles over the empty cartons, sniffing one suspiciously. By the time I get back to the sofa the baby has his eyes open. When I put the bottle to his mouth, he thrashes his head and tries to swipe it out of my hand. He succeeds on the third try and it rolls with the tilt of *Mnemosyne* to the far side of the room. He wails with gusto.

'You should sing him a lullaby,' Rene says, helpfully.

'I can't think of one.'

I go downstairs to find the nappy bag and a change of clothes. I pause at the top of the stairs, heart pounding. I mustn't stop. The baby grow is difficult. Even when it's done there are spare poppers and bits of fabric are bunched up, but he's dressed and clean.

It doesn't fix the crying.

For five minutes I stop, leaving him with Rene. I drink a glass of tepid tap water and eat chicken in white sauce from the tin. I take tablets for my back. I know there are other tablets I should be taking, but Abigail is the one who doles them out in my weekly organizer.

Still the baby cries.

Using cushions and a blanket from the sofa, I make a sort of crib on the floor, enough that I know he won't roll away. The water has dried in the sun by now. I put him down; I need to think. Thinking is hard enough, but with the constant wailing it's impossible. Rene is sitting on the sofa with a guitar in her lap. I'd forgotten about it until now. She is struggling to reach the frets with one hand and get her other arm over the body.

'This one's bigger than mine . . .' She plays a few wobbly notes, the beginnings of 'Frère Jacques', then gives up. 'Can you play?'

'Perhaps, a little.'

'You should play us something. The baby might like it.'

I take the guitar. I don't want to admit I can't remember any songs. I can't even remember the one I played last night. But there are others like that one. Seven of them.

I remember a line from somewhere . . . *The seven ancient modes are not scales in the true sense. They do not specify particular notes. Rather, they are patterns, spacing the notes we can play closer or further apart like the notches on a key. And that is what the modes are — seven keys to this earlier music.*

With that, I remember the second song. I sit on the sofa, position the guitar while Rene scoots closer, and start to play.

The opening bars see-saw between A minor and B minor. The tune I'm humming rises and falls gently like waves.

The baby stops crying. He watches us, me playing and Rene pressed into my side. I reach the end of the tune and circle back to the beginning, closing my eyes.

'When did you get so good?'

I ignore Rene's question. I have a familiar feeling. We are going down. The sea is draining, like water in a lock. It feels like being in a descending lift. It gets stronger as I play, until I daren't stop playing.

Down, down, down, into darkness.

The Maiden

1948

ELLA IS SITTING AT her window, with Rene's guitar resting on her knee as the sun rises over Springburn. There's steam curling up from the back court, where Mrs Kerr has lit a fire in the building where they wash their clothes. It takes a while for the cast iron tub to heat up, but Mrs Kerr rises every morning before the cockerel, and the little shed is puffing like a traction engine.

Ella plays and sings, looking through the rising clouds to the grey city beyond. She likes to start the day by practising. Ella never had music lessons like Rene did. She taught herself from books that her dad bought at the big music store on Sauchiehall Street. This tune, called 'The Maiden', is from one of those. She knows it so well, it's like she's been playing it her whole life.

It's eleven years since Rene died. Ella wonders what her

friend would have made of the last eleven years. It seems strange to her that Rene never saw the war. She wasn't there when they announced it over the radio, or when they built the timber scaffolds in front of the tenements to protect the entrances. The wood was rough-hewn from pines and much of it still had the mossy bark left on. It looked like something out of a picture book, like *Robin Hood and the Sheriff of Nottingham*.

And of course, Rene wasn't there when their fathers left. She wasn't there when the bombs fell, intended for the ship-yards on the Clyde but often straying into quiet streets. She wasn't there to keep Ella company on the half-days when school was closed in the mornings. She wasn't there when they'd gathered them in the gymnasium under the school to sleep the night. Ella remembers thinking that, if Rene had been there, it would have felt like an adventure. Without her, it was more time to be scared on her own.

Now the war is over, though much of the city lies in ruins, and her childhood seems further away than a mere decade. Her father hasn't returned yet, because it takes time to put all the pieces back in the toybox. Rene's father, who she called Pa, won't be coming back at all, killed in Africa not by tank or grenade but by a tiny, biting insect that gave him malaria. At least her friend didn't have to read that telegram, didn't have to watch her mother fade to a ghost.

All these thoughts pass fleetingly through Ella's mind as she plays, because playing familiar tunes does not require thought. Playing feels like opening a door to a private room where she can go and collect herself. That's why she does it – not to get better or impress anyone, but only to feel free for a while, a bird in flight.

Ella hadn't started playing the guitar straight away. Before the funeral, she'd put the guitar in its case under her bed, pushing it right to the back and filling in the space with everything she had – a box of wooden dolls, tangled skipping ropes and the teddy bears she already considered herself too old for.

Ella didn't mind being the keeper of the instrument, so long as she didn't have to look at it. She couldn't bear the thought of anyone else seeing the guitar, let alone playing it. It would feel like a betrayal to let anyone else have it. She told her parents she wouldn't be learning the instrument, and they had agreed with a shrug.

All the time, the guitar lay silent in its case under the bed. Or at least, it *should* have been silent. At night, when the house was quiet, Ella would turn over in bed, and the creak of the iron springs was answered by a hum. The noise was so soft she could never be sure if she had really heard it. Not a plucked note, but the gentle buzz you would hear if you opened the case. Ella would turn over again, to see if the noise repeated, but it was never clear enough to be sure. The guitar was mocking her.

Finally, she'd had enough. Ella didn't want to look at the guitar, but if she got it out, she could lay an old blanket over the strings, so they would be muted. After the lights had been turned out, but while there was still enough of a glow from the fire to see by, Ella had gotten out of bed, pulled everything aside and dragged the case out. She lifted the lid and sat staring at the guitar. The blanket she'd intended to put over the strings was next to her, and Ella felt suddenly guilty, as though it were a sack for drowning kittens.

The next morning, before she'd even been out to visit the second-floor toilet, Ella told her parents she was going to learn guitar. Her father had given her a lecture about not wasting money only to change your mind later, but she had promised. He didn't seem to believe her, but they'd gone to the biggest music shop in town, where he asked a sales clerk for a guide.

Left to herself for a moment, Ella had scuffed her feet and looked around the shop. Along one wall were booths where you could play the latest records on big headphones. Three young men were bobbing their heads to different tempos. She had gone to look through a rack of music books. There were a lot of books about music, Ella thought – who had time to read them all? They were the size of sheet music, no thicker than a quarter inch. They had titles like *A Theory of Harmony*, *Patterns for Improvisation* and *A Repository of Melodic Ideas*. Sitting among them, one title caught her eye.

The Songs of the Dead
by
Jack Shapiro

Was it that word, 'dead', that made her stop? Or the whole title, like a puzzle to be solved, for how can the dead sing? She thought of Rene, who had liked to sing. Ella had reached the book down from the shelf. There were more words than notes in this book, which contained just seven songs, or 'exercises':

1. The Child (Ionian)

2. The Maiden (Dorian)

3. The Lover (Mixolydian)

4. The Rebel (Aeolian)

5. The Matron (Phrygian)

6. The Mother (Lydian)

7. The Crone (Locrian)

'Ah, these books aren't primers, Miss.' The sales clerk has reappeared with her father, carrying a book called *The Complete Guide to Guitar*. 'They're for the advanced player.'

Ella ignored him and held the book up to her father. 'Can I get this one?'

Her father looked at the clerk, who had pulled a face. 'That one is rather esoteric, sir. I think your daughter might be better . . .'

Her father had flipped the book over, read the title, and looked at Ella with something like understanding.

'That's all right. We'll get the both of them.'

Ella plays 'The Maiden' through for the fourth time, watching the steam from Mrs Kerr's washing. She wonders what she thought she would find in *The Songs of the Dead*. It's full of strange ideas about life and music, with hand-drawn pictures that look like they belong in a spell book.

'Eleanor! Come get your breakfast,' her mother calls from the next room.

Being an only child, Ella has always had her own bedroom. But now, with just her and her mother, the house feels almost luxurious with space – a room each! Her mother says that being left to her own devices made Ella wilful, but Ella isn't sure. She gets up and smooths her new dress out. She likes the fabric – little white flowers on a blue background – but can't help feel the cinched waist would look better on someone with actual hips.

'Come on love, before it gets cold.'

Her mother has made pancakes, once a treat, though the milk used for the mixture is so watered down that they are leathery, and there's no sweetness to be had. At least there's a little butter to spread. Ella was always scrawny, but the last few years have been especially lean. Hunger hasn't stopped her upward growth, and she feels like a malnourished house plant, grown too tall in the search for sunshine. At least she has a job. She can afford to put a bit more food on the table, when the ration book allows.

The pancakes are gone in a minute and they sit in silence,

sipping the tea. Ella looks at her father's shoes, which have been propped on the rail around the hearth since he left, so that they're inclined towards the fire. Every week or so her mother will take the shoes and polish them, if only to get the dust off, but then they go back in front of the fire as though he will put them on any minute and needs them warmed.

'You better get off. Don't want to be late.'

'Want me to pick anything up on my way home?'

'You're all right, love.'

Eleanor looks over at her mum, in her floral pinny and hairnet. She is only in her early forties but looks like an old woman. Ella wonders if she'll look like this in twenty years' time.

'Bye, Mum.' She kisses her on the head, then goes to fetch the satchel that she wears to work.

* * *

It's a quiet morning in the bank – the worst kind. By the time Ella has ridden the tram into town and walked to St Vincent Street, she's ready to lose a few hours to work. Ella is grateful for her job but that doesn't mean she has to enjoy it. It's better than a munitions factory or sewing uniforms till her fingers bleed, but that doesn't make it any less dull.

The main hall is grand – a wide checkerboard floor, curving wooden counters polished until they shine, and a glass dome in the ceiling to flood it with light. The grandeur of the dome is reduced only slightly by the crosses of brown tape over every pane to stop them shattering in an air raid.

Ella takes up her place at the counter. She deals with an update to a pension book, serves a small withdrawal and helps an elderly gentleman make out a cheque. But there are gaps between all of these, and the gaps are the worst. There are three other tellers, all of them men too old to go to war. There's no music, and they're not allowed books either, or magazines. Not that Ella can imagine any of her colleagues reading anything as frivolous as a magazine. They are allowed to talk to one another, if there are no customers to serve, but the men never stoop to make small talk with Ella. Sometimes she wonders whether they think that, if they are unpleasant enough to her, she might leave and be replaced by a man. Mostly she thinks they're just rude.

She wishes she could listen to some music. She knows she could do anything if there were music. Her fantasy which recurs the most – more often than tables piled high with food or beds piled high with silken sheets – is endless music. The fantasy is vague, almost abstract. Sometimes she imagines the music following her, like the soundtrack of a film. Other days she imagines disappearing into the music altogether, floating away into a lifelong song.

Today Ella has fixed the handle of a rubber stamp with her attention and is trying her best to let her mind wander when she becomes aware of a customer standing on the other side of the counter. She snaps to attention.

'Good morning, sir, how can I help you?'

'Hey.'

'Hello? Oh!'

She didn't recognize him at first, perhaps because he has grown, or perhaps because she hadn't expected to see him here. It's Rene's brother, Robert. She wonders if Rene would recognize her brother now, changed from a scrawny nine-year-old to a young man, broad-shouldered, with his curly auburn hair cut short enough that it can be gelled and neatly combed down. A single curl stands in rebellion near his temple. He's holding a parcel under his arm, wrapped in brown paper. He still looks like he has something on his mind.

'How are you, Ella?'

'I'm fine, fine.' She nods, not used to making small talk. 'You?'

He bobs his head agreeably. 'Fine, aye. Nothing to complain about.'

'You got a job at the docks, Mum said?'

'Got myself an apprenticeship as an electrician. But they sent me on an errand to head office, so I'm in town . . .'

The explanation seems to suggest something else. Ella becomes aware of her colleagues turning their heads to look. She hopes the manager isn't lurking in the background somewhere.

'How can I help you, Robert?'

'Oh, I don't have an account here.'

Ella frowns. 'Would you like to open one?'

'Oh, no, no . . .'

If she once felt intimidated by the two-year difference in

their ages, Ella has forgotten. Her anger, never at the end of an especially long fuse, flares.

'What do you *want*, Robert? This is a bank, not a dinner dance.'

Does she hear one of the men snigger? Robert's eyebrows rise, but he looks more amused than offended.

'I was just wondering when you take your lunch? I wondered if you fancied something to eat? I'll pay.'

Ella feels several conflicting emotions at once, primarily embarrassment but also fear, curiosity and residual anger.

Her stomach growls.

'Something to eat?'

* * *

By the time the hour hand of the main hall clock has crawled to one, Ella is so nervous that she steps out and immediately accepts Robert's offer of a cigarette. He lights it for her with a brass Zippo. She takes a quick drag, appraising him properly for the first time. Smart shoes, trousers pressed, but his burgundy tie is askew. He doesn't look out of place in his beige electrician's coat – even at twenty, there is something of the absent-minded professor about Robert.

They walk in silence through the city centre, which is quiet even at lunch hour. Sometimes it feels as though the city is being slowly deserted and nobody is telling them. Ella feels she will wake up one day and find herself alone in this crumbling maze. She's light-headed from the cigarette. There's a cold wind blowing down Buchanan Street and they hunch into it, drawing a little closer together.

Miss Cranston's tea room is warm and brightly lit. The air inside is steamy. A girl at the door takes their coats and shows them to a table.

'Have you been here before?'

'No, I haven't . . .' Ella puzzles over her menu, because she can't think of a single thing to say to the man across the table. While not exactly scandalous, this meeting will inspire gossip. The sort of thing a young woman should avoid if she wants to maintain her good name. Ella feels that, through no fault of her own, she's never had a good name to tarnish. Everyone in the cafe seems to be side-eyeing them.

'You should order something.'

Robert nods, gets the waitress' attention, orders a pot of coffee and afternoon tea. The waitress nods and retreats.

'Coffee *and* tea?' Ella asks, incredulously. 'I thought we were having something to eat?'

Robert smiles, not unkindly.

'Afternoon tea *is* something to eat – sandwiches and scones and little cake things. You'll like it.'

'Oh.' Ella reddens. 'That sounds nice.'

They sit in uncomfortable silence for a long minute. Just as earlier at the bank, Ella feels she needs to say something to move things along.

'Look, Robert, this is very nice . . . I'm flattered . . . But don't you think I'm a bit young?'

'Young?' Robert rubs behind his ear, a habit of his when he's confused.

'Yes, I mean . . . I'm eighteen, you're what? Twenty now?'

Realization seems to dawn on Robert and he panics. 'Oh! No that's not . . . what I mean is . . .'

Ella watches him fluster for a minute, completely lost.

'What I mean to say is, I'm not trying to court you.'

At this exact moment two waitresses appear, bearing coffee and a tiered silver stand, laden with sandwiches and cakes. Robert clears his throat and looks up at them.

'Sir?' one of them asks, eyebrows raised.

'Yes,' he says, sounding as though he's being strangled by his necktie, gesturing to the table in front of them. They set to work laying out everything.

When they are gone, Ella and Robert sit looking at each other. Her mouth twitches with a smile, which breaks into a full-blown grin, and then she's laughing. Robert smiles, then breaks down, suppressed laughter shaking him. In the quiet of the tea room, the moment is amplified so that Ella cannot stop herself from laughing, gripping the table with one hand, wiping her eyes with the other. People are *definitely* looking now, but she doesn't care. This is the best lunch break she's ever had.

When they've calmed down, they take a breath and look at each other again. Robert takes the coffee pot in hand.

'Shall I?'

'Please. Mind if I . . .?'

'Go on, you must be hungry.'

Ella puts a few of the little triangular sandwiches on her plate – ham and cucumber, egg and cress, something fishy that might be salmon. She starts to eat. The white bread is light and fluffy, the inside spread thickly with butter. She pauses to add a generous serving of cream to her coffee and three spoons of sugar. The tension has gone between them, as they go about the little rituals of serving themselves.

'God, I wish I worked here instead of the bank.'

'You must make more than a waitress?'

'Not by much, I reckon. They don't pay me anything like what the men get. If I worked here, I could take some left-overs home.'

Robert smiles.

'I see what you mean. Come to think of it, I think I'd rather be a waitress than an electrician.'

'You'd look very fetching in that black and white pinny.'

'I don't think I've got the legs.'

This makes Ella grin as she's biting down on a cream scone, and her resulting imprecision makes jam spurt onto her hand.

'Bugger,' she mutters under her breath, licking it off and reaching for a napkin. A man in the corner audibly tuts.

'You're going to get me kicked out of this place.' Robert laughs.

'Now that *would* be a memorable lunch break.'

'I think you're supposed to save the scones for after you've finished the sandwiches, no?'

She shrugs. 'They looked too good; I couldn't help myself.'

'Here, you should have one of mine.'

'You sure?'

'I'm not that hungry.'

Without waiting to be told again, Ella slides the scone onto her plate and gulps some more coffee.

'Shouldn't you be telling me why I'm here?' she asks.

Robert's eyebrows rise for a moment, as though he had forgotten he was the one who asked her here. 'Oh, yes. So . . . you still have the guitar?'

Ella stops midway through the miniature chocolate cake she's stuffing into her mouth and swallows hard.

'Look, I know it belonged to Rene. And I wouldn't blame you for wanting it back . . . But I've grown very attached to it.'

'No, that's not what I mean.' Robert spreads his hands on the table. 'Thing is, your mum was talking to my mum, and she said that you got really good. At the guitar, I mean.'

'No.' Ella shakes her head. 'I mean, that's nice of her to say. I'm not bad, I guess, but I taught myself.'

'She said you could play along with anything on the radio, just by listening.'

Ella shrugs, not confirming or denying.

'The thing is, I play a bit of saxophone, and I've got a band.'

'Oh?'

'Well, it's not really *my* band. The guy whose band it is fell off some scaffolding at the docks a couple of weeks ago.'

'That's awful!'

'He's okay. Well, not okay, but he'll be okay. He's all in casts at the moment, and he'll not be playing guitar any time soon . . .'

Ella starts to put things together.

'You're asking *me*? I've never played in public, not even in a talent show.'

'Well, I'd want to hear you play first. If you're interested.'

Ella pours herself another cup of coffee and catches a passing waitress. 'Can we have some more cream please?' She takes her time stirring in the sugar.

'What do you think?'

She takes a deep breath. 'Can't you get anyone else? I can't be the only guitarist around our way.'

All of Springburn is musical, she thinks. In their close alone, Ella can think of two trumpeters, the hermit in the single-end who plays the C melody sax and a drummer in the basement. The family upstairs all seem to play piano and violin.

'I am not saying you're the only choice, I just thought . . .'

'There's Mr Mactaggart up the road.'

'Bill Mactaggart must be in his sixties – he doesn't want to go around with a bunch of teenagers playing residentials in a badminton club.'

'You have a residential?'

Robert shrugs by way of downplaying the term. 'Once a week at the club on Keppochhill Road, you know the one?'

'Never been there, but aye.'

'Well, it's okay. We play every Wednesday and we get the takings on the door. But the owner says we have to replace Jimmy on guitar if we want to keep our spot.'

'How do you split the takings?'

'Evenly. It's not loads, but the other night we took home three and six each.'

Ella pauses in ferrying the last cake to her mouth.

'When can I audition?'

Robert grins. 'What are you doing tonight?'

* * *

The men's changing rooms of the badminton club are unheated, so Ella sits on a wooden bench with her coat still on. The air smells like BO and talc. Resting on her lap is the heaviest guitar she's ever held. It's an Epiphone, an American import with a sunburst finish and violin cut-outs. Ella has never played on a full-sized guitar like this, only on a three-quarter scale bought for a seven-year-old. She has no time to get used to stretching her hands over the wider frets.

Worse still, there's a cable running from the guitar to a menacing metal box at her side, with the words 'HIGH VOLTAGE' stencilled in red on the back. Another cable runs from this box out of the room, to where Robert is searching for a plug socket. Apparently, he made the amplifier himself from spare parts. Ella keeps her hands off the guitar strings to avoid fatal electrocution.

There is a sudden hum from the box.

'There you go!' Robert shouts from the hallway.

The two other boys eye her. They seemed amiable enough when Robert introduced her, but it's clear she'll have to win them over. Willie Barr sits on the opposite bench a little further down, with his bass drum, cymbal and snare arranged in front of him. Sandy (no surname given) stands, warming up with scales on his double bass. Robert strides back over.

'Well? You should try something.'

Ella takes a deep breath and gingerly places her fingers on the strings. The humming goes expectantly quiet. She holds down G major and strums. In the small, tiled space of the changing room, the sound from the little box is enormous. It rings in her ears like a bell. She looks to Robert, who is grinning at her surprise. He turns a dial on the amplifier and the volume is tamed.

'You ready to try something?'

*   *   *

Despite the combined weight of the amplifier and the guitar in its case, Ella floats home. She can't remember feeling more exhilarated. Perhaps when Rene was alive, perhaps all that time ago. What has she been doing since? What the hell has she been doing for eleven years, when she could have been doing this?

Her fingers are stinging, her ears are ringing. As of twenty minutes ago, she is a proud member of the Jimmy Grey All Stars. When Ella is more established in the band, she will suggest changing their name to someone who was actually playing in it. She races up the stairs of their close and fumbles the key into the lock.

'Mum, I'm home! Sorry I'm late, I—'

Before she can finish her sentence, a man steps from the door to the front room, his face half obscured by the shadows. He stands there, unspeaking.

'Dad?'

She puts down the guitar and amplifier just inside the doorway and steps closer. The man who might be her father stands his ground.

'You're late.'

'Yes, I . . . Dad?'

Ella moves forward, pulling him into a hug. He's no taller than she is now, which strikes her as very odd. He puts his hands on her shoulders and pushes her back to arm's length, looking her up and down. Her mother is standing in the doorway to the front room, smiling uncertainly. She looks like she's been crying.

'Come on, the both of you. I'll make a pot of tea.'

Ella's father grunts and lets go her shoulders. She stands in the dark of the corridor, listening to her parents talk to each other for the first time in years. She feels as though she has forgotten how to walk, how to move. She has waited so long for his return, so why this weight in her stomach? The man in the next room looks like her father, sounds like her father, even smells like her father – coal soap, Brylcreem and Ogden's pipe tobacco in a precise ratio. But for all that, the man in the next room fails to unlock any of the memories Ella has of him. She can't shake the feeling that he's a doppelganger.

A dark reflection.

* * *

It is the third Wednesday night they've played the badminton club, and Ella has never seen it so busy. She wouldn't be big-headed enough to suppose this was anything to do with her if Robert hadn't said so himself.

'They're coming to see you, Ella!'

'Pfft, no way.'

'They are too. There aren't any other bands with a girl on guitar.'

Ella smiled. 'So, I'm a circus attraction? The bearded lady, that kind of thing?'

'No, not like that. I mean, name me another band that has a girl in it. Not a singer, I mean.'

Ella knows he's right – she can think of women who sing, and the music halls have plenty of women who play piano, or niche instruments like the harp. There are no dance bands with a woman.

'Well, let's just hope the novelty doesn't wear off too soon.'

Robert rolled his eyes. 'Well, I think it's great.'

Tonight, they've run through their repertoire of dance tunes, foxtrots and waltzes, with the occasional tango as an 'exotic'. Robert has been sharing his gramophone records with her so that she can learn new tunes at home. She's even learned to sing a few of them, though she knows she's a better guitarist than a singer.

When everything is done, she packs away quickly while Robert goes to talk to the manager about getting paid. She helps Willie disassemble his drums, which live in the back room of the club unless they're needed for another gig.

'Thanks, Ella. Will you join us for a dram?'

The manager lets them buy beer if they drink it in the back room. Ella shakes her head quickly, not meeting his eyes.

'No, I should get home. My dad will be waiting for me.'

Sandy looks up from the chord chart he's frowning over.

'That's a shame,' Willie says. 'He should let you stay out a bit later.'

'I'll walk you home, if you like,' Sandy says.

Ella is taken aback. Sandy never speaks, to her or anyone else, unless it is to ask a question about the music.

'Yeah, all right.'

Robert comes back, bearing a plate of sandwiches from behind the bar. He puts it down and turns out his pocket onto the nearest beer-stained table, then sorts the coins into four piles.

'Good news – we can all retire. Five and two.'

Willie rubs his hands together in exaggerated glee.

'Five and two! A few more nights of this and I'll be able to buy the radio instead of us shelling out the rent every month. Jimmy falling off that scaffold is the best thing that ever happened to us!'

Robert punches him on the shoulder, but Willie just laughs. Willie has three younger sisters and no dad. He makes a joke out of everything, but Ella knows that he isn't doing gigs for the fun of it.

'Want to fritter some of this hard-earned cash on a drink?' Robert turns to Ella.

Whenever Robert talks to her, the other two turn away, as though it's a private conversation that needs to be respected.

''Fraid not; I need to get home. Sandy's going to walk me back.'

Robert rubs behind his ear. 'All right then. See you on Friday for practice?'

'See you then.'

'I'll let you know if we get any other gigs, of course.'

'Of course.'

'Right, well . . . night then.'

Ella turns to grab her gear.

'Oh! You should have my half of the sandwich.'

'You sure?' She smiles.

'Aye, Mum always has something waiting for me.'

'I'll have it, if it's going wastin',' Willie teases.

Ella grabs the half of ham sandwich before he can and shoves it in her mouth with a grin.

*　*　*

It's cold out, but the sky is scattered with stars which shimmer in the black pools of rainwater. Ella and Sandy walk in silence.

Her shoulders ache from carrying the guitar and amplifier to-and-fro, but none of the All Stars owns a push bike, let alone a car, so all gigs must be within walking distance or they'd need to scrounge a lift.

She shouldn't complain, of course – with his double bass strapped to his back, Sandy looks like a skinny-legged ant carrying a leaf several times his weight. He seems nice enough, and plays well, but Ella knows almost nothing about him. He has a good job at the docks – an apprentice draughtsman. He's older than the rest of them, stayed in school longer. She thinks they're going to walk the whole way in silence when suddenly he pipes up.

'Your dad giving you trouble for staying out?'

'He . . .' Ella isn't sure what to say, though she sure wants to talk to about it. 'He just got back from service, I think he's a little . . .'

She trails off, not knowing how to express it.

'My dad got back a couple of months ago.' Sandy looks straight ahead.

'Oh?'

'Rob and Willie don't understand – Willie never had a dad, growing up, and Rob . . . well, you know.'

Ella isn't sure where this is going but lets him talk.

'I'm just saying, I know how it is.'

She isn't sure that she does know what he means, because it hasn't occurred to her that there might be something in common between the families of men returning from war. To her, it's just her dad. His problems are his own. The way he won't say anything as they sit around eating breakfast. The way he will slope off to the pub as soon as it opens. The way she hears him through the walls in the night, shouting in his sleep.

'I think . . . I think it'll be better when he gets a job.' She looks at Sandy, who looks back, briefly.

'Yeah, I'm sure it will be.' He doesn't sound very sure. 'I guess what I'm saying is, when they left they were our dads, but now they're back they're soldiers. They're used to routine and being given orders and giving orders. And they're used to excitement and being surrounded by other soldiers. They're used to . . . I don't know.' He shakes his head.

They're getting close to Bedlay Street now, and Ella doesn't know what to say, but she feels that something is going unsaid.

'Are you all right, Sandy?'

He looks at her, a little startled perhaps. 'Oh, yeah, of course. I'm just saying, if you ever need to talk . . . If there's ever trouble . . .'

He trails off. Ella is home. She puts a hand on his shoulder. 'Thanks.'

'No bother. See you Friday.'

'Aye, see you Friday.'

* * *

'I can't believe they fired you!'

A month has passed since they were last in the Buchanan Street tea room. This time, Ella is paying.

'Ach, I was expecting it, as soon as the men started coming back.'

The bank hadn't marked Ella's leaving in any way. Just a final pay packet and a letter from the manager. She wouldn't mind if her dad was bringing in anything, but he still hasn't found work at the docks. At least she's been saving up. The Robert Mauchlen All Stars (*Fresh from a successful tour of Clydebank and Yoker!*) have gone from strength to strength. The residency at the badminton club still brings in a good amount every week, and a few of the town halls have been curious enough to book the band with the girl guitarist. Robert is talking about expanding the band, looking for another horn player so they can get bigger slots.

Ella, to her surprise, loves playing. She only started for the money and expected to hate sharing her music with other people. But she likes seeing people dance to what she's playing. She likes the fleeting moments when the four of them manage to lock together, like four parts of the same machine. She likes being part of a group, for the first time in her life.

'So, what'll you do?' Robert pours her another cup of coffee.

'Oh, I'll find something. My dad wants me to find a nice boy to marry and forget about jobs.'

Robert smiles. 'Must be good to have him back?'

Ella nods, but the gesture is automatic. Since her conversation with Sandy, she can't stop thinking about all the families all around her who have suddenly got their husbands, fathers and sons back. Men who had done unspeakably brave, unspeakably awful things to defend those same families. Every time she wakes to her father's night terrors, she wonders what he did, and what it has done to him.

'How's the apprenticeship going?'

'I dunno. Fine, I guess, but I don't want to be there forever.'

'No? You seem good at it.'

He shrugs. 'You should see it, Ella – these huge skeletons of ships, half in shadow, and all these men crawling around like insects.'

'Sounds impressive.'

'Aye, well it is. But it makes you feel small. And the noise!'

'Worse than practising in the changing rooms?'

'Such a din. Rivets being hammered and sheets of metal slamming together. I've met men who've been working there thirty years and they can't hear what you're saying right next to them.'

'You should pack up and get a plane to Hollywood.'

'Not Hollywood, perhaps.' He shrugs, stirring his coffee. 'But London, maybe.'

'Oh, aye?' She pokes his shoulder, making him grin shyly.

'Well, not right away. I'll finish the apprenticeship. Something to fall back on.'

She bites into a scone, staring past Robert through the clouded windows to Buchanan Street, all shades of shiny grey in the rain.

'That's what I should want, I suppose,' she thinks out loud.

'Something to fall back on?'

'Yeah. But I just want to play.'

Robert smiles. 'I'm glad I talked you down from your tower.'

'I just wish it was enough to pay the bills.'

'If you moved to London, maybe it would be. They have all the big shows, more dance halls than you can count . . .'

He trails off, looking at her intently.

'Well, if you ever go to London, give me a call.'

He nods once. 'I will.'

They eat in companionable silence, Robert having most of the coffee, pushing most of the sandwiches and cakes to Ella's side of the stand.

'I was going to ask . . .' he begins.

'Yeah?'

'You and Sandy?'

The question, if it can be called one, doesn't surprise her. She and Sandy have walked back from most gigs since that first time. She could say that he lives close, but of course Robert lives closer.

'I like him, but there's nothing going on. We don't even talk, really.'

Does she imagine that Robert looks a little relieved?

'No, of course. I just wanted to check he wasn't bothering you. And he's been real quiet recently, I wondered . . .'

She shakes her head. 'No, he's nice. Is it just him and his parents at home?'

'Aye, same as us. He's an older brother that got called up, but he's not back yet. I guess his dad got priority with being older.'

'What's his dad like?'

Robert frowns, puzzled by the question. 'I only met him once or twice. Not a big music fan but seemed nice enough. Why?'

'No reason. What records have you brought me today?'

* * *

Over the weeks, Ella spends more and more time with Robert. She might feel self-conscious if they hadn't clarified at the outset that they are not dating. Robert is a friend.

They go to the cinema a lot, mostly the Oxford on Keppochhill Road, a converted part of the Corporation Tramway Building. Ella prefers Prince's, where Harry Houdini performed years ago, but it's closed for refurbishment. Sometimes they go to the Kinema instead, which is nearest to Bedlay Street and is cheap, but it never shows the new releases. They call it 'The Coffin', either because it's shaped like one, tapering toward the screen at the foot end, or because it's so close to Sighthill Cemetery, where Rene is buried.

They buy lumps of nougat with nuts in and sit respectably near to the screen. They watch cowboy movies and gangster movies and epic movies with lots of men in togas. The pictures glow with a Hollywood light that Ella has never seen shining down on Springburn. She's never gone to the cinema this much in her life, happy to sit at home with the radio, but her mum doesn't complain about the expense.

At weekends they see black and white films at the Communist Meeting Hall, which feature bombed-out tanks in snowy fields and men marching across a frozen landscape.

As propaganda goes, they're pretty obvious, but Robert talks earnestly about the redistribution of wealth and seizing the means of production and Ella smiles and says she'd like to see him do that.

Robert is interested in everything; he's like a walking museum. Most times Ella sees him, he's got a book he's ferrying to or from the public library. She's seen him reading books about German philosophy, the history of perspective in Western art, and how to forage wild food. Willie takes the piss, but Robert just smiles and shrugs as though it's a harmless addiction like cigarette smoking.

One evening as Ella's walking back with Sandy, he says:

'You like Robert, don't you?'

'I like him fine . . .' Ella knows she sounds defensive.

'It's all right,' Sandy says, looking straight ahead. 'I like him too.'

Later, she will wish she had talked to him about it. But Ella says nothing and Sandy says nothing in return. When they get to her close, he looks as though he's ready to run.

'See you soon, Ella.'

She sets down the guitar and amplifier, pulls him and his double bass into a hug, and pecks him on the cheek.

'See you soon, Sandy.'

He looks at her, smiles, and nods once in acknowledgement. She watches him walk down Bedlay Street and disappear.

* * *

Sometimes Willie joins them at the cinema, but most of his money goes on his sisters. If he comes along, they buy his nougat for him. Sandy never comes along. Ella always puts money aside but starts to feel the gigs are just paying for the movies. She doesn't mind. A couple of months pass this way. One evening, Robert and Ella are walking down Gourlay Street on the way back from a screening of *The Wizard of Oz*, which has finally made its debut at the Kinema.

'You should come see the shipyard sometime.'

'Where'd this come from?' she asks, handing back the cigarette they're sharing. Cigarettes are a luxury, so it's not strange that she's sharing one with Robert.

'I dunno. I work there. Sandy and Willie work there. I thought you might be interested.'

'What are you going to do, get me a welding job?'

Robert's lips curl around the cigarette, holding the smoke to extract as much goodness as possible. He exhales his answer:

'I'd say you're built more like a riveter.'

She punches him on the shoulder. 'Shut it, Mauchlen.'

'I just thought you might be curious, that's all.'

Ella shrugs, accepting the cigarette back. 'Maybe I am. But it's not going to work if I show up in overalls, is it?'

'I might know another way.'

* * *

The sun has set over Glasgow. It's a dry night, broken clouds scudding in a high wind that doesn't reach the ground. The moon is a couple of days from being full. The kind of night the army avoid for daring raids and ambushes, Ella thinks. She's holding a bundle tied in a piece of old tablecloth while Robert inspects the chain link fence.

'I swear it's around here somewhere . . .'

'Maybe they fixed it.'

'It's been here for ages and they didn't . . .'

Her parents think she's at a rehearsal. She didn't dare invent a concert in case they found out otherwise, though her dad had questioned the need for a rehearsal when they play so often.

'We need to learn new songs, Dad, or people get bored.'

'You can't learn on your own?'

'We have to learn how to play them together.'

'You'd think you didn't want to be in the house with us.'

'Don't be like that, Dad.'

She had gotten out eventually, after more guilt tactics. Now she's wondering if it was all for nothing.

'Maybe we should give up. We could see if Willie's up for going to the pictures.'

'Hang on a minute . . .' Robert shines his tin torch on a new bit of fence. 'Ah! Here we go.'

He raises the corner of fence like he's raising a curtain for her to step through. Ella hands him the bundle and crouches down.

'You're sure we're not going to get shot?'

'The security guard is sixty-five if he's a day. All I've ever seen him armed with is a truncheon that looks like it's from a Punch and Judy show.'

'Fine. But if we get arrested, I'm saying you abducted me.'

She ducks under, only slightly snagging her coat on a loose wire, and holds the fence for Robert as he does the same.

'Okay?' He dusts himself off.

'Yeah, let's go.' She grins.

The shipyard is different to how Ella imagined it. The picture in her mind was of a cramped space, filled with the enormity of the ship. Instead they are in a wide clearing, gently sloping down to the Clyde. By moonlight she can see several low buildings. Further off in the gloom she can see . . . something.

'That's the shop where I work.' Robert points to one of the squat buildings. 'All your electrical supplies there. Over there is Sandy's hut . . .'

The abandoned space is dreamlike. Ella can see evidence of activity —the ground is muddy or spread with crushed rock. The only grass grows at the edges of things, where it cannot be trampled by workers or vehicles. But it's all as quiet as the surface of the moon.

They walk a little further, and the shadowy shape in front of them starts to resolve. Ella can see the spiny outcrops of scaffolding, the platforms at different levels. Under it all, sleek and shadowy, is the ship itself. The lower hull is painted black, or a colour too dark to detect. The upper half shines ghostly white. They pause.

'Wow . . .'

'I know. Weird, isn't it, seeing her stranded there?'

'Her?'

'Ships are all female. It's a convention.'

'Well, what's "she" called?'

'*Dumra.*' Ella feels Robert's shoulder brush close to hers.

'Funny name.'

'I think it's a place in India. That's where she's headed.' They start to walk a little further.

'Funny, that's my first memory,' Ella says.

'Oh?'

'They shut down the streets from the Caley works down to the docks, and all the kids went to watch. I was too small to understand, but I tagged along. They were taking an engine on a flatbed truck, to be shipped to India. I remember it was so huge, the tractors pulling it just crawled along. Even I could keep up with it. We followed it all the way to the docks.'

'I don't remember that . . .' Robert says.

'You probably had your head in a book.'

He chuckles. 'Aye, probably. I wonder where that engine is now . . .'

'I don't know,' she pulls her coat around her, 'but I bet it's a lot warmer than the banks of the Clyde.'

'I'd like to go one day.'

'To India?'

'Yeah. A totally different world, y'know?'

'Maybe once we're established at the badminton club the international agents will take note.'

They pick a spot near to the ship, but not so close that they can't look up. It's a bit like being at the cinema and not wanting to be too close to the screen. Robert unwraps the bundle, handing Ella a flask and a couple of sandwiches wrapped in paper. He spreads the tablecloth on a dry patch of ground and they sit on it. The cloth is small, so they sit close by necessity. Robert opens the flask and pours milky tea into the cap. It steams in the cold, wreathing up into the dark. They eat their sandwiches – corned beef and pickle – staring up at the ship. From this angle it's silhouetted against the sky, a jagged outline cut from the starry fabric.

They eat in silence, taking turns to sip the tea. Ella can smell Robert's aftershave and the soap he washes with. She's aware how easy it would be to bring her hand up and brush the stubble on his neck where he's just had his hair trimmed. Perhaps she says it as a way of getting away from these thoughts.

'I never said this . . . not properly . . . I'm sorry. About Rene.'

Robert breathes in and out, still looking at the ship.

'It wasn't your fault.'

Ella takes another sip of tea, holding it in her mouth until her tongue tingles. 'It's silly, but I often feel like she's still around.'

'That's not silly. I feel the same.'

'I know, but it's eleven years. I thought I'd have stopped by now.'

'I don't think she's really gone . . .' Robert hesitates. 'I just think we can't see her any more.'

'What do you mean?'

He straightens up, then hunches forward on his knees.

'I was reading this thing by St Augustine . . .'

'I didn't know you're religious.'

'I'm not, really. But he wrote some pretty good stuff. There's this bit where he's talking about time, and how it's just an illusion.'

Ella frowns. 'Then what are clocks doing?'

'They're measuring the teeth on a cog, or the number of times a pendulum has gone back and forth . . .' He looks at Ella's frown. 'I don't know, it's hard to explain. But what he's saying is, there's no such thing as the past or the future, just this big, eternal *now*.'

Ella tries to get her head around this, craning her neck so she's looking right up through the gaps in the clouds. The stars flicker.

'Nope, I don't get it.'

'Well, he compares it to a poem . . . but you could imagine it like a record.'

'A record?'

'Yeah, imagine a seventy-eight.'

Ella closes her eyes and pictures the record.

'So, you put it on the turntable and listen to the first verse of the song, then there's a chorus, then another verse. While you're listening to the second verse, the first verse is still there, spinning around on the record, but you're not listening to it any more. St Augustine said that the record is like a human life, or all of human history.'

Ella thinks for a moment. The idea is starting to take shape in her head as she imagines the shiny black disc, spinning on its axis. She's not sure if it makes sense or not, but the idea is attractive. She thinks of all the people who have gone before them, their lives still spinning through infinity like silent songs.

'So where's Rene, in this metaphor?'

'She's like . . .' Robert thinks for a moment. 'She's like a clarinet solo in the first verse. A beautiful solo, harmonizing with the melody. And then she stops, and she doesn't repeat again for the rest of the song . . . but she's still there, on the record.'

Ella feels stopped. For a moment she can believe that time is an illusion, because it no longer seems to be moving around her. There is a moment, in this stillness, where she could reach out, touch his cheek with her hand. Would he kiss her back?

'We should get going,' Robert says at last. 'I'm getting cold.'

She has waited too long, but the idea is planted in her mind. There will be other chances. Next time, she won't hesitate.

* * *

Often, they will go back to Robert's house and help his mother knead bread or mix fruitcakes. They never go to Ella's house. Mrs Mauchlen treats Ella like a child, but not in a bad way. She seems to assume they're just friends, which is true of course. Even when Ella and Robert go to his bedroom to listen to records, she seems unconcerned. Since Rene died, Mrs Mauchlen has had a hands-off approach to raising her son. Some people would call it indulgent. If Robert wasn't so fundamentally good, Ella thinks, he would be spoiled by his freedom. She knows *she* would be.

Ella is waiting for her moment. In truth, there are many times when she's tempted. But the moment in the shipyard was so perfect, she feels she can't settle for less. Of course, she wonders whether Robert might make the first move. The thought that he might, out of the blue, gives Ella a kind of excited indigestion. Sometimes, over dinner with her parents, she will fall silent for minutes on end, and when her mother comments on something on the radio, Ella will have no idea what she's talking about.

*   *   *

'Where the fuck is he?'

The Melody Ballroom is empty except for a man sweeping the floor, but it's not long until the doors open. Ella, Robert and Willie were here an hour ago to get some practice in the unfamiliar space. The new trumpeter – Calum Stewart – arrived soon after and ran through the set list. But it's half an hour until curtain up and Sandy hasn't arrived.

'I'm sure he's on his way,' Robert says, pacing. 'He's got a long way to go with that double bass on his back.'

'It's a long way lugging these fucking drums, but I'm here, aren't I?'

Ella's never seen Willie this angry, but she can't blame him. The Melody isn't the biggest venue in town, but they're still punching above their weight. If tonight goes badly, there won't be any more big gigs. People talk. People have long memories. Calum Stewart is looking mutinous. He's older than the rest of them, and they've only practised a couple of times. He's better than they are, and knows it, but is canny enough to see they are on their way up.

'Look, I don't want to be *that* guy, but I didn't agree to this.'

'What are you talking about?' Robert turns on his heel, mid-pace.

'I mean, if he's not going to show up, I'm not going to stick around and make a fool of myself. There are other bands I could've joined.'

'You stay where you are,' Willie growls, pointing a drumstick at Calum Stewart.

'Or what, y'wee prick?'

Willie gets up from his stool and makes toward him, but not before Ella can position herself between them.

'Stoppit, you idiots! He'll be here in a minute, and we'll play the gig. He's never been late before, he won't be today.'

'We could play without him,' Robert says, without conviction.

'Easy for you to say, Saxophone,' Willie says. 'I'm not up for being the entire rhythm section.'

'Guitar is part of the rhythm section,' Robert points out.

'It'll sound ropey – you know it will.'

'This is daft.' Calum Stewart is shaking his head. 'I'm off.'

'Don't you fuckin' dare!'

'Lads?'

The four of them spin around to see a face peeking around the doorway that lets onto the dressing rooms. It's the manager, who somehow hasn't noticed up to this moment that they're short a bassist. He looks angry now, though. Robert clears his throat.

'Yessir, how can we help?'

'There's a call for you.'

'A call?' Ella asks. She's never been told she has a call waiting. It's something that people say in movies. She doesn't even know anyone who owns a telephone.

'Aye, well . . .' the manager puffs his chest out, 'it's from the hospital.'

They look at each other. Like a beat in a song they're all playing, Ella feels the moment they realize. Willie is the first to find his voice.

'Ah shit.'

*   *   *

The ward is quiet. Sandy is in a room with four beds, but he's the only one in there. The All Stars arrive, out of breath from running. They got a lift most of the way after Ella jumped in front of a car and begged the driver to take them. In the end, Calum Stewart was the only one who had stayed at the Melody, as much to look after their gear as anything else.

Sandy is sitting up, wearing blue and white stripy pyjamas, reading a magazine. His right eye is swollen almost shut but, other than that, he seems himself. He looks up as they enter.

'Oh no, you didn't . . .' he starts, and winces. He tries again: 'I didn't mean for you to come. I just wanted to let you know I wouldn't make it.'

'It's a bit late for that,' Robert says.

Ella frowns at him.

'How are you, Sandy?' She sits in the chair by the bed. Willie sits on the edge and Robert stands.

'I've been better.'

'Your own dad . . .' Robert says. Sandy seems to shrug, but the movement is so small, Ella's not sure. His whole body seems tensed up, as though he's holding it in position. His breaths are shallow.

'It's been coming a while. He kept going for my mum and I kept getting in the way.'

'They said you had to have an operation.'

'He punched me in the belly. Doctor said I was bleeding inside.'

'Christ . . .' Willie looks to the ceiling for divine intervention.

'You look all right though . . .' Robert smiles, trying to lighten the mood. 'I thought you'd be all laid out.'

Sandy doesn't respond.

'Is it a big operation?' Willie asks.

Sandy looks at the light, where a moth is flickering inter-mittently inside the yellowed glass. Ella follows his gaze.

'Oh, they already did it. Got it out. They said they'll see what I'm like in the morning . . .' He pauses, tries to take a deep breath and fails. 'I'm really sorry I messed up the gig.'

'Don't be daft.' Robert shakes his head. 'There'll be other gigs.'

'It was only the Melody, for Christ's sake.' Willie smiles. 'Not like we bailed on the Locarno.'

Once more, Sandy makes a tiny motion that may be a shrug. There's a long silence.

'Well . . .' Robert begins. 'We should leave you to rest.'

Ella looks at him sharply, but he doesn't seem to notice.

Sandy frowns. 'You don't have to rush off, Rob.'

'No, you should get some sleep. We'll visit in the morning.'

The air of discomfort is palpable. Though Sandy must be in shock, and in pain besides, there's something unsettling in his manner. Sandy smiles thinly.

'All right then. Sorry again for the gig.'

'Not your fault,' Willie smiles. 'Take it easy.'

'Aye, take it easy.'

Ella goes in to kiss him on the cheek. 'Are you sure you don't want anyone with you? Me and Robert could stay . . .'

'That would be nice.' Sandy looks to Robert, who is hovering uncertainly, halfway to the door.

'I should probably get going. Early start in the morning.'

Sandy looks at him for a moment and nods once.

'Night then, Robert.'

Ella huffs and sits herself down on the metal chair next to the bed. 'Well, I'm staying.'

Robert looks back at her and something unsaid passes between them. They leave, and the room is quiet. Ella watches Sandy, who is watching the moth trapped in the light above them. In the quiet, she can hear the tiny noise its wings make against the glass, like someone flipping the pages of a book.

'Are you okay, Sandy?'

His eyes move to meet hers, too slowly. He's moving at the wrong speed, a forty-five played at thirty-three. She supposes it must be the pain medication.

'I'm all right, aye.'

'I'm really sorry.'

'What for?'

'For everything. For your dad, for this.' She points vaguely to his stomach. 'For not stopping it.'

'How could you have stopped it, Ella?'

She shakes her head. 'I feel like you warned me . . .'

'I warned you for your sake, not mine. My dad was never like this, before the war. You've got to be careful.'

Ella thinks of her father. She doesn't think he's capable of hurting her or her mother. But isn't it possible that he has done the same as Sandy's dad, or worse, in the war? Isn't it possible that those nightmares could blur the line between family and enemy?

'Do you mind if I sleep, for a bit?' Sandy asks.

'No, of course. I'm not going anywhere.'

He smiles, closes his eyes, and quickly she can tell by his breathing that he is asleep. Ella watches his breath gently rise and fall for a minute, then picks up the magazine he was reading when they arrived – *Golden Age* – a magazine about Hollywood stars and Hollywood movies. She's been trying to focus her attention on a piece about Humphrey Bogart's holiday retreat for five minutes when a suited man in a white coat appears, presumably a doctor.

'You can't be here, young lady. Visiting hours are over.'

His accent is Edinbugger; most refined. Ella squares her jaw, unconsciously leans back.

'I'm not leaving; I promised I'd stay.'

The doctor looks from her to the unconscious Sandy, then his eyes return to roam over Ella. She's still wearing the outfit she picked for the Melody Ballroom, a red chenille number that's more fitted than anything else she owns. She remembers her gleeful thought when buying it – *Dad will hate this* – and her stomach clenches. The doctor nods once.

'All right. But the nurses aren't as nice as me, you better watch out for them.'

Ella nods in return. The doctor comes over and places his hand on her shoulder. 'Your boyfriend?'

Ella resists the urge to ball her fists or shrug him off. She needs to stay here for Sandy.

'Just a friend. Will he be all right?'

'Ah . . .' The doctor takes his hand away for a moment to

flip through his notes. 'Let's see now. Blunt trauma necessitating full splenectomy . . .'

'What does that mean? Splenectomy?'

'It means they had to take his spleen out, probably because it was damaged by the blow. It would have kept bleeding.'

He goes and prods Sandy in a few places on his stomach. Ella would dearly love to punch this man.

'But it seems to have done the job – no obvious accumulation of blood, so he's not haemorrhaging any more.'

'Don't you need it?'

'Need what?'

'Your spleen. What does it do?'

The doctor does something like a shrug using just his face.

'Yes and no. The Romans used to take them out of their runners so they could go faster. But it's part of your immune system. Fights off bugs. If he pulls through, he'll always be more susceptible to infections than you or me.'

'*If* he pulls through?'

He's back now to pat Ella on the shoulder.

'Can I get you anything? I could fetch us some cocoa from the nurses' room.'

This time Ella does shrug him off.

'No thanks.'

'Suit yourself.' The doctor curdles. 'Remember what I said – the nurses won't be as lenient.'

With that he disappears, and Ella goes back to her vigil.

* * *

She does not remember falling asleep. There are bodies moving around her, a confusion of voices. The light has changed, becoming brighter.

'Who's she?'

'The girlfriend, I presume.'

'Unmarried? Look at that dress . . .'

Ella opens her eyes. There are two women and a man around Sandy's bed, all of them unfamiliar.

'What are you doing to him?'

The three of them startle at the noise, before the man speaks for them.

'Young lady, we are trying to help your boyfriend here.'

Ella sits up. 'What's wrong with him?'

'Keep your voice down, this is a hospital. He has an infection. Common after surgery like this. We're going to give him some . . .'

But Ella can't hear what he's saying any more. She's looking at Sandy – ash pale and clammy – and there's a ringing in her ears.

Through the next few hours nurses and doctors come and go. They must recur, though Ella cannot recognize any of them. She's dishevelled in her red dress, make-up smeared, hungry and thirsty. She's sore from sitting on a wooden chair all night. Her parents must be looking for her. None of it matters.

Sandy does not move except for breathing. She holds his hand, which is warmer than hers. She holds onto that warmth.

Several times she feels his pulse, though it's hard to find. When she pins down the fluttering for a moment, she guesses it must be about a hundred and fifty beats per minute. She thinks of the metronome her mum got her for her tenth birthday, winding it up and sliding the weight right to the bottom of the needle so that it ticked back and forth as fast as it was capable. Sandy is ticking even faster than that, faster than any song the All Stars are capable of playing. She imagines the music that would pump along to his fevered heartbeat, reeling figures in double time, too fast for anyone to dance to. She lets go of the music.

Ella is not so selfless that she doesn't realize her future is wrapped up in this moment. She's only been playing in the band a couple of months, and they've been the best months she's had. She thought she might get a little longer.

Time passes. Sandy doesn't move, Ella doesn't move. The hospital breaks around them like water. She goes to find his pulse again, but it's not where she left it. She catches broken moments, a triplet beat, a staccato pulse, a single clash of cymbals.

She asks what they are going to do.

Nothing – there is nothing they can do.

She watches and waits. Life moves through its final changes, a succession of strange chords and discords.

Sandy stops breathing.

* * *

They're sitting in the tea rooms again. So much time seems to have elapsed since the first time. A lifetime. They didn't speak during the whole time the waitress took their order, returned with silverware and plates, and finally brought coffee and sandwiches. It's not an angry silence. They're not 'not talking' to one another. Ella can't speak for Robert, but the air in her lungs seems so used up, so spent, she can't imagine breathing it into words. There have been no gigs since Sandy died, but Ella is certain she couldn't sing if she tried.

This shouldn't be the moment, Ella knows. This is not like the moment in the shipyard, where time waited patiently for her to change their destinies. This is just an ordinary moment. But since Sandy died, she has been too aware of these ordinary moments. She wants to make them extraordinary. She doesn't want to waste any more time, thinking it will never run out.

'Robert . . .'

He looks up, and she half-stands. Ella leans over the table and kisses him. It's not a perfect kiss. Their teeth clash a little. But his lips are warm, parted with surprise as much as desire. He doesn't pull away. She sits back down at last, satisfied at least that she has done something, chosen for herself instead of letting others choose for her.

'Ella, I . . .' Robert says, eyes wide and uncertain.

'I should have done that a long time ago,' she says quickly.

Without reply, Robert reaches into his jacket and takes out an envelope. He pushes it across the table.

'What is it?'

'Just read it. Please.'

Ella picks the letter up, expecting it to be written by Robert. Talking is difficult, so he has written his thoughts down. So, when she turns the envelope over and sees it is addressed not to her, but to Robert, there's a moment's confusion. She looks to him for explanation, but Robert closes his eyes.

She takes the letter out. She notes the official stamps, the language of bureaucracy, the use of Robert's full name. She sees the word 'conscription'.

Robert opens his eyes and looks at her, looking at him.

'You're being called up?'

'Air force.'

'Flying planes?'

'Doubt it. They'll have me wiring things together. Ground crew.'

There's a crushing weight on Ella's chest, but she's determined to keep talking. This isn't as bad as she feared it might be. It's another obstacle, not the end of the road.

'Well, you'll have leave, right? And you won't be going anywhere. There's no war . . .'

Robert says nothing.

'We'll write lots of letters. And when you're on leave, we'll catch up with everything. It's only two years, after all.'

'Ella.'

She stops. The tears are forming before she knows what's coming. She will not cry.

'I think . . . I think we should take a break. From one another.'

At this moment the waitress arrives to ask if everything is all right. She realizes, too late, that she has stepped into something, and things are absolutely not all right, and backs away with a painted-on smile.

'Take a break?' Ella manages to say at last.

'After Sandy . . . and now this . . .'

'You're giving up?'

'No.' He looks annoyed for the first time.

'Why?'

'Does there need to be a reason? I can't do this right now.'

His face is clouded over. He looks like a completely different person to Ella, all shadows and hollowed eyes. She feels a flare of anger, bright relief from all other emotion. She lets it fill her.

'You're a coward.'

Robert flinches. 'That's not fair.'

'No? Because I thought I was more important to you than a little inconvenience.'

'It's not about—'

'He loved you.'

They are silent for a moment. Robert is confused.

'Who?'

'Sandy. He loved you. He told me, but you should have known. You should have seen it. He didn't hide it from you.'

Robert can't seem to say anything. His eyes are wide as he

tries to reimagine his friendship with Sandy as something else. A thousand moments, all seen from a different angle.

'And you . . . you didn't stay with him.' Now the tears are falling, and Ella doesn't care. 'You didn't stay with him. Just me.'

'Since Rene . . . I don't like hospitals and doctors.'

'So what? So what, Robert? If it had been you in that bed, he would have stayed for you, no matter how much it scared him.'

'I didn't know . . .' Robert says, and Ella doesn't know if he means Sandy's love or his death. He sounds so lost, Ella almost takes pity on him. Almost. She takes a deep breath, wipes the tears on the back of her hand and stands.

'You're a coward, Robert. To me and to him.'

She walks out of the tea rooms without a backward glance.

3.

The Lover

I WAKE.

Is this waking? Has time passed? We used to record music to magnetic tape. If you were clever, you could cut the tape up and stick it back together in a new order. Splice two songs together, slow one down and speed one up until tempos and keys matched. You hadn't performed the music that way, but you could press a button and it would play from beginning to end as though you had.

My life is playing in a new order, and I can't stop it.

I'm holding something I guess is Sandy's hand, grown cold, but it's just the neck of the guitar. I open my eyes. I'm on the sofa in the saloon. Outside the weather has changed again. It's late in the day. Dark clouds have hidden the sun, drizzle is falling, and wind is whipping the waves into foam. The baby is asleep on the floor, Rene asleep on the sofa opposite, curled like a golden-haired mouse.

I get up and hobble to the kitchen, knowing I should eat something. *Mnemosyne* pitches under my feet. I stop in the doorway, because Sandy is looking at the microwave, turning the plate inside with his finger and frowning. He looks up at me.

'Hi, Eleanor. I was just looking at this thing. I think it's some kind of display case . . .'

'It heats food.'

'How?'

'You put the food in, close the door and turn this dial . . .'

I perform the actions.

'Aye, and?'

'Well, there's no power . . .'

Sandy frowns. 'What's wrong with the power? Fancy boat like this.'

'I don't know.' I shrug. 'I don't know boats. You're the one who worked at a shipyard.'

Sandy sighs. 'Aye, all right – do you know where the engine is?'

I shake my head. 'But I know the way downstairs.'

I have a rare, clever thought and grab the torch from the worktop. Sandy stops by the sofa, looking down.

'Whose baby is that?'

'I'm his grandma.'

I say it with confidence, but for the first time it occurs to me that this doesn't seem right. I'm eighty-seven, and he's a wee baby . . . I try to do the maths to make it work, but I can't quite keep it in my head.

'And the girl?'

'That's Rene Mauchlen.'

'Robert's sister? I never met her, but he mentioned her sometimes. What's she doing here?'

I shrug. 'What are you doing here, Sandy?' I look at him, in his blue knitted tank top and fishtail trousers, not a day over twenty-one. He never looked so young when he was alive.

'Good point,' he half-smiles. 'Come on then, let's find this engine.'

We go downstairs. The dirty water comes almost halfway up my shins now.

'Where'd all this come from?' Sandy, still on the stairs, is rolling his trousers up as though about to go for a paddle at the beach.

'I think it washed in during the storm,' I say. 'So that's my room, and the baby's room,' I point to the doors on the right, 'and that one belongs to . . . to . . .' I search for the names but cannot call them to mind. 'It belongs to the baby's parents.'

'And that one?'

'The baby's playroom. You can't go in there. It's locked.'

'Okay, so none of those are the engine room. What about back there?'

Sandy points around the back of the stairs.

'I don't know what's back there . . .'

I turn the torch and see the hallway carries on. I walk through the cold water and Sandy follows.

'We'll need to do something about the water,' he says.

I reach a door, now on my right. I open the door and shine the torch into a small bedroom like my own, the bed made with clean linen, the blind drawn down over the window. There is no luggage in here; the room is empty.

'If we get the water cleaned up, you could have this room for yourself.'

'Looks cosy.'

I close the door and we turn around to the final door. This isn't another bedroom. It has metal shelving on three sides, bolted to the walls. There are boxes of supplies, though I don't see any food. A pack of kitchen roll lies bloated in the water; plastic spice jars bob around one corner in formation.

'Ah, lamps!' Sandy says, laying hands on two storm lamps. 'Now I just need to find some matches . . .'

'Is that the engine?' I ask, pointing my torch to the back of the room where there is some sort of metal tank with a lot of copper piping. Sandy laughs.

'That's not an engine! Might be something to do with the fresh water. Best leave it be.'

He looks around and pulls out an object that looks like a cross between a vacuum cleaner and an engine, with coiled lengths of rubber hose going in and out of it.

'This might come in handy.'

'What is it?'

'Looks like a bilge pump. If we can't get the power back on, at least we can pump some of this water out.'

Sandy finds matches and lights one of the hurricane lamps, levering up the glass cover and holding a match. It reminds me of the gaslights in our Bedlay Street house. He turns the wire wheel until the filament glows.

At random I grab candles, a jar of honey and a roll of bin bags, shoving them in my dressing gown. We leave the storeroom and wade to the back of the boat, but there are no more rooms, just a big wooden step that leads up to nothing.

'If the engine isn't here, where is it?'

Sandy hooks a hand under the step and lifts. The step is actually a box with a hinged top. I shine my torch.

'Here we go . . .' Sandy says, though he already sounds worried.

I look at the engine. It seems to go back further than we can see. It's black, streaked with grease.

'Can you fix it?'

'I don't know . . . some of these parts are familiar. These are the cylinders, and you've got the spark plugs on either side . . . This is some kind of cooling duct, I think . . .'

'You've not seen an engine like this?'

Sandy shakes his head, wiping dirt from a metal number plate.

'That explains it,' he chuckles, straightening up. 'This was built in 1981. The last engine I saw was this engine's great-great-grandad.'

It's the first time Sandy has mentioned being dead. We should talk about it, but this doesn't seem the time.

'You can't fix it?'

'It looks like water has leaked into the compartment, so it might just be that we need to dry it out. There's no visible damage . . .'

'Ellie, come quick!'

We wade back to the foot of the stairs. Rene stands, peering down at us. The baby lets out a cry to let us know he's awake.

'What's the matter?' Sandy calls up.

'Who're you?'

'This is Sandy. He's Robert's friend.'

Rene squints suspiciously. 'Well, whatever. Come see. Quick!'

Sandy rushes up the stairs, and I haul myself step-by-step. I remember what it's like to have an eighteen-year-old body, but that doesn't make this one move any faster. When I reach the saloon, out of breath, Rene and Sandy have their faces pressed to the window by the kitchen.

I go to the window. 'What are you looking at?'

Rene points over the waves. In the gloom, sea and sky are the same colour. On the horizon is a grey mass.

'Is that . . . land?' I ask.

'I don't know about "land",' Sandy says. 'A big rock, more like.'

I look at the island. It looks like the grey waves set solid. No houses, no lights, no people who might save me from my memories.

'Rene says we're getting closer to it.'

'We *are* getting closer to it. At first I was just watching it 'cause I've not seen anything but the sea for aaaaages. But then it was tiny, just this big.' Rene shows with thumb and forefinger how tiny the island was.

'What do we do?' I look from the baby to the island.

'Let's not panic,' Sandy says, sounding panicked. 'Fancy boat like this must have a nice big anchor we can drop, even if the engine's bust.'

'The engine's bust?' Rene squeaks.

'Hush now,' I say. 'Rene, look after the baby. Me and Sandy are going to find the anchor.'

Wide-eyed, Rene nods and goes to the baby to stroke his head. I smile – I'm starting to remember how to boss my friend around.

I go to the doors at the back of the cabin and step into the rain. Wind tugs at my dressing gown; I wrap it closer and brace against the wooden rail which runs around the outside of the saloon. Sandy steps out and closes the door.

'Are you okay?' I ask.

'Aye, fine . . . I've just never been to sea before, you know?'

'What, never? You were a ship's draughtsman!'

'*Apprentice* draughtsman. I've never been on a ship. We went to Loch Lomond on holiday once and went on the paddle steamer . . . but it was calmer than this.'

I squeeze his shoulder.

'So, where's the anchor?'

'Well, there'll be a control in the wheelhouse, but it might not work with the power out.'

'Oh . . .'

'Aye, but there'll be a manual crank near the windlass. Come on.'

He edges his way along the deck, holding tight to the railing. I follow after, gritting my teeth. Though I can't see the sun, it must be setting. The light is fading fast. The endless space that surrounded us in the day has become close, looming around the little boat. Sandy is clutching tight to the storm lamp and I follow the glow. We're halfway there when *Mnemosyne* jolts. I stumble and fall to my knees.

'What was that?'

'I guess we hit something. But we're not grounded yet.'

We reach the bow and I see the pair of running shoes, in a different position now. Second time around I remember they belong to Abigail. Where did Abigail go? I hope she'll be back soon. I need to rest.

'Here!'

Sandy crouches down, putting his storm lamp next to something set into the deck. It's a chain, wrapped around a cylinder like cotton on a bobbin. The chain goes to the bow, through a metal trench, and disappears. Crouched low, Sandy edges to the bow and leans over with storm lamp extended.

'What can you see?'

Sandy runs back. 'Some eejit already dropped anchor, but they mustn't have extended it very far, or we wouldn't be drifting.'

Crouching next to the windlass, he runs his fingers around the deck. He hooks his finger around a brass catch. The hatch lifts. By lamplight, a handle gleams.

'Help me with this.'

We put our hands to the crank. It goes click-click-click as we turn it. There's not much resistance. We wind for a minute, though it feels longer with the looming island. Suddenly, all tension goes out of the crank. The final length of chain skitters toward us over the deck.

'What?' Sandy yells. He scrambles over and picks up the end of chain. The final link, a figure of eight, has burst open at one end. The metal is jagged.

'No anchor?' I ask.

Sandy sits down on the deck, legs crossed, runs a hands over his rain-slick face. The lamp burns white, casting his features into shadow.

'This is a motorsailer, right?' He peers up at the mast, stretching into the gloom, its sail all wrapped up. 'So, we need to sail her.'

'What? You've never even been to sea before!'

'I haven't got any better ideas. Unless you want to hang over the edge with a broomstick and poke us away from the rocks.'

I think this might not be as bad as unfurling that huge sail.

'All right then, let's do it. But if you get swept into the sea, I'm not jumping in after you.'

That makes Sandy smile at least. He picks up his lamp and together we struggle to the sail. The mast is as broad as a torso, tangled with all kinds of ropes. The ropes lead down to the deck, through junction boxes either side, fastened to moorings and winches.

'Which rope releases the sail?' I ask.

'No idea. We'll just try them. You take this side, I'll take the other.'

I take the first rope and pull, but nothing happens. I try another with same result. There's no give at all. I run through several before I get to a blue rope. There is movement in this one. I plant my feet on the deck, grip the rope and lean back. Somewhere above me, a knot releases.

One moment the sail is trussed, the next it has come alive. In the wind it curls and whips like an animal trying to defend itself. I try to grab the lowest corner, but the sail strikes me with a full-body slap. I don't fall, but I stumble back. Sandy wrestles with another edge, but he can't make sense of it. I grab the sail, but the wind catches it and throws me in the direction of the railings. For a moment I think I'm going overboard, but I fall back on my bum.

I watch Sandy for a moment in the half-light, trying to grab the sail. I see a rope trailing on the deck which goes along the horizontal bit of the mast. I crawl over the deck, grab the end of the rope and pull. My hands are stinging. Something at the other end of the rope struggles like a fish on a hook. The sail becomes less complicated. A triangle inches toward me, attached to the rope.

'Sandy! Come help me.'

Sandy scrabbles over, gripping the rope behind me.

'Heave!' I shout. I saw someone say that in an Errol Flynn pirate movie. I wish he were here now. Movie star or not, he'd have more of a clue than we do.

'It's working. Look!' Sandy points up. The sail billows fatly like a bedsheet drying on the line. I improvise a knot to tie the rope to a mooring on the deck. It feels like we tethered a huge white bird to the boat.

'We did it!' I shout, though I'm scared.

There's a sound. Not a new sound, but a sound raised in volume. The sound of water rushing. *Mnemosyne* is racing forward, hooked into the wind. We're racing toward the island. Sandy seems to have the same thought.

'We need to steer, or we're going to run ourselves aground.'

'What do I do?'

'Go to the wheelhouse. The power's off, but the wheel should still turn the rudder.'

'Okay. Stay here and mind the sail.'

I keep one hand on the railing, fumbling in my dressing gown pockets for the little torch. I click it on just as I reach the stairs and start to climb. My hands are on fire. The railings on the deck are polished wood, but the railings up to the wheelhouse are cold metal, flaked with rust.

I'm almost at the top when the boat shudders. Not as big as the last one, but enough to make me stumble, dropping the torch through the gaps in the stairs. It hits the deck below and bounces high, the beam of light somersaulting before it disappears into the sea.

It's dark now. The light of the lamp doesn't reach me here. I'm not good in the dark. My memory doesn't tell me what things look like in the light. There's nothing for it but a leap of faith. I race up the remaining stairs until I crash into the door, feeling for the doorknob. The rain whips around me, and I am cold and wet and numb.

My head swims; I'm going to fall . . .

My hand closes around the doorknob. The door swings out and I swing in, slamming it behind me. I fall into the chair. With the door shut, everything is calm and still. I shiver in the warmth of this little room.

God, I could sleep . . .

My eyes droop.

I come to my senses, remembering what Sandy said. I lean forward, grip the wheel, and start to turn clockwise. The island was just to our left, wasn't it? So, if I swing us to the right . . . At first, nothing seems to happen. Another thing on this boat that was broken before I got to it. Then, all at once, the dark room tilts.

It's not like when a car swerves. A car is a small thing. I feel *Mnemosyne* under me. I feel her momentum shift. I don't know how far I turned us, but if I keep the wheel turned, we'll run around in a circle and hit the island anyway. So, after a minute, I turn the wheel back to where it was.

I wait.

The cabin is dark but, as my eyes adjust, I can see a clock

in front of me. It has glow-in-the-dark hands. I watch the seconds tick around.

A minute passes.

Two minutes.

Five minutes.

The boat keeps going. There are no more impacts. I close my eyes and lean back in the chair. I'm soaked through, bruised and grazed all over. My hands burn from the ropes and cranks and handrails.

I say a silent prayer, over and over – *I am eighty-seven; I'm too old for this . . . I am eighty-seven; I'm too old for this . . . I am eighty-seven; I'm too old for this . . .*

A light grows behind my closed eyes. Is my prayer being answered? Perhaps the doors of heaven are opening. Or maybe my heart isn't pumping enough oxygen to my brain. Either way, I'm ready to go gently. Instead, the door opens and Sandy leans in with his storm lamp.

'You did it! Swerved us right out of the way!'

I look at him through half-closed eyes. I feel I can't raise my head from the back of the chair.

'You must be tired.' Sandy looks worried. 'Let me help you down.'

His hand takes mine. I rise from the chair, allow him to usher me into the rain, down the stairs, back into warmth.

'Is everything going to be okay, Ellie?' Rene bounds over. 'Did we miss the big rock?'

'Aye, it's fine,' Sandy says. 'Out of the way now. Eleanor needs a lie-down.'

He guides me to the sofa. If I had my eighteen-year-old body I would flop down and pull the cover over myself. But I'm not eighteen now. If I throw myself down, I'm afraid I'll shatter. Sandy helps me lie down, pulls the blanket over. I'm soaking wet, but there's nothing to be done about that now.

'The baby?' I sigh.

'He's fine; I've been watching him. He doesn't do much, does he? He doesnae even suck his thumb.'

'No,' I smile, 'he doesn't.'

'You should get some sleep.' Sandy kneels down. 'Get warmed up.'

'What about the boat? What if there are more islands?' I can feel the tug of sleep like a sail that's about to catch the wind.

'I'll stand at the bow with my storm lamp. If I see anything, I'll come get you.'

'But you'll freeze . . .'

Sandy makes a sound like a shrug. 'I'm dead, Ella. You don't really get cold, when you're dead.'

'Oh. All right then . . .'

* * *

I wake to the sound of the baby crying. It's some time in the night. Rene is curled on the sofa opposite, blonde curls over her face. The baby is kicking his legs. I wonder how I can see him, then spot the second storm lamp Sandy brought up from the storeroom, hanging from one of the ceiling beams. He's turned it down, so the light is soft and yellow.

My body still aches, but I feel lighter. Slowly, I get up to standing and shuffle to the kitchen. Rene rolls her head and mumbles something but doesn't wake. I feed the baby, change his nappy and outfit, then feed myself a tin of cream of tomato soup and some oatcakes. He watches me eat until he falls back to sleep. I watch him back, for a minute. There's nothing to do and nobody needs me. I go to the window but there are no stars. The darkness seems painted onto the glass.

Treading softly, I go to the window to the right of the stairs, looking forwards. At the bow, silhouetted by his lamp, Sandy keeps watch. I can just see the sail, curved into the wind. There's no ripple in the fabric. Everything is peaceful, but we're surging forward.

A memory.

I feel the shape of it before I know what it is. Something winding around itself . . . turning like a wheel . . . not a thing but a sound, not a sound but a song . . .

A waltz.

I remember words, from the introduction to *The Songs of the Dead*.

Greek myth tells of Orpheus, who travelled to the underworld to win back his lover, Eurydice. His means of transport was music – music that made the gods weep to hear it. The Hymns of Orpheus are lost to us now, but their voices are still ours to use, that we may each try to bring back our own Eurydice . . .

I take a last look at Sandy, then go to find the guitar. I take a muslin from the nappy bag and stuff a corner under the guitar's strings near the bridge, to mute them. Quietly I retune, then make a barre chord – an F – feeling the raw skin of my palm stretching. I strum the first eight bars before the melody comes to me.

My voice struggles with the small steps as much as the big ones. But I sing it through, and through again, feeling the snaking tune wind in and around me. The tune is called 'The Lover'. Its modal melody is as evocative as old perfume. The room does not spin or drop this time; there is no whirlpool, picking us up and hurling us around. *Mnemosyne* speeds forward, with Sandy holding his storm lamp to the dark.

Still playing, I race forward into the past.

1954

THE COACH HAS BEEN travelling through the night. Nobody has said anything in that time. Ella thought she might be able to doze, but the leatherette seat is unforgivingly firm, and she can't stop her mind turning. They stopped at a lay-by in the Midlands at half four, and a few people stamped to the concrete facilities to pee. Ella had gone to stretch her legs, watching her breath curl up into the darkness. She had walked around to the back of the coach and read –

NORTHERN ROADWAYS Ltd
20 RENFIELD STREET
GLASGOW C2.
PHONE CITY 7501/2

129

Renfield Street had felt a world away, separated by much more than seven hours on a coach. At a call from the driver they had traipsed back inside. Everyone except Ella seemed to go to sleep. Occasionally one of them would wake and smoke a cigarette, walk up and down the aisle or unwrap another sandwich. Ella's packed lunch was eaten hours ago, and she'd probably be hungry if she weren't so nervous. With every mile that passes, she's increasingly sure she's made a mistake. Robert's call had been so unexpected, so perfectly timed to coincide with a low ebb, it had overcome her common sense.

'You said if I ever came to London, I should give you a call.'

'I said that, didn't I?'

It had been a strangely stilted conversation, not least because she was standing in Willie Barr's front room. Willie had moved to the new development in Barlanark at the same time as Ella and her parents, and lived a few doors down with his wife. Bedlay Street is gone – knocked down by the council for 'redevelopment'. When Willie had tapped on their door, she had thought something was wrong.

'It's Robert on the line. He wants to chat with you.'

'What for?'

Willie shrugged. 'Better find out.'

It has been six years since Sandy died. Robert was conscripted into the air force not long after the funeral, and that put paid to any question of getting the band back together. Robert wrote her letters. Sometimes it was two a week. They would be full of what he was listening to, the radio show he hosted at the airbase, the books he had scrounged from the mobile library. At first, she hadn't replied, but he just kept on writing.

'Ella? It's Robert.'

'I know, Willie told me. It's weird hearing your voice.'

'Yours too.'

Ella doesn't remember what she said to Robert, but he had sounded enthusiastic. A flat in Brixton for three people with a spare room, an upright piano in the living room. The rent was more than she was used to, but Robert's flatmate had the big room and was paying extra. Their friend had skipped out after a month of living in London and they needed someone to fill the spot.

'I've got a fixer who gets me gigs all over London. I could introduce you. And there's so much work, Ella! Dance halls all over the place, not just in the centre. All these sixteen-piece bands, and a lot of them are six-nights-a-week. Plus, the front bit of the flat is over a wee shop that does sweets and tobacco, so once Mr Jacobs has packed up and gone home for the day, you can make as much noise as you like. I can blow my sax at two in the morning and nobody cares!'

Ella had said polite nothings and hung up, but she already knew she would say yes. The vision Robert had painted in that five-minute conversation was one of paradise. A city of music. As much money as you could be bothered to work for. Fellow musicians coming and going in a flat where it was always possible to play. Of course, she played her acoustic in the house, but not after eight at night, or Mrs Tolbert would be round to complain in the morning. The walls were thin, and Ella had given up on plugging in the electric she had bought with savings from working at the post office. The thought of having friends around – trumpet players, piano players, drummers . . . She's aware it is a sort of cliché, but it sounds perfect anyway.

She should probably be less confident about her playing, she knows. But there's little else she's worked on for the last six years. There's little else in Barlanark to occupy her mind. When her dad died – felled on the way back from the pub one evening – his dislike of her practising in the house died with him. She practised alternate tunings that allowed her to play cluster chords. She got so good at fingerpicking that people said it was like two people playing together. She bought the records that Robert recommended and learned bebop by ear. She has confidence in her playing. She wants to show off.

And, although Ella doesn't admit this to herself, she is going for Robert. She is going because Robert called her, and perhaps that means that things are not hopeless after all. After Sandy died, it felt like their moment was over. She had returned the guitar and amplifier to Jimmy on his release from hospital, and he had proceeded to form a new band who had taken the slot at the badminton club.

But now the smoke-filled coach is driving through the labyrinthine streets of an outer city. For the first time since they departed Glasgow, Ella feels tired, her eyelids heavy. As the city grows up around her like a black forest, there is an answering light in the sky. Day breaks over London in shades of rose and liquid gold. The rest of the bus sleeps on.

They pass through Golders Green, and Ella sees a pair of elderly Jewish men walking down the road in their long black garb, with their wide-brimmed hats and curling sideburns. It's the first time she has seen Orthodox Jewish people, and it reinforces her sense that she has come a long way from home.

By the time they pull into the coach station, the rest of the bus seems to have woken up to an unspoken signal, lighting final cigarettes to add to the cloud that they have dragged down from Scotland with them. In the station it is dark and the air smells of grease. They mill around the side of the bus, waiting for their luggage to be disgorged.

Ella retrieves her sailor's duffel bag, which she bought from the army surplus store, then her electric guitar in its hardcase and the Selmer amplifier. It weighs a tonne, and she hopes none of the valves have bust on the way down. Weighed down, Ella turns to find the exit and comes face-to-face with Robert.

'It's you!' She surges forward, laughs at her laden arms, and puts everything down in a hurry. She throws her arms around Robert. Her heart leaps. He has perhaps grown another inch, and in some indefinable way looks more adult, almost sophisticated.

'Oof! It's so good to see you, Ella.'

He hugs her back, but Ella is aware of a presence behind him. She looks at the girl, who is looking at her, and draws back from Robert. He half-turns his body to bring her into the conversation.

'Ella, this is Olivia.'

The girl nods her head once as though to acknowledge that this is indeed her name. She is platinum blonde, fat ringlets tumbling over her shoulders. She has one immaculately pencilled eyebrow raised. Ella cannot force her face into an appropriate expression and dips her head instead. Olivia smiles thinly.

'Pleasure to meet you, Ella.'

Without breaking eye contact, Olivia puts her arm through Robert's in a smooth motion. Robert smiles, almost as though he is unaware of what he has done, but Ella knows him well enough.

He rubs behind his ear.

'Shall we get you some breakfast before we head to the flat?'

* * *

'Sweet Jesus, this is how I die . . . one last puuush!'

A fortnight has passed since she arrived in Brixton, but it feels like much longer. The flat, as lovely as Robert described it, is let down only by a lack of furniture. So, having seen a perfectly good settee sitting out on the side of the road on his way back from a recording session, Lester had fetched them immediately.

'Turn it a bit . . .' Robert yells from underneath the sofa. 'I'm caught on this banister.'

Lester turns to Ella and grins. 'Perhaps we should put this down and leave him for a bit? We could have a cup of tea.'

'I can hear you, you swine.'

If half her hopes had been dashed as soon as Ella got to London, it seems the other half have grown in scope to make up for their loss. Much of that is down to Lester, Robert's flatmate, who is like no one she has ever met.

Lester is from Buffalo, New York. He's a fellow guitarist, he is black, and he seems always to be laughing. He dresses snappily, most often in waistcoat and trousers, shirt sleeves rolled up, with silk ties and two-tone brogues. He almost gives the impression of being rich, though Ella knows this is not exactly the case. There was some sort of accident when he was a kid. Lester got a big insurance pay-out, which he's spending.

'And *down*!'

The settee, duck-egg blue with only minor staining, has made it up to their humble abode. Lester drags it across the sitting room until it's under the window, next to the upright piano, and proceeds to spread himself out on it, head propped on one arm like a Hollywood starlet reclining on her chaise longue.

'Good work, team. I've got eggs and bacon – let's have a celebratory breakfast!'

Robert has his hands on his knees, still puffing a bit from exertion.

'Not me, I'm afraid – rehearsal.'

'What do you need a rehearsal for?' Ella asks, aware that

she's sounding like her dad. 'Aren't you playing six nights a week?'

Robert shrugs. 'He wants to try out some new things, some bebop. With that trumpet section I'm just glad we're not doing it live for the first time.'

Lester laughs, sitting up and running a hand through his short hair.

'Man, you are wasted on that crew.'

'At least it pays well . . . and it's nice feeling like the guy who knows what he's doing. I'm sure something else will come along. It's not like there's a scarcity—'

He stops abruptly, aware that for the last two weeks Ella has been searching for work and not finding any. Lester does a good job of not noticing.

'Okay man, see you later! Let's get you some breakfast, Ellabelle, you poor waif.'

By the time she hears Robert close the downstairs door, Ella is sitting in the kitchen (what luxury, to have a whole separate room for cooking, with enough room to sit at the table!), listening to the eggs sizzle in bacon grease. The coffee-maker, an all-in-one Italian contraption which still seems magical to Ella, is starting to percolate on the other ring of the cooker. Lester has taken off his waistcoat and is prodding the rashers with a wooden spoon. At the sound of the door, he turns to her.

'You know you're going to find work, don't you?'

She's taken aback by the direct question.

'Yeah, sure . . .'

'But you're having doubts?'

She sighs, throwing her head back.

'I just keep getting knockbacks. Someone tells Robert that they're *desperate* for a guitarist, but as soon as they hear my name the position is mysteriously filled.'

Lester smiles gently. 'I know that feeling.'

'You're not a woman—' Ella blurts, before realizing what she's saying.

Lester puts his hands up before she has a chance to apologize. 'Don't worry about it. You don't even think about it and I like that. But it's true – I had the same thing. All these people desperate to get a guitarist, until *my* black face turns up. Suddenly it ain't so urgent.'

'What changed?'

Lester shrugs, then turns to take the spluttering coffeepot off its ring.

'Nothing changed. I just kept turning up. And eventually I found people who didn't care what colour I was, so long as I could play to their tempo.'

'That's your advice? That I should just keep turning up?'

Lester grabs the coffeepot with a tea towel and brings it over to the table, pouring them both a large mug.

'I know it's not much. But it's the best advice I've got – some people care and some people don't. If you keep turning up, day after day, eventually you'll find the people who don't care.'

Ella smiles. 'Thanks, Lester.'

'No worries, Ellabelle. I'll keep asking around for you. Us nonconformists gotta stick together.'

She likes that.

She likes 'nonconformist'.

* * *

Another fortnight passes. Ella keeps getting up early in the morning, keeps introducing herself to new people, keeps waiting for the phone to ring. She signs up with the Musicians' Union, even though the fees sponge up the last of her money. She looks for waitressing jobs. Despite her lack of work, or perhaps because of it, she's having the time of her life. There's a sense that all this cannot last. She's not supposed to be here – a Scottish girl from Springburn with no formal training. So, she might as well enjoy it.

Ella likes Lester, but he's still something of an enigma. He plays gigs like Robert does, and is even good enough to get session work. But he turns down gigs too – Ella hears him on the phone saying no to opportunities when she knows for a fact that he isn't busy. Unlike Robert, he doesn't have a regular engagement, so every day is different.

Sometimes she hardly sees him for days and gets the sense that he doesn't come back to his room. Other times he's never out of the flat, playing music in the front room or in the kitchen, chatting with her and Robert for hours, or with whoever he has brought back as a houseguest that day. Other times he spends locked in his room, sometimes putting on the radio but mostly silent. It's one of these times that she asks Robert about it.

'Is Lester okay?'

Roberts shrugs as though to dismiss the question, but he hesitates a moment before answering.

'Yeah, it's nothing. He just likes to do things his way.'

As promised, the flat is open all hours, especially after the shop downstairs has closed. They host trumpet players and pianists, boys who sing the blues or sing sea shanties or sing Frank Sinatra. People turn up bearing every conceivable instrument – cor anglais, bongos, a French horn, even a concert-scale glockenspiel.

The space by the window, the space over the shop, is where they play. Someone at the piano, two or three people on the blue sofa, others on wooden chairs or standing. The size of the ensemble swells and diminishes with arrivals and departures – duet to trio, trio to quartet, quartet to quintet. One night, everybody is about to go home when three horn players arrive, back from a gig on a West End show. Quintet becomes octet. It feels as though, with players coming and going, they could keep playing endlessly. The fabric of the building seems to shake, but nobody knocks on the door to complain. They drink whisky and beer, smoke cheap cigarettes.

But for all this, Ella's favourite time is when it is just the three of them. In addition to saxophone, Robert has learned clarinet. They will sit, Lester and Ella alternating between playing rhythm on Lester's acoustic and fills on Ella's electric, while Robert plays smoky melody lines. In these long moments, she feels they understand each other far better than when they use words.

*   *   *

Another week goes by. Lester offers to pay Ella's rent and she doesn't say no. He doesn't even tell Robert. Though her room is barely decorated, she starts to pack away the few keepsakes she has on the dresser. She makes a call to enquire about the cost of a ticket to Glasgow.

She says nothing to Robert.

She's sitting in the kitchen one morning, watching the rain stream down the window. She has a headache from the night before, when a bass-playing friend of Lester's had arrived, fresh back from a tour of American military bases in Germany, bearing two large bottles of schnapps. She is contemplating going back to bed when the phone rings and Lester pokes his head around the door.

'Call for Miss Campbell.'

'Who is it?'

'I think it's the union.'

She picks herself up and gets to the phone.

'Hello? Yes, speaking.' She listens for a moment. 'Well of course I can read!'

Somewhere behind her, she hears Lester snort with laughter. Putting one hand on her back, he whispers in her other ear – 'He means, can you sight-read music?'

Ella blushes at her mistake, but the person on the other end of the line is already talking. It seems haughtiness may have worked in her favour. She scrabbles for the pencil and paper they keep on the table.

'Yes . . . yes . . . okay, I will do that. Right. Goodbye.'

She put the phone down and turns to Lester, wide-eyed. 'Well?'

'The big band at Streatham Locarno. They need a replacement after their guitarist got in a car crash. He said he'd already gone through five people in the directory and none of them picked up. They need me tonight.'

Lester scoops her up and spins her around and hugs her so tight she thinks her throbbing head will pop like a cork. He puts her down, but her head keeps spinning.

'This calls for a celebration! Is any of that schnapps left over?'

Ella groans and hugs Lester again, breathing in his cologne.

* * *

The Gerry Whitfield Big Band plays five nights a week at the Streatham Locarno. Saturdays they play a matinee tea dance. Ella turned up on the first day and found Gerry Whitfield pacing the dancefloor, trailing plumes of cigarette smoke. After a few pert questions, he had taken her to the stage and got her to run through ten charts, accompanying her on the piano.

By this time, fear had curdled Ella's hangover into stomach-churning doom. She stumbled a few times over the charts, lost his tempo a few other times. But she gritted her teeth and clung on, feeling more as though she was driving a runaway car than playing guitar.

At the end, Gerry Whitfield had nodded a few times.

'You're good. Good enough for us. I do usually ask if you have a black suit.'

'I have a black dress . . .' Ella stammered. 'Knee-length, cinched at the waist . . .'

'Yes, yes, I am sure it's lovely.' He nodded a few times more. 'Fine – get back here for six thirty and we'll have a quick run-through with the band.'

A month has passed since that impromptu interview and Ella is still in the band. The original guitarist has recovered from the car crash but hasn't got back his place. She gets on well with the rest of them, even gets invited to other gigs they're playing.

The pay . . . She's sure that there are musicians making more in London. There must be. But the fact that she is making so much, above her rent and the bills, all for playing music, seems beautifully absurd. She will remember it while walking down the street and burst out laughing.

Her role in the band isn't difficult, because guitar is never a featured instrument in their arrangements, where the saxophones and trumpets do the soloing. For now, this is a small qualm. Looking out at the whirling bodies, all those sharp suits and bright dresses, dancing to the music she's playing – that's enough.

* * *

Spring passes into summer. Ella's fear, that her new life would prematurely end, wanes with the heat. One Saturday night, she's sprawled out on the blue sofa after a sweltering gig at the Locarno. Robert is in the broken wingback armchair, frowning over a book called *Advanced Polyrhythms in Improvisation*. Olivia is sitting on a chair near him, painting her nails and reading a magazine propped in her lap.

She doesn't visit often, which Ella is thankful for, but will turn up without warning and hang around until her distaste for their flat gets the better of her. Ella has heard her nagging Robert to move out, though she leaves the 'and in with me' unspoken.

Lester bursts in through the front door and takes the stairs two at a time. He's wearing cream linen trousers and a waistcoat with a sky-blue shirt.

'Right! Who wants to go on the town?'

Robert raises his head, squinting at this radiant apparition.

'It's eleven at night, Lester. We're knackered.'

'Aw, don't be a killjoy. If you were going to bed, you'd have gone already.' He comes and leans on one wing of the armchair, peering down at the theory book. 'What're you doing, your math homework?'

'Pretty much.' Ella smirks, raising her head from the settee.

'Well, I think we should go to The Nucleus.'

'What's The Nucleus?' Ella asks.

'It's a coffee shop in Monmouth Street where the beatniks hang out. It's open till six.'

'In the morning?' Olivia frowns.

'We should go!' Ella says, impressed. She's not a hundred percent sure what a beatnik is, but she knows they fall under the umbrella of nonconformity. 'They have music, right?'

'Of course.' Lester grins. 'You should bring your instruments, they'll let us play.'

'They'll let anybody play free of charge,' Olivia pouts. She doesn't play anything except people's nerves, and though she claims that she adores music, Ella has seen little evidence. Robert throws his theory book down sulkily.

'It'll be ages to wait for the next night bus, and I can't be bothered to trek all the way uptown.'

'Oh, but we don't need to get the night bus. I'll give you a lift.'

Robert and Ella exchange a look. Lester can be a bit . . . impulsive, at times.

'You'll give us a lift? In what? Did you buy a couple of tandem bicycles?'

Lester just grins, turns on his heel and walks back down the stairs. With another glance at each other, Robert, Olivia and Ella follow after him. A warm breeze is blowing through the open front door, the air smells smoky. Lester steps to one side with a flourish.

'Ta-da! What do you think?'

Sitting on the side of the road is an enormous car. There

are prominent rust patches fringing the bodywork, the style old and boxy. The paint job is white and custard yellow. Ella thinks that if they added some raspberry racing stripes, the car would look like a tremendous, wheeled trifle.

Robert looks around the car, eyes wide. 'A Hummer? What *year* was this made?'

'Nineteen thirty-two, baby! Great year for cars.'

Ella can't stop herself laughing. 'What do you know about cars?' She nudges him in the ribs.

'Not much, but what's to know? Just look at her!'

'I can't help but look,' Ella smirks, 'it's taking up most of our road. I am not sure if you bought a car or a conservatory.'

Robert straightens up from inspecting a loose bit of running board. 'What did you spend on this monstrosity?'

'The low, low price of twenty pounds.'

Ella raises her eyebrows. It's not much money for a car, but it's still a lot of money.

'Does it go?'

Lester throws his hands up in mock offence. 'What kind of question is that? Of course it goes! I drove it here myself. Now come on, get your glad rags on and let's take a trip. We'll drink some coffee and play some good music.'

'I take it this coffee bar doesn't serve drinks?' Olivia asks.

'Strictly unlicensed premises, Miss, but no rules about taking your own.' Lester pats the breast pocket of his waistcoat, which has a hip-flask-shaped bulge. 'So, we'll Irish up those coffees and dance the night away.'

He grabs Ella's hand and twirls her in a pirouette. She laughs, as much at Olivia's obvious disapproval as anything.

'Well, I'm in,' she says. Robert is still staring at the gigantic car, smiling and shaking his head.

'Oh, all right. Who am I to say no to the owner of London's biggest car?'

Olivia nods once with a pout.

* * *

Admittedly, the car starts like a dream. They've loaded the guitars and Robert's tenor sax into the boot. In the ancient automobile, each of them dressed up, Ella feels like they're off to rob a bank. They drive down through Brixton Hill, the roads all but empty under the lamplight. There are a few stars in the sky, but the sky never really gets dark at this time of year. They cruise up to Stockwell and follow the river. London lies across the river, glowing gently like a golden hoard. In the car they chat over the thunderous sound of the engine, smoking cigarettes out of the rolled-down windows.

Ella sits in front with Lester at the wheel, Olivia and Robert bouncing around in the back. Robert passes a hip flask forward to Ella and she takes a long swig. Ella looks sideways at Lester, with one hand on the wheel, the other arm slung over the open window, so casual that you wouldn't know he was manoeuvring two tons of rusty car.

They cross the river at Westminster Bridge. Though the night is warm, the air over the Thames is hazy, and the lights of Parliament smoulder to their left. Ella pokes her head out of the window as they pass under Big Ben, grinning up at his expressionless face. They hang a right up Whitehall, heading in the direction of Piccadilly Circus with its advertisements for Bovril, Wrigley's Chewing Gum and Lemon Hart Rum. Lester is talking loudly about some kind of drink with eggs in it called an Orange Julius, saying he would pay *fifty bucks* for a cup right now, when the engine makes a strangulated noise.

They look at each other. The engine chokes and falls silent and the gigantic car cruises to a halt. Lester guns the ignition a couple of times, but it splutters and dies.

'Shit.' Lester bangs the wheel.

'Twenty pounds well spent,' Olivia drawls.

'You'll have to get out and push.' Lester looks around at them.

'Us? What about you?'

'I'm driving.'

'Uh, Lester, there are a couple of coppers over there.' Ella points sideways to their left, where two policemen are standing sentry. They keep looking at each other, then back to the car, as though talking about what to do.

'Where are we?' Robert says, then – 'Oh no . . .'

'What, where are we?' Ella asks, swivelling round to face them.

'Oh, we've just broken down outside Downing Street, is all.' Olivia has her arms crossed. 'They're probably discussing what to do if this car turns out to be a gigantic bomb . . .'

'Oh no, oh shit . . .' Lester starts to panic.

'What's the matter?' Ella shakes his shoulder. 'You do have the documents for this car?'

'Yes, yes I have those . . . just no insurance . . . or driving licence.'

'Lester!'

'You don't have a licence?'

'I have *a* licence,' he shrugs, 'it's issued by the State of New York Commissioner of Motor Vehicles.'

'Jesus Christ, Lester—'

Ella cuts Robert off. 'They're coming over. Both of them.'

'Okay, look casual.'

One of the policemen comes to the open driver's window, while the other inspects the vehicle. Lester smiles.

'Trouble with your vehicle, sir?'

'Good evening, officer. I'm afraid we've got a spot of engine trouble.'

'I see, sir. And where are you off to at this time of night?'

Lester opts for being more or less truthful.

'The Nucleus coffee house on Monmouth Street – we're jazz musicians on our way to a late gig.'

The officer crouches closer, looking around at the rest of them, and seems to decide the explanation is plausible. Ella smiles and raises a hand.

'Good evening, Miss. Is there anything we can do to help you get on your way?'

Lester looks from the policeman to Ella as though searching

for inspiration. 'As a matter of fact, I think it is just a problem with the battery. If you wouldn't mind giving us a bit of a push start, I reckon I can get her going again.'

The policeman's eyebrows rise for a second, but he nods.

'All right – if you wouldn't mind winding down your window all the way, Miss, me and my companion will see what we can do.'

The two policemen put their shoulders to the frame of the car. One, two, three . . . They start to push and, remarkably, the car starts to move forward. Ella looks at the man beside her, Brylcreemed hair neatly short under his helmet, a bulge of neck escaping from his collar turning red with exertion. Lester guns the ignition. The car is barely moving, though she can hear the slapping of the policemen's shoes either side of them.

On the third attempt, Lester turns the key and there's a belch from the engine. For a moment, Ella thinks it has died again, before it roars into life and the car jolts forward. The policemen let go as the car speeds faster than they can run. Lester lets out a triumphant whoop and Ella leans herself out of the window, waving to the policemen. They have their hands on their knees, catching their breath.

'Thanks! See you next time!'

'See you next time?' Lester laughs. They're all laughing as the car races up Parliament Street, except for Olivia, who has her arms firmly crossed over her chest.

'I have never been so mortified.'

At this moment, the car chooses to noisily backfire, causing Olivia to scream and the rest of them to erupt into fresh peals of laughter.

*   *   *

The Nucleus is just as Lester described – a smoky, poorly lit basement full of teenagers in smart sweaters, drinking little cups of coffee. Some of them are talking, some of them are reading – Ella sees Jean-Paul Sartre and Nabokov in the hands of young men – but all of them seem to be flirting.

The room is full of enthusiastic affection. Nobody is smoking regular cigarettes where they can be smoking a corncob pipe, or gold-tipped Sobranie. Though there is no licence for alcohol, it seems many of them have had the same idea as Lester or are indulging in less visible vices. They drink two rounds of Irish coffees and talk about everything and nothing, half listening to the band – a quartet of French horn, trombone, clarinet and drums playing something which may have been intended as New Orleans jazz.

Soon enough the trio have exhausted their repertoire and, after Lester gets the nod from the man behind the bar, the three of them excluding Olivia take to the stage.

They launch into a series of dance tunes, with Lester singing and providing rhythm on his acoustic. It is not a big sound, but the three of them know how to get people dancing. Within a minute of them starting, heads have turned their way, people are nodding to the beat. Before they can start the second tune, the drummer from the previous band asks if he can have a jam. With the thump of the bass drum, couples get up to dance.

They play for forty-five minutes. Olivia, who has sat the whole time they're playing fending off amorous attacks from teenage boys, collars Robert and asks him to take her home. Ella can't blame her really, but she's having too much fun to let it get her down.

'You sure you won't stay?' Ella touches Robert's shoulder for a moment, retreats at a glance from Olivia. For a moment he looks undecided, before Olivia places her hand on the small of his back.

'Nah, we should get back. I've got a full day tomorrow.'

They leave to get a taxi.

'You wanna keep going?' Lester asks.

Ella nods. 'Sunday is supposed to be a day of rest.'

'Atta girl.'

He fetches two more coffees, they drain the last of his hip flask and clink them together.

'To insomnia.'

'To staying up past my bedtime.'

* * *

Lester swings it that they can leave their instruments in the back room of The Nucleus. He stops a guy meandering around the tables, apparently muttering to himself, and buys a bottle of cheap whiskey. It emerges from inside the man's mackintosh.

Lester seems at home anywhere. You wouldn't know he wasn't born within a square mile of Monmouth Street. Ella wonders if he was this natural back in New York, or whether 'out of context' is where Lester feels at home.

She wonders if she can do the same, away from Glasgow. Can she fashion a new way of being? She looks around the room of teenagers smoking silly cigarettes and reading existentialist tracts. Perhaps reinventing yourself isn't so difficult. Perhaps you just move on, try something new and, if you can't forget the bodies you left behind, pretend you've never grieved.

Lester returns with two more cups and they slug whisky from the bottle until the coffees are brimming. They sit close, facing each other, and Ella is dimly aware they must look like they're on a date.

'So, who is Ella Campbell?' Lester asks, as though he has read the last minute of her internal dialogue written on her face.

'Who am I? Like, where did I grow up and who are my friends? What lessons did I enjoy at school?'

Lester shrugs. 'Sure, I guess. But no, that's not what I meant . . . Who do you want to be? What do you want to do?'

'Those are big questions. How about you tell me first?'

Lester straightens up and looks for a moment at the ceiling.

'I want to be famous.' He nods slowly. 'I want to be a singer with my own band, who writes his own songs.'

'You want to write your own songs?' The thought strikes

Ella as novel. It's not that singers or musicians don't ever write their own songs, but it's uncommon. Songwriting is done by the songwriters, music is done by the musicians. 'Have you written any already?'

Lester looks comically bashful. 'Maybe. Maybe I'll play them to you one day.'

Ella smiles. 'I'd like that.'

She puts one hand on top of his.

It must be the coffee, but Ella is barely aware of time passing, that it's the middle of the night. They talk about everything, it seems. She tells Lester about ambitions she hadn't thought of before which, in answering the question, seem real and important to her. She wants to be well paid. She wants to be a session musician. She wants to see more of the world and make people dance who don't speak her language.

Lester smiles at that.

'You have a way with words. Maybe you should be a lyricist.'

They drink more of the whiskey and Ella tells him about her past, about Rene and Sandy, about the world she left behind. He tells her that Glasgow doesn't sound so different to Buffalo in some ways, though he doesn't say what those ways might be. They seem to tell each other everything, though in the days that follow, Ella will wonder if the whiskey robbed her memory of Lester talking about his childhood. She tells him about her school, about her parents, but she will have no memory of him mentioning these things in return.

Finally, it's nearing five in the morning. There's almost no one left in The Nucleus, and the cafe nightshift are preparing to go home to their own beds. Ella and Lester stumble up from the basement into an empty city. The streets around them are wide and blank. She feels as though London is a complex mechanical toy, put together by an ingenious toymaker, not yet set in motion.

She looks at Lester. 'Are you going to drive me home?' she slurs.

'Even if I weren't drunk, I doubt I could get that car running again.' He smiles and takes her hand. 'Mind if I walk you back?'

She nods. Above them the sky is awash with colour, striated silver clouds over a background of pink, leading up to watery blue. The moon is visible to the south, wafer thin. They cross back over Westminster Bridge and look out over the gunmetal grey waters, flowing down to the sea.

Ella feels breathless, not from walking but from the sense of what she's about to do. What is she about to do? She does not know until she's doing it. She turns to Lester, puts one hand on the small of his back, draws close and kisses him.

He freezes for a moment, but only for a moment, then sinks into the kiss. His breath smells of coffee and cigarettes, but so does hers. His skin is soft and warm and smells of soap. They pull away and he is smiling uncertainly, dark eyes reflecting the twinkling light of the river.

'Really?' he asks.

Ella pauses for a second, not breaking eye contact, allowing her thoughts to catch up with her actions. She thinks of Robert. But why? Robert isn't thinking of her. She nods.

'Yes, really.'

They kiss again.

* * *

By the time they've walked back to the flat in Brixton Hill, they're too tired to talk. They go together to Lester's bedroom, which has the only double bed. They fall asleep side-by-side, fully dressed, and sleep until four in the afternoon.

Over the next fortnight they orbit each other, closer each time. Ella is busy in the evenings and Lester often has gigs, but when they're in the flat they will sit and play music or listen to the radio. When Robert is out with Olivia, or when he has said goodnight, they will go to Lester's room and kiss on the bed. They don't sleep together. Ella doesn't hold back, but Lester seems to want to be courteous. Or he is as nervous as she is, Ella thinks, though this seems unlikely.

They go places together on Sundays. A trip to the Leicester Square Odeon; the putting course at Finsbury Park; the penguins at London Zoo. They do not tell Robert, though Ella suspects he knows something is going on. She catches him watching.

Ella's not sure if this is love. She's not sure she cares. She wants to be with Lester and he wants to be with her. It's easy. It's fun.

After three weeks have passed, Lester plays Ella his songs.

She listens to them, hands clasped in her lap like an anxious parent at a school talent show. The songs are deceptively simple. He strums the chords; his voice never makes any great leaps. Yet Ella thinks there is something wonderful about these songs. She can't place the style – there's American blues in there, something folky about the melody, influences of jazz or even show tunes in the harmonies. But the songs belong to Lester, in a genre he alone occupies. They are like masterful paintings, executed with the fewest brushstrokes required.

He records demos of the songs on his latest purchase – an Argyll Minor reel-to-reel tape recorder for fifteen shillings. Housed in a fabric coated suitcase that might belong to a child, the recorder comes with a single microphone. Lester asks Ella to play guitar fills on the demos, and though she accepts, the task makes her more nervous than getting up in front of three hundred people at the Locarno.

They do the five songs together, and because the single microphone must be placed somewhere between Lester's voice and guitar, Ella's electric is pleasantly in the background.

Ella shows him *The Songs of the Dead* by Jack Shapiro and plays the tunes for him. He smiles and says that he can hear her style in some of them. He especially likes one of the waltzes, 'The Lover', and they record a demo of it with Ella playing the melody line on her electric. The six songs – five of Lester's and the wordless tune by Jack Shapiro – fit on one tape. They listen back to the demos over and over and agree they are good.

'Maybe I don't need a band,' he says, after a couple of repeats.
'Maybe I just need you.'

She kisses him on the forehead.

*   *   *

A month after the night they visited The Nucleus, Ella and
Lester are lying side-by-side in his bed. She's tired from playing
the Locarno, he's tired from a day of trudging around Denmark
Street, convincing producers to listen to the demos.

She turns and puts a hand on his chest.

'Lester?'

'Yeah?' He sounds distant, staring at the ceiling as though
it isn't there and he can see all the way to the stars.

'Do you . . . do you want to . . . ?'

She gets his attention but doesn't know how to say it. She
undoes the top button of her blouse. All night she watches
couples dancing. Couples flying apart and coming back
together again. Couples engaged in a dance that isn't *just* a
dance. Lester looks her in the eyes and nods twice. Her heart
skips a beat.

'Okay, so—'

'Ella, look . . .' He turns to her. 'There's something you need
to know about me.'

No, no, no.

He doesn't want her that way.

So stupid.

'Look, I understand,' she says, flatly.

'No, you don't.' He flops back to look at the ceiling again. 'Did Robert ever tell you about the accident? The reason I got my pay-out?'

' . . . No.'

He stares at the ceiling for a long time, and Ella begins to suspect that he'll say no more. When he speaks again, the words come in a rush.

'I was at school, when I was seven years old, back in Buffalo of course, and we were just sitting down for Geography when there was this funny sound. Like a bang but not quite like that . . . Anyway, it was one of the boilers that heated the school. It exploded. Or else there were some rags near to the boiler that might have caught fire. Anyway, it doesn't matter, but . . .'

He peters out. Ella puts her hand back on his chest and, without looking at his face, gets closer, encouraging him with her proximity.

'Go on.'

'Well, whatever it was, the school was on fire in under a minute. Faster than they could get us out. I don't remember it so well, maybe I tried to forget it, but I just remember a lot of smoke and shouting and not being able to see where anything was and being so scared that I wouldn't find the exit, and then . . .'

He laughs suddenly, and it makes Ella jump, but she tries not to show how scared she is.

'And then it was like a cartoon. Like one of those cartoons

where the devil comes and gets them. Suddenly I could see flames, and they were under my feet, poking like tongues between the floorboards. And I ran around, but I couldn't get away quickly enough . . .'

Ella glances at his face and sees that he is crying. They are silent for the longest time.

'Five of my classmates died there, two died later at the hospital, and one of them was . . . my friend . . . I called her my girlfriend . . . Her name was Mary Ann.'

'I am so sorry, Lester. I had no idea.'

'Anyway, it's fine.' He wipes his eyes roughly. 'I made it out and they didn't, and I should stop feeling sorry for myself when I got to live my whole life.'

'That's not fair. You shouldn't be unkind to yourself.'

Lester shrugs and looks away for a second. He takes a deep breath and then looks back to her.

'I was in the hospital for a couple of months. That's when I started playing guitar. They brought one to my bed. And the insurance pay-out when I was twenty-one meant that I could come to England, meant that I could meet you. So, I'm not sad about it . . . but I . . . I . . .'

He swallows nervously, gestures vaguely to his body. Ella understands. She gets up on one elbow, pulls his face towards hers. She kisses him, her tears falling onto his face and mingling with his own.

'I don't care. It doesn't matter. Whatever it is. It doesn't matter. Only you matter.'

He takes a deep breath, and this time he seems calm. They get off the bed so they're standing next to each other. Ella can tell that he wants to turn the light out, because he keeps looking over at the switch, but she stays between him and it, and they say nothing about it.

He takes off his shirt and Ella sees the smooth brown skin of his chest, sees the point where it becomes rough and bobbled, like something that has melted and re-formed. She sees the burns that spread down his back, down one leg, slung over his shoulder like a sash. She steps out of her own clothes, heart stammering. She steps forward and puts her arms around his waist and kisses the burnt skin on his chest above his heart.

'You're beautiful,' she tells him.

*   *   *

Summer turns into autumn.

Ella and Lester are official. They couldn't keep it from Robert any longer. Olivia seems to think it's faintly ridiculous but is friendlier toward Ella. They go places on weekends, looking at the sarcophagi in the British Museum, the vast, murky oil paintings in the National. They visit vast, suburban churches and look around like tourists. Lester will make notes in a little book that he keeps for songwriting ideas. Ella wonders what songs he could write about the graves of people he never knew.

Autumn turns to winter.

Everything is wonderful and then, abruptly, it isn't. If Ella had forgotten how cold the flat gets, she soon remembers. They keep the fires going as much as they can, but it never seems to get warm.

Robert is always busy, always tired, and always too tired to play when he's around. He spends more and more time with Olivia and talks about moving in with her.

Lester seems to take fewer and fewer gigs, spends more time knocking on doors in Denmark Street, or sitting in the lobbies of recording studios, waiting to be seen.

The demo tape is played many times, but nobody offers him a contract. His mood changes like the weather. He keeps to his room or disappears for long spells. When he returns, he won't tell Ella where he has been.

*　*　*

It's half one in the morning. Ella is sitting at the kitchen table, easing high heels off her swollen feet, when she hears the door go. She knows it's Robert as he's walking upstairs. Perhaps it's the burden of carrying two saxophones, but he has a certain lope. He puts his cases down in the hallway, stretches with a quiet grunt, lets himself into the kitchen.

'Oh! I didn't realize you were up.'

'Just got in.'

'Gig okay?'

'Mm, yeah. The orchestra pit in that place is tiny, but I like the arrangements.'

'You wore heels for the pit?'

'Someone warned me about the conductor. Doesn't like his women too "casual".'

Robert moves over to the sink and makes a noise between amusement and sympathy. He runs his hands under the cold tap and splashes his face.

'And you're just back?'

'We went for drinks after.'

'Ah. You want a cup of tea? Cocoa?'

'Okay.'

Robert finds the milk pan, fills it from a fresh bottle of blue top, rummages in the cupboard for the powder.

'Back in a minute.' Ella goes through to her bedroom carrying the heels in one hand, tosses them across her bed, struggles for a moment to unzip herself. Stepping out of the dress, she allows the cool air from her window to blow over her for a second before taking her dressing gown from the back of the door and putting it on. When she comes back to the kitchen, Robert is taking the milk off the hob. She sits and watches him add the milk to two mugs, stirring methodically, pressing the lumps out with the back of a teaspoon.

'I never thought we'd be here,' Ella says. She's so sleepy, and still a little drunk. She feels like she's talking to Robert in a dream.

'Here?' Robert asks, still stirring.

'Here in this kitchen. Here in London. After all this time.'

If Robert seems to stiffen, it's almost imperceptible. 'Life's a funny thing, isn't it?'

'Yeah. But it seemed pretty unlikely, not long ago.'

Robert brings the mugs of cocoa to the table and sits across from her. The table isn't big. Their knees could brush together under it, if they weren't careful.

'You're right. I didn't see this coming.'

'Well, you invited me.' Ella takes a sip of cocoa, but it's too hot. She blows steam from it.

Robert smiles. 'You're right. But . . . well, I suppose I didn't see that coming.'

'You surprised yourself?'

He nods. He smiles slightly, but it is mostly in the eyes. A rueful kind of smile.

'Well, I'm glad you did,' she says. 'It's good to be here.'

'I wish I'd done it sooner.'

'Invited me here?'

'That's not what I mean. I wish . . .'

He trails off, but she knows what he means. She doesn't want to think about that. About what would have happened if Robert had acted sooner. She changes the subject, but immediately regrets it.

'How's Olivia?'

Robert looks away, toward the window, though it is dark and there is nothing to be seen.

'I don't know. I think she's mad with me.'

'Mad for what?'

'I don't know. Most of time I don't, until after the fact. Sometimes I don't find out, even then.'

Ella has never heard him talk this way about Olivia. She sips cocoa and lets him go on.

'She just . . . she gets emotional about things, I guess. And she'll disappear for a few days. Won't answer my calls. I get so worried, but then she's back as though nothing was wrong and—'

He stops himself, mid-flow, sensing he has said too much. Ella knows she shouldn't keep talking. She should make her excuses. She should go to bed.

'Lester is like that too. He just disappears . . .'

'Mm.' Robert makes a sound of partial agreement. 'But I don't think he's making a point about anything. Lester disappears because sometimes Lester just disappears.'

Ella nods, though it's an oversimplification. She wants to say that, making a point or not, the effect on her is just the same. She worries. She has no idea where he is right now. But she feels that, if she can keep going, keep everything normal, she can rescue Lester from his bad dreams. She has heard him in the night. She hangs onto the hope that she can get the other Lester back. As his mood changed with the season, maybe it will change again, come the spring.

They sit in silence and sip their drinks for a minute. Ella can feel sleep rising up in her. The warm drink isn't helping. She forces her eyes open. She wants to say something. She has wanted to say it for weeks, but the right moment was never there. She won't waste this one.

'I'm sorry . . .' she begins.

'What for?'

'For what I said . . . in the tea rooms.'

Robert is frozen. If Ella has doubted how much she hurt him for the last six years, it's plain to see on his face.

'I'm sorry I called you a coward.'

'It's all right,' he says, robotically.

'No, it's not. I shouldn't have said it. I've hated myself for it.'

He looks at her, unable to say anything for a long moment. Then –

'Was it true what you said? About Sandy?'

She nods slowly. 'That's what he told me, in his own way. He could never have said . . .'

'No, of course.' Robert nods. He wipes tears from his eyes briskly, stands up. 'Well, it's late. I should get ready for bed.'

'Okay.' Ella nods too, sadness and relief mingling. 'I won't be long myself.'

Robert hovers for a moment, puts his mug in the sink and goes. Ella drinks the last of her cocoa, quite cool now, and listens to him brushing his teeth. Sleep curls around her and, before she knows it, she's asleep. She's not sure how much time has passed when someone shakes her by the shoulder.

'Ella, time for bed.'

'Mmpf? Geddoff.'

She scrunches her eyes more tightly shut. She knows she would be more comfortable if she weren't sitting on this kitchen chair, but there's no way she's getting up now. Ella drifts back to sleep.

An arm is slung around her shoulders. Another arm goes under the back of her knees. She's lifted from the chair. She keeps her eyes closed. This is less weird if she's asleep. Robert carries her through to her room, places her on the bed and pulls the cover over her. Ella thinks he has gone when he bends down and kisses her forehead. She feels him sitting on the edge of the bed. Her heart speeds up, then slows again. She feels peaceful with him there. At last she sleeps.

When she wakes in the morning her bedroom door is shut, and Robert is gone.

*   *   *

It's Friday morning. Ella and Robert have been quietly moving around the flat for a couple of hours. They've eaten separate breakfasts and shared a pot of coffee. Robert ironed some washing off the creel and Ella scrubbed the chipped polish from her nails and painted on a fresh coat. They shine like the poison apple in Disney's *Snow White*. She shouldn't bother, given how quickly they get chipped when she's playing, but she knows that when it comes to live gigs, people don't book her just based on her playing.

There's no sign of Lester, though Ella heard him moving around in the night. Last night some friends of Robert's stayed late and jammed for a while, but Lester hadn't come out. He's said no more than a dozen words to Ella in the last week.

She blows on her nails until she's sure they're set, drinks the last of the coffee and gets up from the table. Robert watches her but says nothing. She walks into the hall and knocks on Lester's door. No response. She hesitates. There's no lock. She pushes into the room.

Lester is lying fully clothed on top of the bedclothes. His shirt is so crumpled he looks like a deflated balloon.

'Hey.' His eyes fix on her, but his body remains inert.

Ella sighs and closes the door behind her.

'What's going on?'

'What do you mean?'

She goes and sits on the edge of the bed. Tentatively, she reaches out and touches his shoulder. Since when did she get cautious about touching him? Even before they were going out, Lester was always so tactile, it never felt strange to hug him or ruffle his hair. They were more like siblings, then.

'You can talk to me.'

'I know.' A curt nod, the most movement so far.

'Then why don't you?'

Ella counts eleven breaths in and out before he replies.

'Because there's nothing to talk about. I get like this some-times . . .'

'It's been a long time, Lester.'

'I know. Sometimes it's short, sometimes . . .' he trails off. He barely seems to have the energy to finish a sentence.

'Maybe you should see—'

He doesn't wait for her to finish the sentence before he's shaking his head.

'No. I'm not seeing anybody, okay? I'm not crazy.'

'I didn't say—'

'I'm like this sometimes, and then I'm not. I don't know how long it will be. If you're not up for that, if you can't *handle* that—'

'Hey, I did not say that.'

'Good . . . *fine.*' He goes back to staring at the ceiling.

She waits for something else. Anything else. But the broadcast has ended and there's just the hiss of static in her ears. She bends, kisses him on the forehead, and goes to get on with her day.

* * *

Ella looks around the cramped room. The walls are pale beige, flecked with brown stains at coffee-cup height and smeared yellow at ceiling level by cigarette smoke. The air is thick with it now, as the horn section exhales steadying puffs like an idling engine. There are many other performance aids littered around the room in addition to the half dozen brands of cigarette on display – decongestant nasal sprays and inhalers, menthol chewing gum, glucose tablets, chapsticks, liniments and moisturizing creams for sore mouths and fingers. Studio work, Ella gathers, is a marathon not a sprint. There is something about it all that makes her feel uneasy, like she has stumbled into the male locker room and everyone is about to strip off for a shower.

She fingers the fretboard nervously. It's not her guitar, but a much nicer model, given to her by the producer when he saw her battered Vega Duo-Tron. This is a Gibson jazz hollow-body with a lemon-yellow maple top that shines like a tiger's eye gem. Ella wants to play and play this lovely guitar, but she has had no chance – it was straight into the studio with the rest of them.

She wishes she had a cigarette, because at least she would have something to do with her hands. She could watch it burning down and it would look cool and contemplative. Instead she studies the chart in front of her as though trying to work something out, but she suspects this makes her look rather stupid, because the chart is the easiest thing in the world – five chord changes in the key of B flat, with an instruction for the guitar to play rhythm on the second and fourth beats. Hardly Beethoven. Still, she mustn't mess this up. She's been waiting for too long.

There is some signal that break time is drawing to a close. Ella isn't sure what the signal was, but she's aware of the hastily dragged cigarettes, the application of Vaseline to chapped lips, the shaking out of spit valves.

The song they are recording is for a toothpaste commercial. Ella knows this because her chart has 'Tootpaste Comercial' written on it. There is no extra information about what brand it may be, or whether the advert will be on radio or television. Ella is wondering if she will hear the tune, hear her own playing, maybe when she is least expecting it, when the voice of the producer crashes her thoughts.

'Miss? Are you ready?' She glances around and realizes that

everyone is sitting attentively, waiting for the take. They are not smirking at her exactly, but there is something in their expressions. It's not that she isn't welcome. She can stay, so long as she's content to be an amusing plaything. After all, she's no threat.

'Yes, I'm ready,' Ella says.

* * *

When the session is over, Ella goes to return the Gibson and reclaim her ancient Vega. It's going to be difficult to go back to the worn frets and wobbly tuning of her old guitar. Maybe if she gets a few more sessions like this one, she can have a look around the instrument shops of Denmark Street.

The other players file out of the studio, chatting to one another and paying her no attention. She sees the producer at the back of the room, coiling a length of cable like a cowboy with his lasso. He's wearing a white technician's coat, and with his pale blond hair it gives him an almost ghostly look. He can't be much older than Ella.

'Hey, this isn't mine.' She holds up the golden instrument.

'Oh, sure. Yours is just at the back there . . .'

'Thanks.' She goes to swap the guitars.

'Actually, do you have a moment?'

'Me?'

'Yes. My name's Peter.'

'I'm Ella.'

'Hey Ella.' He combs his floppy hair to one side with his

fingers. 'I just want to show you something in the control room.'

Ella frowns, putting the guitar down. She's wary of accepting this offer from a stranger but is curious to see the control room. Everything about this place is novel. She follows him up the stairs with a backward glance to the empty studio.

The control room is warm — even more so than the stuffy studio. There's a whirr from cooling fans in the machinery. If Ella looked inside the console, the tape machine, or the banks of compressors, she would see row upon row of glowing valves, big and small, like ranks of seraphim. The room is cramped and Ella, not usually claustrophobic, feels an implied threat at being in such a small space with this man.

'Look, don't take this to heart, okay . . .' he starts, but does not finish, swinging himself into the booth and past her, landing in the chair like a pilot settling into his cockpit. He leans over to the tape transport console and presses a button. There's a heavy click. The jingle they just recorded starts to play out of the speakers which flank the window looking out over the empty studio.

Ella waits for the thirty seconds of the tune to play out. It sounds good over the speakers. When it's done, Peter presses buttons to stop the tape and rewind it. He turns to her, looking apologetic.

'What? What's the matter with it?'

'This is your first session, right?'

She can feel herself getting angry, needs to hold it together. 'Yes.'

'It's just that you're rushing a bit. Very common with new session players . . .'

He presses play again. Ella listens to the tune and realizes, with horror, that he's right. It's not much, but she's coming in a fraction ahead of the beat every time, as though she's trying to drive the band to a faster tempo. He clicks the tape off again.

'Look, don't worry about it – the conductor didn't notice, so if anyone mentions it he'll say it was intentional.'

'Do you even play?' Ella asks, feeling immediately childish.

'No,' he smiles, 'I just listen to music all day.'

'Well, I think it sounds fine.'

Ella rounds on her heel and leaves Peter to his control room, knowing very well that she will go home and practise with the metronome until her fingers are sore. She's in the marble reception hall of the studio, buttoning her coat and getting out her mittens, when she hears her name.

'Ella?'

She turns, half expecting it to be the conductor, ready to condemn her inability to play to tempo.

It's Robert.

Ella knows something before she knows it. She feels drunk – the dimensions of the room stretch and tilt around her. She leans forward and grasps his arm.

'Why are you here?'

'I'm sorry . . . something's happened. I couldn't tell you over the phone.'

* * *

She doesn't take off her coat. Winter clothes are ideal for this sparse, tiled room. The lights are as dim as the winter sun. Robert stands close by with one hand on her back. She considers shrugging it off but does not.

Her anger towards Robert is fierce but unaccountable.

The policeman opens the metal locker, which looks more like a butcher's refrigerator. He slides out the gurney, where a body is laid under a white sheet. He looks at her for permission to continue. She nods without looking him in the eye, and he peels the white sheet back.

Lester was not in the river all that long, but long enough for it to bloat and distort his features.

For a moment, she has the wild hope that this has all been a mistake. A black man with similar features, of course . . . But then the white sheet is pulled down as far as his chest, and Ella can see the canyon-system of scarred flesh over his unbeating heart.

'Yes, that's Lester Benjamin.'

* * *

Ella doesn't let them cremate him. That's the least she can do. Lester didn't have a will, but she claims the Argyll, the tapes and his guitar for herself. She pays for the funeral with her own money. She feels nothing, good or bad. She's a frozen person in a frozen world. Events shift around her like icebergs.

A couple of weeks pass. She's sitting at the piano in the front room, not playing but looking out of the window at a flock of starlings circling in the grey sky. The keys of the piano are coffined under the rosewood fallboard, where she rests her elbows. She hears Robert come out of his room and hesitate in the doorway behind her. When she doesn't turn around, he says –

'I think I'm going to move out.'

She watches the wheeling birds. Are they catching insects up there? Is it a mating dance? Or do they do it just for the satisfaction of doing it, like playing music?

'Don't you have anything to say?' He walks over and sits on a chair next to the piano. Lester used to sit there, when they played together. Robert is dressed for a gig, his saxophone case in hand.

'You sound like you've made your mind up.'

'It's just, the two of us are paying for three rooms and . . . Olivia found a place for the two of us.'

Ella makes a noise of contempt. Robert doesn't say anything. They sit in silence for a moment. Ella doesn't have the energy to fight. She tries to hold onto this moment, before the two of them fly apart again.

'Do you think we're cursed?' she asks, at last.

When he speaks, Robert's voice has contracted. She doesn't need to speak their names for him to know what she means. People their age should not know so many dead people.

'Just unlucky, I guess,' Robert says. 'Though I'm struggling to see the difference right now.'

She looks at him and forces a smile.

'You should get going.'

* * *

She searches for a flat in town. She keeps playing gigs, keeps making money, making contacts, getting on.

When she comes to pack everything away, to move to her new one-person flat in Soho, she finds *The Songs of the Dead* in Lester's room. She doesn't remember him taking it, though they shared everything. She flicks through the pages and something catches her eye. Lester has underlined part of the introduction in pencil, then circled around it for good measure.

She reads:

Perhaps a professor of musicology could explain the profound effect of music on us as human beings. I am no professor. I cannot say why one song makes me happy or sad, why it reminds me of my childhood or my lost love. But I think perhaps music is part of us all. It is in our cells, our bodies, a memory passed down from our earliest ancestors. The shapes we make with music are tools, the same as hammers or pliers, but subtler. The shapes we make with music are the keys to the locked doors of our past. And if we can open those doors, perhaps we can come to terms with what we have done, who we have been, and the people we have lost along the way.

4.

The Rebel

EVERYTHING IS CALM AND bright. I open my eyes and look at the wood-lined ceiling, the light dancing off the ocean. Like an echo of a dream I hear 'The Lover' repeating. I raise my head. Oh . . .

I'm alone in the saloon with the baby. Was this the dream to wash Rene and Sandy away? I don't want to be alone on this boat. I go to the window and see Sandy, standing sentry, but the storm lamp has gone out. Rene is cross-legged nearby, chatting about something.

Breathe, just breathe.

In the daylight I can see a spider has built his web outside the window. It's hung with dew, or perhaps sea spray. I wonder if the spider knew, when he built the web, that he was going to sea. I check the baby. He wakes as I get close. I rock him around the cabin for a minute while he splutters into my shoulder. I make him a bottle, change his nappy.

I'm getting good at this.

He cries half-heartedly. When I put him in his cushion-crib, he doesn't complain. He's wearing a baby grow past its best, but there are no clean ones upstairs. I don't want to go downstairs, but it can't be helped.

The water is knee-high now.

I go to the nursery and find baby grows. I'm coming back into the corridor when I hear a noise. Holding the clean clothes to my chest, I wade to the spare cabin and let myself in. Lester is sitting on the bed, arranging a few things next to him on the sheets. He lifts his head and notices me in the doorway, then turns back to the things on the bed, worrying over them.

'It's funny – why these things? My fountain pen, a handful of change, half a roll of Polo mints . . . Why did I come back with these things?'

He's not wearing the outfit he was wearing on the day he died. Not the outfit he put on, knowing he was going to climb the parapet of Waterloo Bridge. Not the outfit the mortuary gave me, washed and folded into a neat parcel. There was nothing else to hand over except his wristwatch. Everything else must have fallen out of his pockets as he tumbled through the silted darkness.

No, he's not wearing that outfit – he's dressed in a white linen waistcoat and trousers, with a sky-blue shirt rolled to the elbow. He has taken off his brogues and socks, placed them next to him. The bed is dry, but the water is close to swamping it.

'Come back? Where did you come back from?' I ask. In contrast to Lester I feel so shabby. An old woman in a stained nightgown, hair greasy and uncombed.

'I don't remember. Back from . . . *not-here*.' He shrugs.

'When someone dies, people say they lost them. You know? "We lost my mum last month", and "She lost the baby."'

Lester smiles faintly, as though he's enjoying listening to me.

'Anyway, I used to think it was a silly expression, when I was younger. You don't *lose* someone, they die. They're not lost, they're . . . gone. Gone to bits. But when you died, I felt just like that. You weren't gone, I just lost you. You were around somewhere, I was sure. Maybe not in the flat, but around London somewhere. You were doing a gig or showing someone your tapes. I'd just misplaced you.'

He looks at me. It's the longest thing I've said in years. I didn't know I could say things like that any more. It's easier to talk to the dead than the living.

'You always were the clever one.'

I take a deep breath. I did this already, grieved already. Do I have to do it again, just because he's turned up?

'I've had time to think about it. It was a long time ago.'

'Was it?' He frowns. 'I feel like I just fell into that river and . . . washed up here. Wherever here is.'

I shake my head, smiling. 'The Ionian Sea, maybe?'

'Is that from a kids' book?'

'Somewhere near Greece.'

'Like where Orpheus came from?'

'I think so.'

'Did you rescue me from the underworld?'

I'm embarrassed by the question. I didn't mean to rescue anyone except the baby.

'Maybe. I think I'm just trying to rescue myself.'

He gets off the bed, standing in the cold water, and puts the bits back into his pockets.

'Aren't we all, Ellabelle? I'm sorry you got so old.'

'I am sorry you didn't.'

I think I might have gone too far, but a broad smile breaks over his face. Lester starts to laugh.

* * *

I introduce him to the others. Sandy seems suspicious, not because Lester is black but because he is American. He warms to him when I explain he's a musician. They chat about Count Basie and Duke Ellington for a while, but then Lester tries to enthuse about Elvis Presley, to Sandy's confusion.

'Is he a Welsh singer? I don't know any Welsh singers.'

I explain to Lester that Sandy never heard Elvis. Though Sandy and Rene look younger than him, all their references are older. Rene likes Lester immediately, though I have to explain she shouldn't call him *coloured*, much to Rene's confusion and Lester's also.

'Why not?'

'I don't think it's something people say any more.'

Rene and Lester look at each other and shrug. For his part, Lester is interested in Rene, the long-lost sister of his friend.

'What happened to Robert?' he asks, in a moment where Rene has gone to look at the baby. I search my memory but can find nothing later than moving out of the flat in Brixton Hill.

'I don't know. I wish he was here.'

'Me too.'

* * *

There's a crew now on the *Mnemosyne*. The sail has come loose in the night and flopped down in a tangle of ropes, but I'm in no rush to fix it. Unless we need to dodge another island, I'd rather drift aimlessly than forge at speed into the unknown.

For now, the most important thing is to get the water pumped out of the lower decks. Sandy helps set up the bilge pump on the deck. We run one hose down the stairs and the other overboard. I pull the cord to start the engine. It coughs once then roars. Half a minute passes before a jet of water shoots overboard. Sandy keeps one hose sucking up water below, Lester holds the other over the rail.

It takes hours with the engine running. Sandy found two cans of petrol in the storeroom, and we've gone through all of one. Finally, we all go downstairs. There's still water, but it's not covering the floors. They're streaked with grime and swollen with damp, but the water lurks only in the corners, running along skirting boards to the rock of the boat. We fetch tea towels from the supply room to soak up the last of it.

'All done apart from this locked room.' Sandy points to the playroom door. Water bleeds under it and makes a puddle. My hand brushes against the key in my dressing gown pocket, but I say nothing.

'That's all right,' Lester says. 'It'll dry up on its own eventually.'

Upstairs, the main cabin is like an oven. The baby settles in my lap on the sofa while I feed him. He drinks quickly, but as soon as I take the bottle away he starts to gag, then cough, then brings it up again in a milky puddle on my lap.

'Oh, yuck!' Rene says.

I feel the baby's forehead. Even for this room, he seems hot. I put him down. Lester watches him while I go to the nursery and fetch a thermometer and a bottle of medicine. By the time I get back to the main cabin, Lester has sat the baby up and is rubbing his back. He's been sick again. There's yellow bile all down his baby grow.

'I don't think this kid's very well.'

I've seen Abigail use the thermometer. After several failed attempts, I learn how to press the button, wait as it counts down from three, pressing it to the baby's temple. After a few seconds it beeps, '38.7' flashing up with a red light.

'That can't be good,' Lester says.

'What's the matter?' Rene asks. There's something unconcerned about her concern. Children have a weird trust in adults to make things okay.

'I don't know . . . he has a fever.'

I give him medicine, but he throws it straight back up. I can feel my panic rising. This isn't fair. I don't remember how to be a mother. I barely remember how to look after myself.

'I remember when my baby sister was like this,' Lester says. 'I told you about her, didn't I?'

'She was nine years younger than you. She was born after the fire, when your mum met a new man.'

'Yeah, my little half-sis. Anyway, she got a bug and wouldn't stop puking. The doctor came and gave her medicine and told us to keep giving her liquids, because she'd keep throwing them up, but we had to give them anyway.'

'I just don't know where he got a bug from. We're the only people on this boat. No offence but you're all, you know . . .'

'Dead, I know. What have you been feeding him?'

I point over to the kitchen. 'We have these little cartons of milk. They keep for as long as you want them to keep, so long as you don't open them.'

'Okay,' Lester nods slowly. 'Have you been cleaning the bottles?'

'Of course; I give them a rinse after every feed.'

'But have you been sterilizing them? My mom used to put all the bottles in this special pan on the hob and they would sit in there for ages until the water boiled.'

I feel the blood leave my face. Of course, there's a thing in the kitchen that Abigail used to put the bottles in. You fill it with water and pop a tablet in. The tablet fizzes away and makes the water smell like a swimming pool.

'I'm such an idiot.'

'No, you're not. Come on, we'll get through this. We just need to keep the milk going in, yeah?'

'Okay.'

We fall into a routine. I sterilize the bottles, make them up with milk, and Lester feeds the baby. The baby throws up, cries about the pain, then sinks back into a half-sleep. Lester coos to him; Rene strokes his head. The weather gets hotter and hotter. The ocean shimmers. I realize I haven't changed his nappy for a while. When I do it's barely wet.

'It's happening,' I tell Lester. 'He's dehydrated.'

He nods. 'Then you just need to keep putting the milk in. That's all you can do.'

I take the bottles back, refill them with milk. We're using up all the UHT milk. I feed him, holding a towel under his chin for when he brings it up. Lester picks up the guitar. He plays softly, fingerpicking old American folk tunes I haven't heard since we were last together.

I don't love him any more. Not like that. But hearing his voice trace the outlines of those melodies, I feel a pull to that earlier time. A time when things were simpler.

He sings:

'Hang me, oh hang me, I'll be dead and gone . . .'

My head swims with the heat and walking back and forth constantly. I wonder if it's not so bad, to be dead.

'Hang me, oh hang me, I'll be dead and gone . . .'

I start to feed the baby again, who cries as the milk hits his belly.

'Wouldn't mind the hangin', but the layin' in the grave so long, poor boy, I been all around this world . . .'

The sun is like a bird, fatly perched at the top of the sky. Two hours pass, and three. As I'm holding him, the baby's eyes roll back in his head. His arms are up, in front of his face as though defending himself. His face is red. He starts to tremble, then jerk. I put him down, scared I'll drop him. There's nothing to do except wait for the seizure to pass. For a minute I forget how to breathe. Finally, it stops.

Four hours have passed. Finally, the heat fades a little. It's still warm, and the heat lies over the ocean like a blanket. The baby is sleeping, stripped down to his nappy. His eyes no longer look sunken. His little chest flickers up and down.

'What did you do after I died?' Lester asks.

I haven't looked from the baby for ten minutes. I think Lester is just trying to distract me. I search my memory. I remember Abigail, and I remember this holiday a little. I remember my husband died. Then sometime after that I went into a home. But after Lester died? How did I travel from there to here?

'I don't remember.'

'How come?' He's smiling but sounds a little hurt.

'I forget a lot of things. I have dementia.'

'What's that?'

'It's when you start forgetting things. When you can't remember how to do stuff. It is mostly old codgers like me.'

'You don't seem like that to me. You don't seem like you can't do things.'

I shrug. 'I guess I'm making an effort.'

'You really don't remember anything?'

I take a deep breath. 'I gave them your nice black suit to bury you in, the one you wore the night you played at the Lyceum.'

He nods and smiles. 'Good choice. Though maybe I'd have gone with the white tuxedo.'

'And I remember that Robert moved out . . .' I think for a moment, then shake my head. 'But I don't remember what I did next. I just know I ended up here, same as you.'

Though the heat is waning, just sitting here tires me. The room flickers. Maybe I'm going crazy. Lester sits next to me, slings an arm over my shoulder.

'Don't worry about it. I'm the one who left you. And you're the one who remembered the song that brought me back.'

I nod. 'I wish I could remember the next one.'

'Oh, that's easy.' Lester grins. He hums a tune. The tune is set to a swung rhythm. It slouches and slopes. It sounds like the blues, but not quite right. I pick up the guitar and start to play along. Yes, twelve-bar blues. The Aeolian mode. I know this song, it's called 'The Rebel'. As I play, Lester moves a little further away to give me room, resting his head on the sofa back. Without stopping, I lean back and do the same. Together we stare up at the ceiling. I think of all the times we did this, lying in Lester's double bed, while one of us played and the other sang.

I close my eyes.

I feel it coming – the moment when verse switches the chorus, or chorus switches to middle eight. The moment when two bits of tape, carefully pasted together, overlap. The room shimmers like heat haze rising off the ocean and is gone.

The Rebel

Jack Shapiro

1966

'I SAY, ARE YOU FREE?'
Ella looks up from the coffee she's adding creamer to in the deserted green room. Her session, for a BBC sitcom theme tune, is over after just an hour in the studio. She has nothing on for the rest of the day. She's annoyed – the booking agent had given the impression this would be an all-day thing, and she turned down an evening with a quartet at Ronnie Scott's.

Ella doesn't like her own obsession with making money, but it's good for her to be busy. Money is as good a thing as any to chase after. The voice from the door is the studio manager, Humphrey, an Old Etonian who owns a selection of bowties.

'Nope. Quiet day for once, Humph.'

'Have you ever played the electric bass before?'

She shakes her head. Humphrey wrings his hands for a moment, clearly in a bind.

'But I'm sure I could pick it up quickly. What's the gig?'

A relieved smile breaks over his face. 'Oh, nothing difficult – rhythm and blues number, mid-tempo. Their regular electric bass player ate some bad mussels and they want someone who knows their way around the chords . . . for a demo they're doing.'

'A band, then? What are they demoing?'

'Well, demo might be the wrong word, ahem . . .' Humphrey is the only person Ella has met who actually says 'ahem'. 'They're just playing around. They popped in to develop something. I think they're probably just checking the studio out, to be honest.'

Ella puts down the teaspoon she's holding. Now she *knows* something's up. Regular bands don't 'develop' stuff in the studio, especially not with session musicians. St Augustine might have thought that time didn't exist, but he never filled in a studio time sheet.

'What band are we talking about, Humph?'

'Ah, yes . . .' he shuffles a little. 'Have you heard of The, uh, Rolling Stones?'

* * *

The studio has been set up with sound baffles so it's hard to see who else is in the room, but Ella is sitting opposite the guitarist – what *is* his name? – with the shock of raven-black hair. He's been engrossed in playing something on his unplugged guitar since she got in, so she hasn't even been introduced. He's wearing white-framed plastic sunglasses indoors. A smouldering cigarette dangles from his lips. His T-shirt reads:

hit – house
PN
SCHWABING

Which is hard to argue with.

One of the engineers comes and places the electric bass, a Fender Precision, in her lap. It's heavy, and she quickly realizes how much pressure it takes to hold the strings down. She hopes this session doesn't go on too long, or she fears for her left hand. The engineer plugs her into a nearby Vox and asks her to play something.

'I'll adjust you.'

Ella is wary of being found an imposter. The last twelve years have made little difference to how women musicians get treated, even when they do know what they're doing. Hardly a session passes without a man 'helpfully' writing corrections on a chart that she could have transposed in her head or telling her how the controls on her amp work. The best of them are condescending, the worst outright rude. The only thing Ella can do is be irritatingly competent. The idea of someone finding out that she doesn't know what she's doing brings her out in a sweat.

She starts to pluck the open top string. Like on her guitar, it's tuned to E, but this note is a full octave lower. The sound from the amp is loud enough to make the guitarist look up for a moment, though his expression is unreadable.

The note rumbles in her chest. It feels less like she is playing an instrument than operating heavy machinery. Ella could break concrete with notes like these, and she likes it.

'Cool, you can stop now. Don't change anything,' the engineer says before departing.

Ella is used to engineers telling her not to change anything and is used to ignoring them. She turns the volume down on the amp as far as it'll go and practises the chart. She would hardly call it a chart, even, just a hastily scrawled line of chords with *x1* and *x2* the only instructions.

Ella wants to stop and watch whatever the guitarist is doing, because he seems so entranced doing it. It doesn't look complicated, just a repeating riff, but he's probing it over and over for some subtlety which Ella cannot perceive. She wonders if he will know it when he finds what he wants.

She turns the amp back up and puts her cans on. She listens to some back and forth between the singer and the control room, and slowly the rest of the band are tested for levels. When prompted, she plucks some notes, hearing herself simultaneously on the headphones.

They play through the song once and come to a halting finish. There's no real end to the song; they just play over the chorus a number of times until the parts of the band fall away from one another like the wheels coming off a car in motion.

Ella sits and waits. There's some disagreement among the band, though she cannot see the members who are disagreeing. The guitarist cocks his head as though listening intently, despite the fact he's still wearing his headphones and can hear everybody perfectly well. A faint smile plays around his lips.

Whoever the mystery band members are, they're discussing whether the song should be faster or slower, whether it should have more chord changes, whether it should be in a different key, a different style. Ella is amused by this indecision. She thinks that, if they want a song in a different style, they should write a different song.

Nevertheless, their freedom is refreshing. Usually if there are disagreements in the studio, it's like the moment when a wasp flies into a schoolroom, giving everyone respite from their multiplication tables. Still hidden behind headphones and sunglasses, the guitarist takes out a packet of cigarettes, taps two out, takes one for himself and offers the other to Ella.

'Thanks.' She takes it and leans across the divide, so he can light their cigarettes together. He takes a long drag, exhales a luxuriant plume of smoke, then takes his headphones off.

'Better go see what they're whining about,' he mutters to her with a lopsided grin. She smiles back.

Twenty minutes later the guitarist hasn't reappeared, and the band don't seem any closer to an agreement. Ella doesn't mind that the session is dragging when she's getting paid. Still, it gets boring, sitting with an instrument that you don't know how to play. She looks at the guitar that has been left behind, a Les Paul Custom. It's not best etiquette to grab another player's instrument, but Ella is bored. She puts down the bass and picks up the guitar, searching for something to play that will take her mind off the moment.

Something about the bluesy number they've just been playing reminds her of another tune – a sloping, swung rhythm set to a twelve-bar blues. The Aeolian mode. Ah yes – Jack Shapiro again. She hasn't thought about Jack for a little while. After Lester died, she stopped playing those songs. Instead of breaking the silence, they made her more aware of it. But she feels like playing one now. Like picking up where she left off.

Rolling down the volume, Ella begins. She plays with a mixture of fingerpicking and palm slaps for the rhythm. She plays the tune through a couple of times, half humming the melody that she's outlining on the top strings. Ella has entirely forgotten the band and their disagreement until she becomes aware of someone standing nearby.

'Trying to put me out of a job?' The guitarist is standing nearby, glasses off to reveal piercing eyes, mouth parted to reveal crooked teeth.

'Sorry . . . I got bored.' She decides honesty is the best policy.

'No fucking wonder. I thought you were a bassist?'

She shrugs noncommittally. 'What are we doing with the song?'

'*We* are jacking it in for the day. Mick wants to sleep on it. I thought it was all right.'

Ella smiles and nods, sensing the song was one of his own.

'What was that you were playing? Sounded weird.'

'Sort of folk tune I know. Called "The Rebel".'

He grins, and Ella thinks of the Wolf in Little Red Riding Hood.

'Reckon you could teach it to me?'

*   *   *

It's a couple of hours later. Ella is sitting in the green room of the studio with the guitarist, a man in a leather jacket called Barry, and two girls who seem to have come as window dressing for whatever he is selling. One is blonde, the other has a jet-black bob. They look like an angel and a demon, either side of Barry. Ella's worried about what she's gotten herself into, but this is how she's lived the last twelve years.

Ella never says no to anything unless it's boring. She's toured around Europe, been to the Caribbean, even America. She's done countless recording sessions, dates in the West End, all sorts of bands. The only thing that she wants to do is keep moving forward. The only thing that she's afraid of is standing still. That's what the dead do.

Perhaps there's another reason behind her fear of inaction, though she tries not to think about it. Inaction drove her and Robert apart. She is making up for saying no at the wrong moment by always saying yes.

A brown paper parcel is placed down on the table. Barry then reaches inside his jacket, taking out a silver cigarette case. He pulls out a hand-rolled cigarette.

Oh, Ella thinks, *pot*. She's a little relieved, a little disappointed. She does not especially like the drug. It makes her jittery, paranoid. A lot of players like it, say it helps them get in the groove, get creative. But Ella feels like she's wearing woolly gloves when she smokes it, cannot find her way around the fretboard. Never mind – she will get a drink after this, go home. Maybe the phone will ring. Maybe it's not too late to play Ronnie Scott's.

They light the joint and pass it around.

Ella watches them politely, feeling rather older than everyone in the room. Nevertheless, when it's passed to her, she takes a certain pride in not looking like a square. She scissors the joint between two fingers and takes a long drag, which she holds deep in her lungs. It's only when she comes to pass the joint to the guitarist, sitting on her left, that Ella realizes that she may have miscalculated.

Not pot.

What then? Not something she has tried before. There's the familiar weightiness, the sense that she's sinking ever so slightly into the furniture. But this is stronger, more all-encompassing. A warm tingle spreads through her arms and legs, out to the tips of her fingers and toes. She feels as though she has sunk into a warm bath and has to look down at her dry clothes to double check that this is not the case.

Her heart rate speeds up. Or is it slowing down? Before she knows it, the joint has passed around the circle again, back to her. This time she is a bit less concerned about seeming square, on the fence about whether she likes the drug. She thinks about passing. She thinks about handing it straight to the guitarist.

But then the little voice in the back of her head pipes up – *Boredom is to be avoided.*

Ella takes a deep drag and passes the joint immediately this time. She seems to be able to hold her breath forever. Wonderful – she has learned how not to breathe. It was easy all along, you just have to stop. A sense of profound comfort overcomes her. Ella hasn't felt so *comfortable* her entire life. Sprawled out on a featherbed, with a balmy summer breeze coming in through the window, a tall glass of lemonade fizzing quietly nearby ready for her to drink, she could not feel this comfortable. She is supercomfortable. She is a superhero! Comfort Girl.

It's not just her body, she realizes, but the voice at the back of her head. Perhaps for the first time in a decade, she doesn't feel anxious. She's not worried about what the next gig will be, what will keep her from getting bored for the next few hours, what she will do if that boredom is not alleviated. For the last decade she has chased excitement.

Finally, that's about to change.

*   *   *

It's early June and the streets of Soho are starting to feel close and sticky. After a morning of session work, Ella has retired to a pub on Old Compton Street which is excellent on days like this. It's dark, smells of the gents, and the carpets haven't been changed in so long that shuffling punters have worn furrows into them like sheep tracks. But it's always cool and always quiet. The perfect place to sit back and enjoy the sensation of time coming to a standstill.

This is what Ella has discovered – Slow Time. It took her a long while after that first time to put the experience into words. Robert had told her that time didn't exist, but wasn't that just wishful thinking? Ella had half-listened to a programme on the Home Service about Albert Einstein while making scrambled eggs. The most outrageous claim seemed to be that time moved at different speeds in different places. This seemed sacrilegious to Ella, who is praised for the metronome accuracy of her playing. Time is her occupation.

But now she understands it. There are two clocks. There is the one that the world runs to, the outside clock. It's the clock they set all the others to – Big Ben, the clock over the green-grocers in Goodge Street advertising Guinness, the four million wristwatches all over London.

Then there's the inside clock. The clock that keeps her in time to the music. And, unlike the outside clock, the inside clock could be sped up or slowed down. Ella has experimented with speeding it up, but it's slowing things down that interests her. One second for everyone else's minute. For the first few weeks she had gone around as though she had discovered a great secret, holding it close to herself when she rode the Tube across town. Men in beige coats and dark trilbies had peered at her from behind their newspapers, or from behind the fish-tank glass of their NHS spectacles. She had looked down at her lap and smiled a secretive, catlike smile.

It's not that she's stupid. Well, not *naive*. She knows Charlie Parker didn't die at thirty-four for nothing. It's just that she doesn't care. This is better than what she had before, and she doesn't want to trade it back. Lester is dead, and Rene and Sandy and millions more. Death can't be avoided but living miserably can.

The barman here has an obsession with polishing. He wears a blazer with a cravat and addresses all the men as 'squire'. She knows that he is casting a disapproving glance her way occasionally, in the single-seat booth she's occupying. To her, his frenetic pacing and polishing at the bar resembles nothing so much as the wing beats of an insect that will not live more than a week. Her brain, her metabolism, are more like that of a giant turtle, one of those slow, half-dreaming reptiles that live for centuries. She will be here long after he has gone.

After her first experience, smoking heroin, Ella had been unsure what to do next. She knew it was a cure for an illness she hadn't known she had. The band had packed up and left the studio, Barry and his silent women had vanished in a puff of white smoke. It was only a couple of weeks later, back at the same studio, that she had seen one of the girls – the one with the jet-black hair – hanging on the arm of another client. Ella had sensed something transactional about their conversation and waited, not leaving until the two broke off, the client going into his session, the girl going in the direction of the door, before following after her.

'Yes?' The girl had spun round warily.

'I'm Ella.'

The girl squinted. 'Mella? Like Melody?' She spoke with a French accent.

'No, Ella. With an E. We met the other week . . .'

Her name was Camille. She was indeed French but spoke good English. She seemed suspicious of Ella but eventually remembered her face. Ella hadn't known what to ask for, but somehow convinced Camille that she wanted to be a client to Barry. Camille had taken her phone number, nodded quickly.

'I will talk to him. If he says yes, I will call.'

It hadn't taken long. Ella was barely through the door of her Soho flat when the new rotary phone in her front room started to ring. She never saw Barry again. She was neither rich nor famous enough to warrant his presence before the moment of transaction. Instead, Camille became her salesperson. Except, unlike the greengrocer or the butcher, Camille liked to sit down with Ella and enjoy the produce.

Not that she scrounged – Camille always had her own supply. Ella didn't mind. Neither of them was talkative afterwards, so having her there never felt like an imposition. And her experience was useful. To begin with, Ella smoked the drug. Then, as time passed, and she became more discerning in the effects that she was seeking, she asked Camille to teach her how to inject.

'You are sure, Melody?'

This is what Camille still calls her, based on that initial mishearing. It seems appropriate, and Ella likes having an alter ego. Melody does things that Ella would not.

'I'm sure.'

She never asks whether Camille is getting paid for any of this, but she suspects that the drug itself is payment. It doesn't seem like she can afford to eat. Ella is aware that people find skinniness attractive, even if she's always wanted to be less of a beanpole. Indeed, with their black hair and pale skin, Camille remarks on how they could pass for twins, though she is ten years Ella's junior.

Ella only shoots up back in the flat, to be safe. Camille has taught her about the alternatives freely available in chemists up and down the country. With the first swig of beer, Ella takes a pair of fat Demerol tablets, lights a cigarette and leans back, waiting for her clock to slow down. The next thing she knows, the cigarette has burned down to the filter without her touching it. The incinerated remains lie in a straight line in the ashtray. Her thoughts drip by at a glacial pace. If she sits still for long enough, the tablets will paint a ghostly world inside her skull, another London appearing street by street, storey by storey.

'Ella?'

She looks up. Or rather, she begins to look up. The sound of her own name panics her. There's a man standing in front of her with red hair and a red beard. There's something ferocious about his expression, though slowly Ella recognizes it to be one of concern rather than anger.

'Ella? It's me, Robert.'

'Robert?' Ella parrots, willing her inside clock to speed up a little. Yes, of course it's Robert. The beard threw her. Robert has grown more unkempt as the decade progressed. He's grown out his hair – always unruly but now a mop of curls which overlap with his beard, which he strokes several times a minute. To Ella he resembles nothing so much as an unmade bed, strewn with old books and cigarette papers, saxophone reeds and imported forty-fives.

She has seen him many times since Lester died. She knows that he broke up long ago with Olivia, though she doesn't know who he's been with since. She's been in sessions with him, though he does far fewer, preferring to play live. In twelve years, they've barely spoken. They've exchanged pleasantries, ticked off questions in the category of small talk. It's not that she hates him. He's just an emissary of the past, and dodging the past has become her forte.

She's aware of a group of drinkers somewhere behind Robert who are looking over at him. He must have walked in with them. There's a clutter of instrument cases around the table, marking them out as a saxophone section. Robert is pulling out the little stool on the opposite side of the table, putting down his dimpled glass.

'How are you?'

Again, that look of concern. She wonders if she would see it if she weren't so high. She wonders if he's always had this expression and she never noticed.

'I'm great. How are you?'

She doesn't know how slowly she's talking. She wishes she were facing the bar, so she could time herself to the brass clock that hangs above the optics.

'I'm okay, just doing some rehearsals for a big band.'

Robert has never grown out of big bands. Ella wants to tell him how unfashionable he is, how much money he could be making, if he weren't one part of a sixteen-piece organization playing to a limited audience. But she can't quite bring herself to.

'Are you working much?' he asks. *Tick*, another box checked on the Small Talk for Musicians list.

She looks at him for a long moment, though exactly how long she's unsure. She could answer the question. She could ask another question in return or parrot his. She could go through with the whole charade, but she doesn't really feel like it. It doesn't feel especially important. This feeling of superiority is a feature of Slow Time. It's hard not to watch people scuttle about without starting to see insects.

'Are you happy, Robert?'

He looks at her and does not say anything, does not smile. After a moment, he takes a swig of beer.

'I guess so.'

'You guess so? You don't seem very certain.'

He shrugs. 'I've got a good life, I make good money . . . every day I do the thing that I wanted to do when I was a kid. I have good friends who play the music I love . . . I'm not unhappy.'

Ella sits back in her seat, takes a drag of her cigarette and is unaware of the smirk playing about her lips until Robert narrows his eyes.

'What about you? Are you happy?'

She shrugs his look off. 'I'm doing great.'

He nods for a second, as though deciding how to respond to a statement which he regards as a lie.

'Have you eaten? Can I get you anything?'

'Why should you get me anything?'

'I don't know . . .'

Ella knows she's too thin. She knows Robert is right, but it doesn't preclude her from feeling angry. She's always been thin, but now she needs to punch extra holes in her belts to keep her jeans up, her ankle-high boots seem to have been stretched by someone else's calves. In general, she has the appearance of a street urchin who has robbed the wardrobe of a wealthy woman.

'What do you want to say, Robert?' The anger in her voice surprises her. 'I can tell you're dying to say something.'

Robert glances over his shoulder to see if any of his friends are listening in on the conversation, then leans closer, whispering with something like urgency.

'I know it is none of my business. But I care about you Ella. I know that we've drifted apart since . . .' He leaves it unsaid. 'And I'm sorry, okay? I'm sorry that I moved out instead of staying put.'

He looks right at her, as though afraid that if he breaks eye contact, she will run. Ella tries not to say it, she really does.

'That's what you always do, isn't it? Run away?'

Robert says nothing so Ella carries on, jabbing at him with her words, trying to get a rise.

'You ran away from me in Glasgow and you ran away from me in London. Now you're trying to act as though you're my friend. But you're not my friend, Robert. You don't *deserve* that.'

He clenches his jaw. 'I couldn't take it. When Lester. . . when he. . .' Robert's composure finally cracks, and Ella can't supress a cruel smile. 'When he died, I couldn't handle it. It messed me up.'

'You could have fooled me.'

'I just wanted to move on, okay?'

'Me too.' She punctuates this by stabbing her cigarette into the ashtray, extinguishing it. He sighs like a parent –

'You don't look well. It's none of my business but I'm allowed to be concerned.'

She stares at him for a long time, unblinking. Half-in and half-out of Slow Time, it feels like an hour. He flinches away.

'Fuck you,' she says, gathering herself to leave. 'You had your chance to be concerned twelve years ago.'

She exits the pub and doesn't stop moving until her legs have carried her back to her flat, where she draws the curtains and lies down in the dark to dream.

* * *

Summer turns into autumn and Ella has become unlikely friends with Camille. Over the last decade she's had many acquaintances, many of whom she would have called friends, but with the appearance of Camille she realizes they were nothing of the sort. They were friends who came to parties, or friends with whom she would have a drink. But they were not friends in the way that Rene had been a friend, or Lester. They were not people you told secrets to, had adventures with, invented games with to pass the time.

Camille shows her how to paint her eyes with black kohl so she looks like a heavy-lidded Egyptian goddess. She takes her to buy clothes, after Ella confesses that she has barely bought anything new apart from jeans for years. Camille drags her around the King's Road from one boutique to another, each with a more ridiculous name than the last – Granny Takes a Trip, Hung on You, I Was Lord Kitchener's Valet. She buys thigh-high boots, floral-print dresses, a sheepskin coat with a furry collar. They each buy several pairs of sunglasses to hide behind.

In turn, Ella introduces Camille to culture. They go down to the UFO club, held every Friday night in the Blarney, an Irish ballroom in a basement on Tottenham Court Road. The manager, Joe Boyd, booked Ella for some folk sessions and told her about his new project. They watch Pink Floyd, Soft Machine, and dance to light shows.

In the days they go to museums and bars, theatres and arcades, all the time stoned to various degrees. They punctuate their trips with visits to pharmacies, making reasonable demands for Demerol, Dilaudid and Percodan. They know which maladies to impersonate. They have a variety of real and forged doctors' notes.

They do not talk much about their past. Ella gets the impression that Camille ran away from home, but knows nothing about where 'home' was, or why she might have run away. She does not ask, and in return Camille doesn't ask her. Ella likes the idea that her friend rebelled against something and decides retrospectively that she rebelled as well.

Lester called them nonconformists, which had satisfied her at the time. But it sounds passive now. It sounds like a label given to a rejected component, made too big to fit into the machine for which it was intended. She prefers the idea of being a rebel, of actively rejecting the lousy options offered to her.

* * *

In October, with the weather turning cold, they attend an all-night rave celebrating the launch of the *International Times*, at the Roundhouse in Camden. The inside of the building is grimy and bits of metal stick up here and there. Empty crates of Gilbey's gin litter the floor.

They have queued up for the best part of an hour, with what seemed like thousands of people, to climb the single-file staircase to get in the abandoned building. They see Marianne Faithfull in a nun outfit that's a lot more revealing than any nun's Ella has seen. They start dancing to the live music, trying to keep warm in the unheated Victorian building.

Abruptly, Camille grabs Ella's hand and drags her across the dancefloor to a bunch of kids huddled in a circle. Camille is good at noticing this sort of thing. She elbows them into the circle.

'Hello.' She smiles brightly at the kids.

'Uh, hey,' a lank-haired boy looks at them. 'What do you want?'

'Whatever's going. You're about to share some drugs, right?' Camille positively beams. Ella wants to laugh and run away at the same time.

'No, we're not.' A girl shakes her head so hard her eyes water.

'If you share with us, I won't rat you out.'

The kids look at each other and lank-hair makes the decision.

'I only have one spare.'

'Me and my friend can share.' Camille's smile is positively feline.

The boy reaches into his pocket and, one by one, distributes sugar cubes to each of them like communion wafers. LSD. Ella feels a stomach-jolt of fear. Camille takes hers, bites it in half, and pops the other half in Ella's mouth before she can protest.

'Thanks, friends!'

They make their getaway quickly, laughing uncontrollably. Ella's pulse is racing. She knows she shouldn't let Camille lead her into danger like this, but she doesn't care. Half an hour later they're still dancing. The light shows and the music have become very REAL, all of a sudden, and the crush of bodies is making Ella anxious.

'Hey, I feel like I need to relax,' she shouts in Camille's ear. Camille nods. This is their code.

They push through the crowds until they've found the awful bathrooms, find a free cubicle and shoot up. Ella's anxiety dissipates with the hit and the sweet-wrapper colours dancing in front of her intensify.

'I always wanted a sister,' Camille says, out of nowhere.

'Me too.' Ella looks her in the eyes. Suddenly this sentiment is very true – she has always wanted a sister.

'You are my sister, I think.'

'Yes. Yes, you're right!' Ella breaks into a fit of giggles. 'We're sisters, and we never realized.'

Camille grins. 'Wanna dance some more?'

'Yes *please*.'

They return to the dancefloor and weave strange shapes through the air. Ella watches the shapes of the music in front of her like puppets in a kids' TV show. The bass, made of green felt, jerks and wobbles towards her but never arrives.

The guitar, made of shining blue satin, floats like a ghost over Camille's shoulder. Ella laughs and laughs – after all these years of playing it, she can finally see what music looks like.

In the middle of the hall is a pile of jelly which they're all invited to eat at midnight, while art films are projected onto the walls. The Pink Floyd end the night by blowing the fuses on the entire building and plunging them into darkness. Ella and Camille scream and throw their arms around one another and laugh.

When it's all over they stagger through the biting October winds, numb with junk and giggling as they hunch into a shared cigarette. The stars are glitter-bursting in black puddles and Ella has found her long-lost sister and life is going to be all right after all.

* * *

Ella pulls into the studio with a few minutes to spare. The rest of the band are already getting comfy but she's not technically late. She feels warm and light, somewhere in between Fast and Slow Time. The morning was spent with Camille, getting high in the long grass of Hyde Park and watching clouds roll over them like glaciers. All the leaves were falling in slow motion.

The band isn't huge, but she knows most of them by their faces and it's a good crew. There's piano, bass and drums for the rhythm section, plus a Hammond organ. Ella's so relaxed that the moment she sees him comes as a shock. She stops dead for a moment.

'Hey, Ella.'

Robert is pulling a rag through the valves of his saxophone. She nods, once, but says nothing. The studio is fairly small, the band are all in here. Only the drums are partially separated by a couple of sound baffles. There is a guitar amp set up next to an empty chair. The chair next to Robert's.

Aware of her movements, Ella goes and places her guitar case next to the chair. She takes a look at the chart, an up-tempo rhythm and blues number with a section for soloing indicated for piano, guitar and saxophone. Ella puts the chart down and leaves the room. It takes her a minute to walk to the ladies – a single toilet at the end of a corridor used by the cleaning staff – and locate the pills in her purse.

Unlike many of the things Ella uses, these pills are perfectly legal. Obetrol slimming pills, available without prescription in the chemists. *Active ingredients: dextroamphetamine, amphetamine, methamphetamine.* Perfect for when she needs to be a hummingbird, not a turtle. She swallows three down with water from the sink.

Back in the studio, the producer is explaining the song. It's Peter Fricke, the white-coated producer who called her into the control room to criticize her timing in her very first session. This will be doubly satisfying then. Peter has lost the white coat, and some of his blond hair besides. His cardigan makes him less ghostly. He's put on a little weight, has a few more lines around his eyes.

'We've already rehearsed the rhythm section, so we'll start with a full run-through, no pressure – hey, Ella.'

Ella nods at him and takes her seat, where her electric has been taken out of its case and plugged in for her. Peter goes on:

'So, we're doing a record for a very nice singer, American, it's all a bit of a secret but I reckon she could be the next big thing. "Psychedelic soul music", they're calling it. Something to sink your teeth into. We've got a couple of really great players joining us today – Ella Campbell on lead guitar and Robert Mauchlen on sax. I'm sure you'll make them feel welcome.'

Robert raises his hand in greeting to the room, but Ella spends a few more seconds reading the chart. Nothing too complex, but some nice changes in there. As he said, something to sink her teeth into. As though on cue, she feels the drug starting to kick in, making her jaw clench. She grinds her teeth. Ella runs over options, arranging notes and chords, rhythms and harmonies in her head like a general assembling troops before a battle.

'Let's just have a run-through to begin with, no tape running, and see what we get.' Peter finishes his preamble and goes to sit in the control room upstairs.

Ella sees Robert turn towards her as though about to start a conversation. She turns the other way to get the tuning pipes out of her case. She checks the tuning on her telecaster, finding it all in order. By the time she's done, the band are being cued over the PA.

'Okay, here we go. One-two-three-faaa!'

Ella bides her time, playing quiet arpeggios along with the band, not raising her head above the parapet. The rhythm section is solid. Robert plays some tasteful fills, but they sound so old to Ella. They sound like what they were playing in the flat over a decade ago. What has he been doing since then?

They run smoothly through the chart, without hiccup, and come to the solo section. Again, Ella keeps her head down. There is some nice interplay between her and Robert, with the piano player making contributions here and there. In jazz, one person would take the opportunity to solo at a time, or two people would pass a solo back and forth. With this kind of music, soloing is more competitive. They jostle against each other. But again, Ella keeps cool, lets the saxophone rise and fall in the order of things, lets the piano fill the space left between them.

They finish the song and the PA crackles.

'That was great, guys, we could have run the tape for that one. Just mind yourselves on the transition to that first chorus. I'm going to count you in a touch faster this time, and we'll go for a take.'

The band readjust themselves, take a breath. Robert doesn't turn to her this time. Ella checks her tuning anyway, teeth grinding, hands urgent to do something, anything. She's starting to sweat. It needs to be now, it needs to be this take. She pushes the output knob on her tele up just a fraction, strums a high barre chord, and the amp screams a little.

'Okay, tape rolling. One, two, three . . .'

The band kick in and Ella takes a deep breath. They clear the first couple of verses, the chorus, the second verse and then . . .

The solo section comes around.

One, two, three . . .

Ella rips the telecaster, screaming up the neck and bending the final fret into something wavering and tortured. From there she scrambles back down the fretboard with tumbling arpeggios. She tries blues fills, jazz fills, modal fills. She makes the guitar sob and wail and stutter like a machine gun.

She backs off for a second, leaving a space for Robert to jump in. He's been in the background so far, providing quiet accompaniment, trying to work around what she's doing. But she's been going too fast for him, changing too rapidly. She looks sideways at him for the first time since they started and sees him frowning at the chart, lips pursed around his sax. He toots away for a couple of bars, trying to find something to follow her, before Ella comes back in with a slide down the neck that sounds like Flash Gordon's ray gun.

What she does next, she's barely aware of. The drug is working her, making her so fast and so fluent that her conscious mind can't follow along. Notes and bends cascade out of the amp like a waterfall. And, just as soon as it started, the solo section is over. The piano hadn't played a note of it and Robert may as well not have bothered. They play another verse and cycle through the chorus a few times for the fade out until the producer brings them to a halt.

'Okay . . .' The PA system crackles with the producer's voice.

Ella holds her breath, hoping the gamble has paid off. The drug is becoming too much now. She doesn't want to sit still. If they have to do another take, she knows she'll blow it.

'Wow.' Peter sounds stunned. 'I think, I mean, is there any point in doing that again?' He speaks to someone unseen. 'No, okay, that's a wrap, lady and gentlemen.'

Ella unplugs her guitar, puts it in the case and walks out without saying a word.

*   *   *

Winter has come. When Ella moved into her tiny, single-bedroomed apartment on Greek Street, she had almost no possessions to move in with, so it had been easy to redecorate. The cracked plaster walls were a mishmash of old, musty colours. She had painted everything white, from floor-to-ceiling, leaving only the wooden floor, which is the colour of well-stewed tea. Suddenly the tiny flat had looked twice as big, twice as light, modern and welcoming. She had parties here, had friends around, brought lovers back.

But now the white walls remind her of the white streets. Everything is thick with snow. It's not often that it snows like this in London, and she doesn't like it. It reminds her of that not-Christmas-Day, so many years ago, when she inherited Rene's guitar. Everything since then seems like some strange, clockwork mechanism spinning off that moment, predetermined and unstoppable. Or maybe she's being paranoid. She's paranoid a lot of the time these days.

The flat is cold, and there's nothing she can do to warm it up. She has an electric radiator, but no coins to put in the meter. She cashed a cheque for a couple of hours of session work earlier in the day, bought some groceries with it, calculating exactly what she would have left over. Now she just has to wait for Camille. There's a fireplace in the living room, but she has no fuel. She eyes the bookshelf under the window, wondering if she could get a decent blaze going from those alone. When she goes to the bathroom, her breath steams.

She wonders what time it is. Camille said she would be here by seven, after she's done with a client, but Ella doesn't keep a clock in the apartment any more. If she opens the window wide onto Greek Street and leans out, she can see the clock hanging outside the jewellers five doors down, but she can't bear to open the window and let more cold air in. She had a clock, but she couldn't bear to look at it any longer and pawned it.

That is what she has learned, after a year of exploring Slow Time – the internal clock doesn't want to be slowed down, and after being suppressed for long enough will speed up to compensate. Now she just has brief islands of respite in between ever-widening expanses of time. She keeps thinking of something Jack Shapiro wrote in *The Songs of the Dead*:

Silence defines music. The gaps between the notes, the phrases and the movements give it shape. Without silence, music would just be noise. Each silence is as unique as the song itself, like a fingerprint. For every song being played there is one that is not. We coexist with those stilled voices. Silence defines each of us, just as silence defines the music we play.

When she first read them, Ella thought the words beautiful, in a mystical sort of way. Now she is worried that silence is eclipsing her. She fidgets her way around the flat, picking things up and putting them down. Her brain moves so quick that, if she has a clock or a wristwatch, she will check it three times before a minute has passed. An hour seems like a day. She's managed to keep playing, of course. She needed to, to pay the bills. Or to pay Camille, at least. She was careful about when she took a hit, never turning up to a session under the influence.

But Ella can tell she's starting to lose it. She's playing as much as ever, so it's not for lack of practice. No, it's her inside clock – she has overwound the mechanism and now it keeps uneven time. For playing lead it doesn't matter – she can still reel off loose, improvised solos, and her lack of timing passes for emotion. But playing rhythm, she starts to drift away from the rest of the band. As hard as she tries, she can't lock into the bass drum. She has enough of a reputation that people still want to book her, but she knows it can't last.

The buzzer goes, and Ella jumps fully up from her seat. Three times in the last hour she's checked the buzzer, worried it might have broken and Camille might be stranded out on the street, thinking that she's not in. Ella presses the release button without asking who it is and scurries to the door.

It seems to take Camille a very long time to walk up the two flights of stairs to Ella's flat, and when she appears, she's hunched in on herself. She's wearing a large black coat, with a black fur-lined collar. She looks like a character out of a Russian novel. Ella ushers her into the flat wordlessly and does all the bolts on the door.

'I thought it would be warm in here.' Camille cocks her head in accusation.

'I didn't have enough left over for the meter.'

'You have money for me though?'

'Yes, yes. Come to the kitchen, we can get warm on the stove. I'll make coffee.'

Camille nods jerkily. They walk through in silence. Ella lights the big gas ring on the hob, while Camille sits down at the kitchen table and starts to unpack the contents of her coat. Ella retrieves her works from under the kitchen sink. She puts them next to Camille, knowing that the other woman will prepare for both of them. She goes and fills her coffeemaker with grounds, tops it up with water and puts it on the hob. Making coffee this way always reminds her of Lester.

'Just black, I'm afraid, is that okay?'

'Do you have sugar?'

'A little.' Ella scrapes the crusted remnants from the sugar jar out into their cups of coffee and comes to the table.

Camille has laid everything out in preparation and is smoking. She smokes Gitanes to emphasize her Frenchness.

'What do we have today?' Ella asks, looking at the unwrapped paper parcel on the table. Just looking at the little pile of pure white powder makes her clench her teeth.

'It is new, arrived just today. Very good, they say. Thanks for the coffee, Melody.'

Ella winces at the nickname, but Camille doesn't notice as she sips the coffee down as quickly as possible without burning her tongue. She blinks away tears.

'You mind if I use yours first? Then we can have some of mine.'

'Sure.' Ella nods quickly, eager for things to get going.

Camille takes the matches and lights a candle, lifts the soot-stained dessertspoon with a little powder from the parcel. The candle and the dessertspoon always remind Ella of heating brandy to pour over the Christmas pudding when she was little. She had always been too keen to tip the spoon, so the flames would take the alcohol. But you had to warm it up, otherwise it would sputter out.

Camille starts to cook. Ella can sense them both relax. Something about knowing relief is close relaxes her.

'So, New Year's Eve,' Camille says, by way of conversation.

'Another year gone,' Ella says, automatically.

Camille glances up at her for a second. 'Did you not . . . do you not have anywhere to be?'

Ella shakes her head. 'I could have gone to a party, but I didn't really feel like it.'

They talk like this sometimes, maintaining the pretence that they're living ordinary lives.

'And I don't have any family down here.'

Camille puts the spoon over the flame and holds it there. Without taking her eyes away, she says –

'I wonder what my family are doing now.'

Ella has never heard Camille mention her family before, and hesitates before asking,

'Your mum and dad?'

'And my two brothers. I left them behind when I came here. They have a . . . *farm*? What's the word? They make grapes.'

'A vineyard?'

'Yes, that's right. The countryside near Aix-en-Provence.'

'I never imagined you coming from the countryside.'

Camille smiles. 'Thanks. That is what I wanted – to get away from all that. To come somewhere exciting.'

Ella sips her coffee down to the dregs. 'And what did your family think of that?'

Camille stares at the powder as it starts to liquefy and bubble. 'Not happy. They said I was stupid. I guess they were right.'

'Don't say that – you're not stupid.'

Camille nods once, either to acknowledge this kind remark or to dismiss it. 'I wanted to be a singer, or an actress. I just slept with a lot of singers. It doesn't really count.'

When the hit is ready, Camille takes Ella's needle and draws the golden fluid up into the glass barrel, then inverts it and taps the bubbles out with an expertise that would make a medical student proud.

'What about you? Where are your family?' She puts down

the needle for a moment to tie a short length of rubber tubing around Ella's arm. Her forearm is cold in the kitchen; she cannot wait to feel indifferent to it.

'Just my mum, up in Scotland. I speak to her sometimes on the phone, but she seems distant.'

'Oh?'

'Mm. Sometimes she talks to me like I'm someone else . . .' Ella trails off. The thought has only increased her sense of urgency. 'Are you ready?' she snaps.

Camille's eyes look up to meet Ella's.

'Let's go.'

She prods at the veins with her cold fingers for a moment before finding a site that she is happy with, then sinks the needle. The plunger goes down and the golden hit vanishes within Ella. She stands, with the rubber tubing still tied around her arm, and walks to the front room. She flops onto the sofa in the living room, pulls a mohair blanket over her, and undoes the tubing.

It's a long time since Ella felt any exhilaration at receiving a shot. Familiarity dulls this response, even if the drug still succeeds in having its effect. There isn't the same rush. But now, she feels herself being thrown back in the passenger seat of an accelerating car. For a moment she feels intense pleasure and relief mingled.

Then she feels panic. Something is wrong. This dose was no bigger than the dose she had last time, yet it feels twice as strong, three times as strong. There is something wrong with this junk. Or too right. Ella tries to call out for help, but only succeeds in limply opening her mouth. Her vision stutters. From the kitchen, she hears the sounds of Camille cooking her own shot as though they're echoing down a long tunnel.

She cannot call for help and she cannot warn Camille.

She is frozen, her internal clock slowing and slowing, pausing and then restarting, like a rundown clockwork toy.

She stops.

* * *

When Ella wakes, she's numb with cold. Her body aches from sitting perfectly still for many hours. She feels some confusion, but slowly the events of the night before bleed back. The sun of a new year is blazing through the window. There is a weight pressing down on her right-hand side, and she realizes it's Camille.

Relief washes through her. She is alive and Camille is alive. She came to sleep by her side and keep warm. She sees Camille's own piece of rubber tubing discarded on the floor in front of them. She turns.

Camille is lying, head tilted back, mouth parted, eyes open.

Ella looks at her for a long time before deciding that she is definitely not breathing. Her pale skin has grown no paler with death, but there is something dull about her eyes. Her lips are blue.

Distantly, Ella hears the peal of bells ringing in the New Year.

* * *

The studio is cold as she walks in, five minutes late for the session. It's rare for studios to be cold, because they're in near constant use, but it's that kind of day. The cold seems to have settled in her bones.

The police took their time questioning her. They had taken the body away, taken the drug paraphernalia and the package. Of course, they hadn't found Ella's needles – she had gotten rid of them before calling. As though the junk was still freezing her brain, she acted with an eerie calm that unsettled her.

They had questions for her, of course. But her answers satisfied them. They did not test her for anything, didn't even roll her sleeves up to see the obvious track marks that nestled in her elbow crooks. She had sat in a tiled room in the police station at Vine Street, listening to shouts and catcalls echoing from the corridors around her as people came and went from the cells. She will be called again to give evidence, but she's not a suspect.

This session is a big one – in addition to the rhythm section there are four saxophones, four trombones and two trumpets, a vibraphone and a percussionist on timpani. Some kind of theme tune for a sports programme. She walks in, keeping her head low, but a few of the players already seated nod to her. She knows the drummer.

'Hey Andy, what did I miss?'

'Not much, Ella. They handed out the charts. Jazzy little number but nothing you can't manage.'

She grabs the chart and flicks through it anxiously. She tries to make sense of the chord progression, but it doesn't come right in her head. She can see the shapes of the chords, but not how she's going to move between them. The tune seems angular, jagged somehow. She would need to rehearse for hours to get the hang of this . . .

'Are we all ready down there?'

The voice comes over the PA from the control room. No headphones for a session like this – just a few microphones arrayed around the room. She doesn't want to draw more attention to herself by asking for more time. Since when does she need more time?

A man strides into the room, presumably the composer, and sits down at a Hammond organ, angled so he's facing the band. Ella hurriedly picks up the P-bass in front of her, plucks a few notes just to check it's been tuned, and sits back. The man at the organ straightens himself, plays a bugle charge on the instrument, then turns to them.

'All right gentlemen, take one? A-one, a-two, a-one, two, three . . .'

The horns blare, with an opening drum fill from Andy rumbling the toms. Two bars in and Ella starts to play. Her fingers still feel cold and numb, but that's not the problem. The problem is that her metronome is shot. She tries to listen to what the band is playing but there are too many competing rhythms. She feels the spaces between beats stretching and contracting like living things. Time, once a smooth and regular thing, wobbles and warps like a vinyl record left out in the sun.

'Okay, okay . . .' The man at the organ waves his hand, and the band comes to a stumbling halt eighteen bars in.

'Bit of a wobble there. A bit more from the horns on the opening note, really hit it, okay? Ready for take two?'

Ella takes a breath to steady herself but finds the exhale shaky. She cannot get through this. She must get through this. She'll get through this and then she'll go back to the flat and . . .

The horns blare, the drums roll like thunder, and two bars in Ella does not play. She cannot breathe, cannot move, too frozen even to excuse herself. It's another eight bars before Hammond organ realizes that the bass isn't playing, and everything grinds to a halt.

He turns, searching, and finds Ella.

'Is there something wrong with the chart, Miss?'

She opens her mouth to speak but no noise comes out and she gulps a few seconds like a fish on land. Before her eyes can water she stands, puts the instrument down, and walks out of the session. She makes it as far as the corridor before she doubles over. Sobs rattle in her belly, creasing her up.

Ella doesn't know how long she's there, but nobody from the session rushes out after her. Time bends and stretches around her, and she wonders if it might snap and leave her standing still, apart from time. She wonders if that's what death is like. She cries and cries. She does not remember crying like this for anyone before. She's not sure if she's crying for Camille or for someone else. Ella feels as though she's the one who lived and the one who died.

'Are you okay?' A hand is laid on her shoulder. She looks up, but the face is scattered by her tears. 'Ella?'

'Robert?'

Her heart leaps for a moment. She feels no shame, just a yearning to be held by Robert.

'No, Ella, it's me, Peter. I'm producing the track.' He looks at her uncertainly. 'Do you remember me?'

It takes her a moment to readjust. She remembers Peter, with the floppy blond hair. Peter who criticized her timing. He looks friendly. He smiles, as though in encouragement. 'Come on, do you want a cup of tea?'

She tries to nod but cannot move.

She feels a gnawing hunger in her guts, for food and for junk and for warmth and for love. She doesn't mean to say what she says next, but it comes out like a voice that she has suppressed for the longest time, finally having its say.

'Help. Please help. Help me.'

5.

The Matron

I WAKE TO DISTANT THUNDER. Without raising my head, I look down. The baby is looking back. As he's noticed, a big smile breaks over his face. I smile back. Abigail could get him to smile, but I'm no good at throwing him around or doing silly voices. I stick my tongue out and grimace. He makes a laugh that sounds like 'heeeee'.

At the sound, someone resting against me stirs. I look to my right and see Camille, head on my shoulder like the day she died. I start upright. Camille slumps forward a little and wakes with a catlike grunt.

'Melody? I fell asleep.'

'It's okay . . .' My voice shakes a little. It's not Camille's fault that she's dead. She can't help it. It's not very nice to act startled or scared of someone. I clear my throat.

'How are you?'

Camille yawns, stretches and sits up, smoothing her hair down. Her make-up is perfect and her dress – horizontal black and white stripes – is uncreased. She doesn't look like she was sleeping.

'Glad to be here. Oh, hello baby!'

She smiles and waggles her fingers at him. He coos.

'Whose baby is this?'

'Mine . . . well no, he's my daughter's,' I correct myself, 'but she's not here so I'm looking after him.'

Camille looks at me squarely. 'You had a daughter?'

I nod. 'I did.'

'With who?'

'I . . . I don't know. I don't remember.'

Camille laughs hard, clapping her hands. 'Well, that sounds more like you at least.'

'It does? What I mean is . . .' I begin, but never get to finish.

'Ellie, come quick!' Rene runs through the doors to the outside, into the cabin, with Sandy following hot on her tail.

'Ella – you have to come see this.'

Without saying hello to Camille, the two of them race from the saloon again. Camille just shrugs.

'I suppose we better go see.'

She gets up easily and walks after them, while I take a couple of attempts to heave myself off the sofa. The longer I spend on this boat, the more worn-out I feel. It's warm on deck, the sun halfway up the sky. I guess it must be morning because the air seems fresh. The sky is full of fat thunderclouds;

the ocean is calm. I hobble to where Camille has joined Sandy at the railing. Rene hops up and down.

'Look, over there!'

I have to squint. The horizon is just a blue-white smudge between sea and sky. There's something darker there, a shadow.

'An island?' I ask.

'No,' Sandy says, 'a ship.'

I can see it now – the horizontal line of the hull and the vertical lines of the bridge. My breath speeds up. Images flash up in my mind. Lifeboats speeding across the waves, cups of tea handed around, someone else taking care of the baby.

'What do we do?'

'We need to get their attention.'

I look around for inspiration. 'How do we do that?'

'We could start a fire!' Rene suggests.

'On a boat? Made of wood?' Sandy scoffs.

'Hey! It was just an idea. You come up with an idea if you're so clever.'

Sandy sighs and looks to the sky. Lester saunters onto the deck from wherever he has been, adjusting his rolled-up sleeves.

'What's popping, people? And who's this?' He notices Camille, who tilts her head as though he's a puzzle. Lester squares his shoulders and holds out his hand. They shake.

'Lester Benjamin, Buffalo, New York.'

'Camille. That's a funny name you've got, Lester-Benjamin-Buffalo-New-York.'

Lester opens his mouth to correct her then realizes she's joking.

'You're French?'

She smiles demurely. 'Do you have a cigarette?'

'Lester!' I snap. 'There's a ship over there.'

Lester looks in the direction I'm pointing, a frown forming on his brow. 'So?' He shrugs.

'So? So, they could rescue us!' Rene yells at him.

Lester reaches into the breast pocket of his waistcoat and takes out a slim pack of Sotheby's.

'See, the thing is, I am not so keen on being *rescued*.'

He places a cigarette on Camille's lips, pats his trouser pockets for matches.

'Why the hell not?' Sandy says, shoving his arm.

Lester turns to look at the gangly teenager by his side as though a fly just landed on him. He takes a match out, strikes it, and lights Camille's cigarette first.

'Why don't I want to be rescued?' Lester says, turning to Sandy with the still-burning match held between their faces. 'Because I don't want to go like this . . .' he blows out the flame.

Sandy pulls back from the smoke. His eyes are wide.

'What d'you mean?' Rene asks.

Sandy is shaking his head as though he already understands, but I'm in the dark. Lester takes a long drag and leans against the wall of the cabin.

'Sweetie, I know this is upsetting, but we were all dead, right?'

'I'm not stupid.' Rene frowns.

'Right. So how is it that we're on this boat, talking to one another?'

Rene shrugs. 'How am I supposed to know?'

'Because we all have something in common, don't we?' He turns to Camille. 'At least, I am assuming you are an acquaintance of Eleanor Campbell, Miss?'

Camille folds one arm over her chest, smokes with the other, nods tightly.

'We're all here because of you, Ellabelle. And there's no one else here. So, if we're all a figment of your imagination . . .'

'No, no, no . . .' Sandy is pacing, rubbing the side of his head.

'I'm just saying, it is a possibility, right?' Lester looks around at all of us one by one. Rene has gone pale. Camille, who has had the least time to get used to any of this, looks calm. Sandy is panicking.

'I don't want to think about this.'

'Well, you have to think about this, fella. It's the elephant in the room.'

'If I'm rescued, you're all going to disappear?' I ask.

'I don't know, Ellabelle. I wish I did. I just know that I don't really want to go back to being nothing.'

'So, what's the alternative?' Sandy rounds on him, pointing. 'We stay drifting at sea forever, until the water and the food run out?'

'I'm not hungry or thirsty, I don't know about you?' Lester replies.

'And what about them?' Sandy points to me. 'What about when *they* don't have any food or water? What about when *they* die? Won't we get snuffed out like a candle anyway?'

Lester doesn't respond, rolls his jaw back and forth.

'That's not fair.' Camille steps forward, exhaling into the blue sky. 'We had our chance. We had our lives. Some of them were shorter, some longer, but we all got a lifetime.' She doesn't look at us, just stares at the sea as though thinking out loud. 'If we're only here because of Ella, it is rude to deny her the same, yes?'

They look at her for a long moment. There's nothing to break the silence. I want to turn and see how far the ship has moved, but I mustn't interrupt. Finally, Lester nods.

'I'm sorry, Ellabelle. I wasn't thinking straight. This is your boat – you do what you want to do.'

Sandy lets out a sigh.

'How do we get their attention?' I ask.

Camille shrugs. 'This boat, does it not have, what do you call them? The lights? Ugh.' She looks around at all of us, urging us to give her the right word. 'The fires? The lights in the sky?'

'Flares!' Sandy bursts out. 'Yes, there must be flares somewhere.'

'What are flares?' Rene tugs at his sleeve.

'They're like fireworks that stay in the sky for a long time. You shoot them out of a gun,' Sandy says.

'Where would they be kept?' Lester says. 'This isn't a big boat and I haven't seen them.'

'I guess they might be in the wheelhouse . . .' Sandy says.

I start hobbling toward the back of the boat. I climb the metal stairs. The cabin is like a greenhouse. I cast around. There is a yellow plastic tub under the desk. I unscrew the lid and see four flares, three small and one large. Back down the stairs. I lose my footing on the last steps and almost fall. Lester is waiting and catches my arm.

'Easy now! You've still got time.'

We hurry back to the group.

'You found them!' Rene claps.

'Do you know how to use them?' Camille asks.

'Guess I'll have to learn.'

I pull one of the smaller flares out of the jar and look at it. It says 'AURORA' in big letters. The rest is covered in tiny black lettering which I can't read. I fumble around until I pull a plastic cap off one end. Inside is a nozzle, and I go to pull this.

'Whoa, whoa! Wait a second – what if it explodes?' Sandy says.

'You all stand back then. If I explode, I explode.'

I pull the nozzle. It comes off and I hold the tube to the sky. But, instead of a flare shooting out as I expected, the tube begins to smoke, thick orange fumes which get in my eyes and choke me.

'Here, you take this one.' I hand it to Rene. 'Just run up and down the deck and wave it around, okay?'

'Okay!' Rene takes the tube like it's a relay baton and sprints off.

I pull out the larger flare. When I take the cap off this one, there's a dangling tag, like a giant party popper. I point it up and pull. A shock shoots down my arm and a red flare climbs into the sky.

'Wow . . .' Lester is the only one who speaks, and we all stare up at the sky, open-mouthed.

The flare twists white smoke until it reaches the highest point it can and starts to fall. A tiny parachute opens, and it seems to hover.

'That'll do it.'

Over the next fifteen minutes we watch the ship. We get excited more than once when it seems to slow down or start to turn. We break open both of the other smoke flares when the first one burns out, and take turns walking them around the deck.

The ship doesn't stop, doesn't turn. Slowly, it sails to the edge of our view, until I'm no longer sure if I'm looking at the ship or a wrinkle of cloud.

It's gone.

*   *   *

By the time I've fed and changed the baby and told Lester to look after him, Camille has disappeared. I find her out at the bow, skinny legs stretched in the sun. Her face is covered by a straw sun hat.

'Where'd you get that?' I ask.

'Downstairs. There was a bedroom.'

'Ah, it must have belonged to Abigail.'

I put my back to the wall and awkwardly slide down until I'm sitting next to Camille. Did I ever have legs like that? I don't believe it.

'There's a lot of water down there,' Camille says.

My stomach lurches.

'Oh?'

'Mm. Up to my ankles. But Lester says they will pump it out.'

'Yes.'

We fall silent. I want to tell her about the playroom. I want to give her the key. But there's nothing to be done. We'll just keep pumping the water about. It'll be fine.

'Who is Abigail?' Camille asks.

'My daughter.'

Camille looks at me from under the brim, squinting a little.

'I can't believe you had a kid.'

'I know.'

'And where is she now?'

I search for an answer and settle for changing the subject. 'You'll get sunburn.' I point to her bare legs.

'Maybe . . . I'm not sure I can.' Camille shrugs. 'Besides, I don't think it is going to be sunny much longer.'

She points to the horizon, where the clouds gather into a dark mass. We're not sailing so much as drifting. But we're drifting towards this darkness. All day we've heard distant thunder, sweeping over the ocean like ripples. But we've not seen rain, only fields of dark sea under the clouds. Camille hums a few bars of something that might be 'Stormy Weather'.

'It should have been me,' I say. 'I expected it to be me.'

'Why?'

'Because I was older. Because you seemed more full of life than I felt.'

Camille shrugs.

'I don't think that makes a difference. Anyway, you must have had some life left. You made a family.'

'Not that I can remember them.'

Camille nods slowly. 'Did my family come to my funeral?'

'I don't know, I didn't go.'

A grin breaks over Camille's face, followed by mock-offence. She hits me gently on the arm.

'Melody! I died, and you didn't even turn up for the party.'

I'm about to defend myself but decide she's joking. We settle back to looking at the horizon. I remember this feeling. For all the adventures we had, all the running around London and being secretive, the thing that drew me to Camille was her silence. She was good at being silent, good at sitting with my silences. Wind whips around our clothes and a little spray leaps over the bow, raining down at our feet.

'I better check on the baby.'

'Okay. I'll come in soon. Just don't expect me to be a nanny.'

*   *   *

I eat a dinner of chicken in white sauce from the can. The chicken is cold, but I don't care. Perhaps I'm just tired, but I feel grateful for the food. By the time the first drops of rain patter onto the deck, the light is fading. Sandy has refilled one storm lamp and hung it in the main cabin.

They're magnificent clouds, really. So high and swirling with shadows that it feels like we're sailing into a room. A room big enough for giants to sit in. The thunder has fallen silent, but the air outside is thick with it. Inside, the main cabin feels cosy. Me and Sandy are on one sofa, Lester and Camille on the other. Rene is playing cross-legged on the floor with a plastic train that belongs to the baby. The baby is at the centre of us all, in his makeshift crib. He's been whimpering in the last few minutes but never works up to a full cry. Perhaps he's still weak after his stomach bug. I think he's lost weight. When I change him into a new outfit, his arms and legs look spindly.

Lester is playing the guitar for us to listen to. He plays Delta blues and English folk and even some French chanson. Camille has one arm over the back of the sofa. She watches as he plays. I'm not sure if I'm imagining their flirting, but I'm not imagining my own annoyance. Not that I feel anything for Lester. I just want my past to behave itself.

'Fancy a cigarette?' Lester asks her in a break between songs. Camille nods, and he starts to furnish them both with a smoke.

'Hey! Not in here,' I say.

'Why not?'

'It's bad for the baby. Go outside if you want to smoke.'

They both look at me with mild disbelief. Even Rene frowns up at me from the floor. Still, they let themselves out onto the deck and shelter in the triangular space under the stairs leading up to the wheelhouse. After a minute I see smoke wreathing around the windows.

'You should play one of *your* songs.' Rene doesn't look up from scribbling on a scrap of paper.

'I don't remember any more,' I say. It's the truth. I don't remember the ones I already played. They seem used-up, like matches. One strike and they're done.

'Maybe if you pick up the guitar, you'll remember one.'

I go to pick up the guitar. I retune it and sit, plucking the open E string with my thumb as though it might become a bassline to something. I shake my head.

'It is no good, my mind's gone blank.'

There's a peal of thunder and the baby starts to cry. I put down the guitar and pick him up. Lester and Camille throw open the doors and hurry inside, trailing clouds of nicotine. The drizzle of a few minutes ago has become a deluge.

'Here it comes!'

We gather at a window, watching as the waves are made rough by the rain. As though a curtain is being drawn, the light of day fades. Far off, down the corridors of cloud, I see lightning flicker. I feel a familiar fear which I can't place right away. We're not steering ourselves; we cannot dodge or choose another path. We can only see the danger approaching. I felt like this when the doctor told me I had dementia.

Over the next half hour, the rain doesn't let up, and the wind grows stronger, howling around the cabin. We start to roll with the waves and I feel queasy. At least with the first storm I didn't have to go through this build-up. Every time there is lightning, Rene starts to count *one Mississippi, two Mississippi, three Mississippi*, until the sound of thunder rolls over us. The first time she counted twelve, the next time it's nine, the time after that just three. There's a bright flash and the thunder sounds at the same moment.

'It's getting really close,' Rene squeaks.

The baby starts to cry, high and frightened. To my surprise, Camille gets out of her seat and crawls over, shushing him.

'There, there, baby, don't cry.'

She picks him up, but he won't calm down. The sound of the storm is building every moment.

'What can we do to calm him?' she asks.

'Ella should play one of her songs – that calms him,' Rene says. Camille nods in agreement.

'Yes, you're a good player. You should play something.'

I shake my head. 'I don't remember anything.'

'Not even a lullaby? What did you play to Abigail when she was little? I bet she loved it when her *maman* played for her.'

I pause. There is a shape, just out of reach. Lester hands me the guitar. I sit on the floor with Camille cradling the baby. I strum the opening chord a few times, Fmaj7, trying to remember the tune. There's a crash of thunder. I strum the chord again and hum the first note. Where does it go from there? I'm standing in a doorway but can't walk through. The boat jolts again and throws me forward, into the melody.

The tune is simple, but it takes all my effort to play. The notes weigh me down, strung around my neck like weights, ready to drag me to the bottom of the ocean. For a moment I look up. The baby has fallen silent in Camille's arms and the others are watching him, sitting in a ring illuminated by the storm lamp above. Sandy and Lester hum the tune in unison. Though the storm continues to rage, they each of them look as peaceful as the congregation at a carol service.

There's a tremendous bang as *Mnemosyne* hits something. For a split second the whole boat comes to a stop like a playground swing caught in mid-air. Clutching the guitar, I fly forward into the past. The storm lamp falls to the floor and shatters, plunging us into darkness.

THE MATRON

1976

Ella smooths out her uniform – the pressed beige of an auxiliary nurse. It's not fashion-conscious or flattering, but she doesn't mind that. She checks that she has everything and turns the key on her locker.

The ward is quiet when she steps from the nurses' room. It often feels, in that moment, as though she's stepping on stage. It's a long time since she stepped onto a real stage. There's some truth to the metaphor, she supposes – the ward is a place of drama. Her own role is a performance. The performance of order, the performance of optimism, the performance of calm acceptance.

She goes to the nurses' station and checks the patient list. Nobody needs to tell Ella her duties by now – she knows what needs doing for different situations. Much of it is unglamorous, of course. There's the emptying of bedpans, the scrubbing of bedpans, the redistribution of bedpans. There's a lot of general cleaning, changing bed linens, and the bringing of food, water, cups of tea, magazines and pairs of headphones that plug into a jack on the metal plate behind the bed.

Finally, and giving this ward its unique character, is the winding and unwinding of bandages, the selection and application of salves and creams, the mummification of the living. Five years ago, Ella started on a general ward, then moved to plastic surgery. She isn't squeamish and has been told she has a good bedside manner. Two days ago, she moved here, to the burns ward.

Ella goes around, dealing first with the bedpans. It's early, before any doctors have made it onto the ward, and she likes the peace and quiet at this time of day. Burns patients seem a quiet lot, on the whole. Sometimes they moan or cry out, especially in the night when inhibitions are softened. But mostly they are lethargic, like to move as little as possible, and their pain is a constant drone rather than the staccato stab of appendicitis or an inflamed gallbladder.

She brings a cup of orange squash to bed one, a newspaper to bed three (though someone has done the crossword already and she has to go and search for another). Finally, she comes to bed five and steps behind the curtain.

In the short time she has been working on the ward, Ella has picked up some of the jargon of the doctors' notes and has had them explain some of it to her. There are two big classifications – the severity of the burns and how much of the body they cover. There are first-degree burns that are superficial things, all the way up to fourth-degree burns which affect the underlying muscles and bones. Then there is 'TBSA'. It stands for Total Body Surface Area and tells you how much of the body is covered. Ella knows that the more of the body is covered in burns, the more likely the patient is to die. She knows that, once you get up to fifty percent TBSA, over a third of all patients die.

The body in front of her – she is uncertain if it is a man or a woman – seems totally encased in bandages. She cannot tell if they are awake and, if so, whether they have seen her. She glances at the notes.

85% TBSA, moderate inhalation.

This is as bad as she has seen. Severe inhalation burns kill about a quarter of patients on their own, though at least he's not on a ventilator. Still, she's staring at a death sentence.

'Morning.'

The pile of bandages speaks. Croaky, but not as much as she might have expected. A man's voice, a London accent.

'Good morning.' Ella feels her pulse racing. Ridiculous – she has seen enough patients in distress that this shouldn't bother her. It must be the new ward, the new conditions. Everything takes some time to get used to. She does the mental equivalent of smoothing down her uniform.

'Can I get you anything?'

A throaty chuckle. 'Have you seen my running shoes?'

Ella smiles and decides to be direct. 'Can you see me?'

The bandaged man seems to nod very slightly. 'Yeah, I can see you, love. My name's Ryan, but everyone calls me Rhino.'

'Nice to meet you, Rhino.'

'I'd offer to shake your hand, but I'm a bit tied up.'

'Are you always this hilarious?'

Another wheezy laugh, which turns into a cough. She waits for him to be done.

'How are your pain levels?'

'Fine.'

'You're sure? We don't hand out medals for bravery.' She looks at the line snaking down from the drip, burrowing into the bandages.

'I'm fine, honest.'

'Thirsty?'

'No. I've got a dry mouth though.'

'I'll get you something to drink. Water or juice?'

'Can I have a cup of tea?'

'They say you're not allowed.'

'What for?'

'Because you burned your lungs, and the steam might irritate them.'

'I don't mind having it cold. I always leave it too long on the site.'

'The site?'

'I'm a builder. Carpenter mostly.'

'Ah . . .' Ella thinks for a moment, listening to him wheeze. 'All right, I'll get you some tea. But if anyone asks, I said no.'

'Mum's the word. Three sugars.'

'Three sugars what?'

'Three sugars, please, Nurse . . . ?'

'Nurse Campbell. You can call me Ella.'

She goes and makes the tea and keeps taking deep breaths which never seem to stretch her lungs out. She takes a drinking straw from the pack in the cupboard. It's a joke on the ward that, if they should be asked by the hospital accountants to choose a single resource to keep – heart monitors, petroleum creams, gauze bandages – they would ask to keep the bendy straws. A lot of the patients on the ward cannot sit up or get themselves into a position where they are able to drink. She adds some cold water to the mug, and when it's tepid she takes it back to Rhino.

He drinks a third of the mug through his bendy straw before making a guttural noise at the pain of swallowing.

'Take it easy.'

'You have any kids, Nurse Campbell?'

'No.'

'I've two girls. Three and seven . . .'

Ella feels her lungs contracting.

'You're married?'

'Yeah . . . Lucy. She's an angel.'

'Is she coming in today?' Ella ventures.

'No, I . . .' long pause, just the sound of his airways crackling. 'I told her not to come. When they arrived, they weren't sure who I was. She hadn't been told.'

'You called her?'

'With some help.' He holds up his bandaged hands slightly and audibly winces. 'Said not to come, not to bring the girls.'

'Why?'

'Because I don't want them to see me like this . . .' he says, and the next time he speaks he's barely audible, but Ella has good hearing and catches it over the sounds of the ward. 'I don't want them to remember me this way.'

Ella takes a deep breath.

'Well then, we're just going to have to get you fixed up and back with your family as soon as possible, eh?'

Rhino says nothing.

*　*　*

Ella's shift ends, and she goes home. She looks in on Rhino before she goes and wonders if he'll still be there in the morning. Over the day he's had several interventions from the doctors, trying to slow his racing heart, prevent fluid build-up and stop his kidneys shutting down. Ella doesn't understand all of it, but she understands more than they think.

She thinks about Rhino all the way home in the car. She thinks about him as she empties a can of spaghetti hoops into a pan and pops bread in the toaster. She hopes Peter will be home soon, and they will watch TV and talk about what his session was like. Ella likes hearing about the business, now that she's not part of it any more.

That frozen January day was the last time she set foot in a

studio. Peter had handed over everything to a junior producer, then drove her to his home. Ella couldn't bear to return to her own flat for several weeks. Peter had agreed when she said she couldn't go to hospital, sat with her as she shivered and cramped and puked her way through withdrawal. Twice he had caught her in the act of trying to escape, with money she had taken from his wallet.

She makes herself a cup of mint tea with leaves from the window box outside the kitchen and stares at the grey January sky. She watches as it begins to spit and vaguely remembers someone saying that skin 'keeps the rain out and the blood in'. Now Rhino cannot do either. The only barrier between him and the universe is an artificial one.

* * *

When she arrives for her next shift, Ella doesn't wait to look at the patient list before hurrying to bed five. Rhino is still there, still wrapped head-to-toe, though everything has moved around slightly. He's permanently hooked up to a heart monitor now, and the drip snaking into his arm looks different.

She stands in front of him and smiles uncertainly but gets no response. She can't see him breathing under all the bandages, and if it weren't for the heart monitor, she would be concerned he was more than sleeping.

Ella returns to the nurses' station, looks over the notes and begins her duties. Today, she's in a rush. It's not that it's especially busy, and she doesn't cut corners, but today she feels that everything else is a distraction. When the bedpans are all changed, drinks fetched, senior nurses notified where pain medication is inadequate, she goes back to bed five. A doctor is finishing an inspection, and Ella makes busy rearranging the sheets. The doctor is in early. No, she realizes from his drawn look – he has been here all night.

'Can I get you anything, doctor? Cup of tea?'

He sighs. He can't be very old, perhaps not long out of med school.

'A cup of coffee would be good. I've had about twenty of them, but I've still got to drive home.'

'All right, I'll just be a minute.'

She goes to the nurses' room and makes coffee with an extra half-spoon of granules. When she gets back to bed five, the junior doctor is writing notes on Rhino's clipboard. There's already a thick sheaf of paper there. Ella doesn't usually ask questions, but she thinks this doctor won't mind. She hands over the coffee.

'How is he?'

The doctor exhales, slightly shakily. 'Bit of a wobbly night. Lurching from one thing to the next, really. Low blood pressure and high pulse, then I'd give him something and he'd have high blood pressure and a slow pulse.' He leans closer, lowers his voice. 'I'm glad to be handing over to someone who knows more than I do.'

Ella nods tightly and swallows her fear.

She has never felt this way about one of the patients. She's seen awful facial injuries in the plastic surgery ward, and never felt this way. What way? As though it's happening to family, Ella thinks. It occurs to her now in glorious technicolour how awful the ward is, how dreadful it must be to have these injuries. She thinks of Lester, sitting in the burns ward of a New York hospital, wondering if he would make it out alive. How can she be numb to it?

'Anyway,' the doctor puts the clipboard down and smooths the wrinkles out of his trousers, 'he's stable for now. I'm clocking off, but if the heart monitor goes off, or if you notice anything unusual, get a doctor straight away.'

He gulps down the coffee and nods goodbye to Ella. She wants to ask another question, but cannot do so in front of Rhino, so she chases after him a moment later, just as he's pushing through the doors to the ward.

'Doctor!'

'Is something wrong?'

'No, it's . . . I was just wondering . . . I know you don't like to speculate but . . .' She feels incredibly foolish.

This is the kind of question that new nurses ask, caught up in the drama of their first patients, unable to stop their minds wandering and get on with the realities of the job. But the young doctor seems to understand. Maybe he's not so far removed from those dramas himself after a long night sat next to the burnt man. He rubs his stubbled cheeks as though giving thanks for his soft, unscarred skin.

'It's hard to say. It's a very serious case . . .' He speaks under his breath, conspiratorially. 'But survival isn't out of the question. There have been cases. He'll have all sorts of complications going forward if he does survive, but every day he keeps going, his chances improve.'

Ella nods. It's not that she feels better, exactly. But she feels a new resolve. She must keep him going. One day at a time, painful as each of those days must be, she will keep him moving forward. If Lester could be saved, this man can be saved too. A family can be saved. School plays, Christmas dinners and wedding speeches can be saved.

When she returns to the ward, the other nurses and doctors give her a string of duties to fulfil, and she must strip two beds and put them back together with fresh linen. The ward, always lethargic, is slowly coming to life. By the time she gets back to Rhino he's awake, though she only knows this by his greeting.

'Morning, Nurse Campbell.'

'Morning, Rhino. Can I get you anything?'

'Well, I've had five people in the night tell me I can't have a cup of tea,' he says, voice scratchy. 'At least I think it was five, could have been the same people telling me over again.'

Ella nods.

'Say no more, I'll be back in a minute.' She goes and makes tea with a straw and takes a glass of orange juice as a decoy to bed five.

'I'll just wait for it to cool. Anything else I can get you?'

'Nah, I don't need anything. You could stay and chat, if

you're not busy? I've been surrounded by people all night, but I've barely spoken to any of them.'

Ella smiles and nods, but then finds herself stumped for a topic of conversation. What do you ask a man whose entire life just paused?

'You're a carpenter?' she asks, then realizes it is another wrong question. Of course Rhino is no longer a carpenter. He stopped being a carpenter at the moment of his incineration. But the question doesn't seem to faze him.

'Since I was fourteen. My dad was a builder, but he made his money from kitchen fitting. He got the old boys to teach me.'

'Do you like it?'

'It's all right, you know? It's a good job for me, because I'm a fidget. That's why this is driving me up – sitting still for hours on end.'

'Just don't go escaping in the middle of the night, okay?'

'If I do, you can be my accomplice.'

She smiles and checks the tea, which is still far too hot.

'Did you always want to be a nurse? Seems like a job you were born to do.'

Ella has been asked this question many times and has always lied, to patients at least. When she came to the hospital, she had to tell the doctors and nurses something about her life, if only to explain the fact that she was a junior nurse in her mid-forties. But if the patients ask, she gives the vague impression she's been doing this forever.

'Not always. I used to be a musician.'

'Oh yeah? What did you play?'

'Guitar.'

'I'd love to play guitar, but I'm rubbish at all that. Can't even sing a tune, the boys tell me. Doesn't stop me trying.'

'If you try that here the senior nurses will have you sedated.'

A wheezy chuckle, followed by a weak coughing fit. 'Do you ever play for the patients?'

'I think it might be frowned on.'

'You should. I bet you're good. Music's good for the soul, isn't that what they say? Good for recuperation. You should play for me.'

'I don't think that's going to happen.'

Another chuckle. 'I'll get you to crack, you'll see. We'll have the whole ward joining in for a chorus.'

She looks to change the subject.

'You want to try this tea now? I think it's cool enough.'

'Yeah, quick, before the Gestapo turn up.'

She puts the crook of the straw up to his mouth. Or, at least, she puts it to the break in the bandages where his mouth must be. When he speaks, she can vaguely see his lips moving in the shadows, but mostly there's just a slit formed by the dressings. She wonders when they will be changing him into fresh dressings, and whether she will be able to stand it.

After a moment he gets his lips around the straw and sucks a mouthful of the lukewarm, sugary tea. He pauses but does not let go of the straw, then sucks again. It reminds Ella of a baby on a bottle. How they will suck and stop, still attached, as though exhausted by the effort. Not that she's had a baby herself. Peter and she tried, but they're both getting on. He says it's nobody's fault, but Ella thinks if it's anyone's fault it's probably hers.

The rest of the day goes quickly. Ella can lose herself in her duties, and will sometimes be surprised that hours have passed, as though she had merely existed, performing her duties automatically. Her shift ends but she doesn't leave right away. She's only rushing back to an empty house. She visits Rhino.

'Hello, Nurse Campbell.'

'That's me off for the shift. I'll see you the day after tomorrow, yeah?'

'That's a shame.' He sounds genuinely sad.

'How are you feeling?'

'Can't complain. They've got me on that much pain medication, you could probably saw my leg off and I wouldn't notice.'

'You must be drowsy?'

'Well it's nice to sleep, you know? Not so nice to wake up.'

Ella purses her lips. 'We're going to get you through this, all right?'

It takes him a moment to respond, as though he's mustering the courage. 'What if I don't want to make it through?'

'Don't say that.' It's not a particularly inspired response, and she feels stupid saying it.

'It's just . . . life is life, isn't it? But this . . .'

She sits down on the plastic chair by the bed, waiting for him to go on.

'You know how this happened? My accident?'

She shakes her head. 'Something to do with a car crash?'

'Not quite. I was driving the van back from a job, had ten bottles of pressurized gas back in the cage. One of those blew up, out of the blue, took the rest of them with it. The whole van went up like a fireball. Just this big fireball, still rolling down the street until I came to a stop . . .' He chuckles at the image. 'Pretty funny, now I say it out loud.'

Ella feels like she can't breathe, like she's inhaled burning smoke.

'Rhino . . .'

'My point is, everything was good up to that point. And then it happened, like things happen. People drop dead in the street, they get hit by cars. I had a friend, knew a guy who was sitting outside a cafe when a bit of the masonry dropped off, hit him on the head and that was it. Made the news.'

'But you didn't die.'

'Exactly. I didn't die. And I should have done. It would have been all right. Things happen, I know that. Building sites are dangerous places. *Life's* a dangerous place, ain't it?'

He takes a long, crackly breath.

'But this isn't life. We should enjoy life while it lasts, and when it goes, just let it go . . .'

* * *

Ella makes it to her car, starts the engine and puts the radio on, turning the dial until she gets some classical – a Chopin nocturne, she can't remember the number – and sits in her parking bay until she is calmer. The throb of the engine is soothing. The car is hers, Peter has his own, and she has gotten good at fixing the engine. The car was cheap when she bought it second-hand, but the engine is easy to get into. Her most impressive feat was replacing the carburettor. She wished it were that simple for Rhino – just replacing the broken parts.

She drives. Once she's home, Ella goes to the music room. Peter is doing a session at Olympic but didn't leave until after lunch. There's a message scribbled on the pad they keep next to the phone.

Won't be back until late - don't bother making dinner.

She stands there for a moment, holding herself together like a pressurized container. Then she sits down at the writing desk and takes out her address book. She used to rely on this book for work, but she's barely touched it in the last year. She turns to a well-thumbed page with a long list of crossings-out, new addresses and numbers added and deleted. She picks up the phone and dials the most recent number on the list. It's years since she wrote it down. Has she ever called it? She listens to the dialling tone for five rings, expecting someone else to pick up.

Click.

'Hello?'

'Hey, Robert.'

* * *

They meet in a cafe. Once he had found a home in Soho, Robert had never moved away from the centre. When Ella arrives, he's already sitting at a table near the back, reading the paper.

'Anything good?'

He looks up, a little startled. Time has not changed Robert all that much – he's a little heavier, wears his hair a little shorter, though it's still curly and, apart from a receding hairline, has not abandoned him. His face has the average number of creases, but Ella can't help but think they are in the right places, with laughter lines crinkling his eyes and a line down each cheek where he has been smiling. In contrast, Ella has acquired four asymmetric vertical lines between her eyebrows from frowning too much.

He stands without saying anything, puts the paper down and hugs her. The hug is not so tight, but she still feels as though the air has been knocked out of her. Robert pulls away, perhaps sensing that he has crossed a boundary.

'Can I . . . can I get you a drink?'

'Sure. Um, what was that?' She points to his half-empty cup on the table.

'It's called a cappuccino.'

'Ooh, la-de-da.' She smiles, teasingly. 'Go on then.'

When the Music Stops

She watches Robert while he goes up to the counter. It's been nearly ten years since she's seen him, without the shared business of making music to occasionally bring them together. She has his address and number only because he keeps sending Christmas cards. She doesn't know where he got their address.

It seems strange how well she remembers everything about Robert, how these details have persisted in time without her being there. Like a holiday destination visited once as a child and then again, many years later, Robert seems like a story she told herself, come to life. She remembers how he moves with a certain gracefulness, his big shoulders and hands seeming to take care not to break anything around him. He returns and sits, smoothing out his checked flannel shirt. He regards her as though examining a tricky chart.

'How have you been?'

'Fine, I suppose.' The phone conversation hadn't lasted long; Ella hadn't wanted to talk over the phone. He nods slowly at this piece of non-information. He knows she wouldn't be here if she were fine.

'Peter doing well?'

'He's well. Keeping busy.'

Robert nods slowly. Since Ella left the business, he hasn't stopped working, doing sessions, small gigs and teaching, but making most of his money playing West End shows. Musicals have had something of a revival in the last few years, though she doubts it will last.

'How have you been?' Ella asks.

'I'm fine,' Robert nods. 'Plenty of work. Not all to my taste, you know, but it pays the bills and it's nice to be in a big band again.'

'You always did enjoy a big operation. If you weren't such a pacifist, I think you might have been happy staying in the air force.'

'Maybe.'

'Seeing anyone?' she ventures.

Robert has seen many people over the years, but none of them lasted more than a few months. He shakes his head. 'Still married to my saxophone, I'm afraid.'

'It's better than being married to a vibraphone.'

He laughs at the dumb joke. 'I don't even know what that means.'

'Me neither.'

They fall into silence for a moment. 'Would you ever come back?' Robert asks at last.

'I don't think so . . . I don't think they'd have me back anyway, been out of it too long. Besides, I like it at the hospital.'

'I can't imagine you as a nurse. No offence.'

'I'm a bit surprised myself. But they say I have a good bedside manner, whatever the hell that is.'

'No, I can imagine – you don't take any shit. You don't let people wallow in their own misery.'

Until yesterday, Ella would have been inclined to agree with this sentiment, but now she just looks down. She laces and unlaces her fingers.

'Look, I'm not really sure why I came here . . .'

His smooth, unwrinkled brow furrows. 'Okay?'

'But I've been an idiot. For treating you like an idiot when you were trying to help me.'

Robert shifts uncomfortably, rubs behind his ear. At this moment, two cappuccinos arrive along with a fat slice of chocolate cake. Ella rolls her eyes.

'Still buying me food? I really shouldn't.'

'Old times' sake. And don't be daft – you're still a rake.'

Ella sips her cappuccino. There's a bit more froth than she would like – they're paying for coffee, not whipped air – but it's actually pretty good. She picks up the fork and takes a bite of the cake. She's about to say how good it tastes when Robert says –

'I was just scared.'

'Of what?'

'That I was going to lose you.'

There's a moment of possibility. Ella is very aware of it. A moment when something might happen, if she says the right thing. It is not even an especially brief moment, not a blink-and-you'll-miss-it moment. The moment stretches over maybe thirty seconds, and she has time to think about what she should or should not say. The door of possibility stays open, waiting for her to walk through, but she stays put.

'Anyway,' Robert begins, as the door closes, 'enough of that. It's all in the past.'

Ella nods briskly.

'Tell me what you've been up to for the last ten years.'

They talk for a couple of hours, with plates and cups coming and going from the table. When she stands, Ella blames the buzzing feeling in her head on too much caffeine. But she knows that's not really it. They've shared their recent histories, gone over anecdotes from their early days in London, reminisced about Glasgow, traded memories of Bedlay Street. They talked about records, bands they saw, concerts on the radio. On her own, Ella can't summon these details, but Robert is good at remembering.

There is something expansive, even a little obsessive, about his mind. It's full of curios and relics, monographs on music and reams of sheet music. She feels as though she is wandering around a charming if rather cramped second-hand bookshop. She wants to stay there, browsing through it all, for as long as possible.

As they walk to the street, another moment of possibility opens. This is a different moment, as all such moments are. It's a different flavour, not quite as exciting as the last, but somehow easier to take.

'This was nice,' she says, matter-of-factly.

Robert shrugs on his herringbone winter coat and stares at her for a moment. He smiles.

'It was.'

She hugs him. 'We should do it again, if you like?'

'I would.'

* * *

Spring turns into summer. Rhino is weak but more or less stable. Ella remembers what the doctor said – every day brings him closer to the possibility of survival.

Patients come and go.

Ella often reflects that, if a video of the ward were sped up many hundreds of times, everything would flicker around and change except for Rhino in bed five. She tries to talk to him as much as possible. She will read him magazines, which are all he's interested in – reviews for movies he's unlikely to see, celebrity gossip, true life stories. At some point he's deemed worthy of one of the hospital's limited store of televisions, which sits permanently on a table at the end of the bed. Mostly he listens with headphones on and makes a noise if he wants the channel changed.

His family calls.

Several times a week at first, then tapering off to once a week, then once a fortnight. To begin with they ask if he wants them to visit, and every time Rhino relays the message that he doesn't want visitors. Ella cannot help but think that, if she were in the same position as his wife, she would have climbed a drainpipe to get in.

When they change the dressings on his chest, she sees something mixed up in the boiled, bubbled flesh. It looks like a splash of ink, and in some way that's what it is – two tattooed hearts nestling close to one another over his own heart. Each must have had the name of one of his daughters inside.

Every week, Ella meets Robert. She doesn't talk about

Rhino. Their meetings are the only time she can breathe. She needs to talk, needs to be somewhere other than the house or the ward. Peter makes enough that she needn't work at all. But when it became clear that she wasn't going to get pregnant, Ella had felt the need for something else. She wanted to get out of the house. She wanted to be useful, after so long only looking after herself. Now she feels guilty for wanting more. But when she's with Robert, everything makes sense.

Nothing changes for Rhino, yet everything changes.

Ella remembers when he came to the ward, how he was burned away on the outside but laughing from behind his mask of bandages. She remembers how his voice, cracked by the smoke, was still the loudest sound on the ward. In the orchestra of human voices, Rhino's was the most strident – part of the brass section for sure. Now he is muted.

He gets bedsores, back pains, constipation, endless skin and chest infections. He survives it all, improves some. Then, nine months after he first arrived, he gets another virus. Meningitis. It burns through him for a week, and at the end he is barely alive. It's only a week after that, when he finally wakes up, that they realize he has gone blind.

* * *

Ella pulls up the chair next to bed five. It's late afternoon and the ward is quiet. She will be off duty soon and has arranged to meet Robert in the hospital cafe. She thinks it's ridiculous that he wants to see where she works, but he insisted. It's all she's been able to think about, all day.

'Hey, Rhino.'

'Hello, Nurse Campbell.'

'How did you know it was me?'

'You're the only Scottish voice around here.'

'Oh yeah . . .'

They sit in silence for a moment. Ella is lost for words. How can she make small talk with a man who has no existence beyond this bed?

'Can I get you anything?'

He sighs deeply.

'You could unhook that feeding tube.'

'You know I can't do that.'

'Why not?'

'Because you need it.'

He shakes his head. 'If someone said they didn't want to eat their dinner, would you force it down their throat?'

Ella says nothing.

'No, of course you wouldn't. But I don't have a choice about whether I eat or not. If I could get out of this bed I could go and buy a pack of razor blades, or walk up to the top floor of the hospital . . .'

'Rhino, please don't talk like this.'

'Why not? Why don't I get a choice?'

'Because we have a responsibility for your well-being. I want to look after you.'

'But you're not looking after my well-being. You're just keeping me alive. It's not the same thing.'

He doesn't sound petulant, just tired. Ella cannot keep up the charade any more.

'That's what parents do, isn't it?' She tries a metaphor he will understand. 'They try to keep their children alive, even when that means the children hating them for a while.'

'Yeah. But I'm not a child, and you're not a parent, Nurse Campbell.'

' . . . I know.'

'I'm not even a parent any more.'

'Don't—'

'Don't say that? It's true though, isn't it?'

'They're still your daughters. They still love you.'

He is silent for a moment, and when he speaks again, his throat is tight.

'And I want it to stay that way.'

They are silent for a minute, then two. She wonders if he knows she's still there. Finally, he says:

'Just think about it, okay?'

Another silence. Ella gets up from her chair and smooths out her uniform.

'All right.'

She holds herself together until she gets to the canteen. There is Robert, sitting at one of the tables with a couple of polystyrene cups and a polystyrene plate in front of him. She walks up, not looking him in the face. She can tell the coffee is burnt just by looking at it. The chocolate cake was young a week ago.

'Ready to give me the tour?' Robert asks, as she walks towards him. 'I like your uniform, it's very . . .'

He trails off, realizing something is wrong.

'Ella?'

He's standing before she knows it, hovering uncertainly in front of her. Then his arms wrap around her. There are no words for a minute. Robert just holds her.

'Sorry . . .' Ella pulls back, staring resolutely at his necktie. 'Bad day.'

Robert nods slowly. 'Well, I'll be honest with you – the coffee here is bilge.'

Ella smiles weakly. 'Yeah, it is.'

'You want to go somewhere nicer?'

'Could we . . . could you just drive me?'

'Drive you where?'

'Just drive. My car is outside.'

'Come on then.'

In the car park, it's starting to rain. Robert, practical as always, has a little umbrella with him. They run, hunched over. Ella's car is still warm from the sun earlier and smells of her deodorant and the boiled sweets she keeps in the glove compartment. It feels alien, getting in the passenger seat. Like sleeping on the wrong side of the bed. Then Robert gets in next to her and she pushes thoughts of bed out of her mind.

He starts the engine, finds the knob to turn on the heater,

adjusts his seat and the rear-view mirror. The windows are shimmering cascades, obscuring the outside world. The car feels strangely private, like a cave behind a waterfall. Ella turns and looks at him, frowning as he figures out the switch for the windscreen wipers. Suddenly she has the urge to say something. Something wonderful and terrible. Something which will blow up in her face, and she doesn't care.

'Robert . . .'

'Mm?' He looks up at her, smiling so sweetly. Such innocence, she thinks. Ella folds.

'Um . . . thanks. Thanks for doing this.'

'No worries. You want to talk about it?'

'Yes. At some point. But for now . . .'

'Say no more. Did you have a direction in mind?'

'No.'

'Wherever the road takes us then,' Robert mugs, impersonating Mr Toad. 'Poop poop!'

The car pulls out, weaves slowly through the still and silent cars like patients in their bays, then out onto the road. Ella watches the road for a minute, then turns the radio on low. It's Radio 3. They listen to Mendelssohn's overture to *A Midsummer Night's Dream*, the orchestra crackling and fading as the car weaves through west London suburbs, through Isleworth and onto the Chertsey Road, heading south. The rain doesn't ease up. Ella lets the light and noise and movement overtake her, trusts her course to Robert. She feels unexpectedly sleepy. At last, she says:

'I thought I would be used to grief, by now.'

Robert sighs, changes gear. 'I always think it's like having a cold – when you have a cold you think you can't get another one, but it doesn't work that way. One loss doesn't protect us from other losses.'

'It's a bit worse than a cold.'

'I know, but I like the metaphor. Some losses make you immune to grief, but not all grief. There's always a different kind that can catch you out.'

'Yes . . .' Ella nods her head. Her eyelids are heavy. 'Why is that?'

'Because . . .' Robert pulls up to a red light and turns the wipers up a notch. 'Because there are as many kinds of grief as there are kinds of people. For every person we get to know, every person who makes us feel like only they can make us feel, there's a different kind of grief.'

Ella says nothing. By the time they have reached Sunbury, curving around the river in the direction of Shepperton, she's asleep.

*   *   *

It takes her a week. Rhino still gets a lot of his medication via drip, but some of his pain medication is too corrosive long-term for the vein it's going into, so they give it to him as pills as much as possible. Ella has heard before of patients pretending to swallow these pills then spitting them out and saving them. Sometimes they don't like what the pills do to them, sometimes they like it too much and want a bigger high. Sometimes it's not about the effect at all.

They're supposed to check under the patients' tongues for this reason, but hardly ever do. If she can make it look like Rhino was hoarding pills, maybe she can get away with it. She doesn't have access to the pharmacy, or the drug cabinet in the ward where deliveries from the dispensary are kept. But at the point where the medication is doled out, she has access. Some patients have one of the pills, some have four or five. They're dispensed in little paper cups like some restaurants use for ketchup. Ella knows which patients pick out the contents one by one and which patients throw them back like shots at the bar. She feels bad, causing people more pain than they're due, but it's the only way.

She hides the pills in the pockets of her uniform. If she gets caught, she will be suspended pending review, probably fired, even reported to the police. They would assume she was selling the pills, or hooked herself. She doesn't care so much about that, she finds. She cares that Rhino would be trapped here. She doesn't tell him what she's doing, in case it doesn't come off.

Nobody complains. At one point, Mr Jeffries inspects the contents of his cup and asks why there is one less pill than usual, but she bluffs that they're reducing his dose and he doesn't argue. Another time she thinks Mrs Savidge has seen her putting a pill in her pocket, but she says nothing. By the end of the week she has thirty-five pills. She's not certain about the fatal dose – she knows it depends on the size of the patient – but she's fairly confident this will be enough.

It takes another two days until the right moment presents itself. The ward is quiet and put to bed. She goes to bed five with the pills in her pocket.

'Rhino?'

'Mmf?' He wakes from a half-sleep. 'Who's that?'

'Me, Ella.'

'Hello, Nurse Campbell. Still here?'

'For a little while, at least . . .'

She doesn't know what to say, having thought she would improvise something on the spot. She has never much liked priests and vicars, but she suddenly feels sympathy for them. To be there at such turning points in a person's life – introducing them to the world as a baby, marrying them to their true love, stepping into the room where they will shortly die – and being expected to say something . . . It seems too much to expect of one person, even if some of their lines are scripted.

Rhino senses her discomfort.

'Everything all right?'

'It's just . . . about your request.'

The word sounds stupid, yet he seems to understand her meaning. When he speaks again, his voice is constricted.

'Yes?'

'I have what you need. We can do it now, or later . . .'

Silence.

She thinks he has changed his mind.

Then she thinks he never really meant it, and he's disgusted at her.

'Thank you,' he says at last. 'I didn't think you'd go through with it.'

Ella keeps jumping every time she hears a noise in the ward around her. Though their conversation is veiled, it's hardly coded, especially to someone who may already have heard Rhino talking about his feelings. She leans into the bed, close to his face, as though she is plumping up his pillows.

'So, do you want to . . . now?'

He considers this.

'Are you in tomorrow?'

Ella feels relief and disappointment mingled. She had wanted to get it over with, she realizes, and immediately feels guilty for wanting to do this on her terms, not his.

'I am.'

'Tomorrow then.'

*   *   *

When Ella arrives back on the ward the next morning, with her stash of pills bundled in a tissue, she's carrying a guitar. An acoustic with nylon strings, the softest-sounding instrument she owns. It gets some looks from the senior nurses, but she explains that Rhino requested to hear her play, and whether through sympathy or amusement, they nod. Perhaps it's curiosity – at some point, word got around that she used to be a professional musician, but she has always declined to comment on her ability, let alone play. This isn't *The Sound of Music.*

'Morning, Rhino.'

'Morning, Nurse Campbell.'

'I brought my guitar.'

'You did?' There's a smile in his voice. 'I knew I'd break you eventually.'

'Congratulations.'

Throughout the day Ella's focus is always on bed five, though she tries to conceal this. If she's seen to be paying too much attention, it might give the game away.

She brings him cups of tea with plenty of sugar and makes sure he has his headphones on, so he can listen to the radio when he wants. It shouldn't be possible to sense a change in him, so hidden from view, but he seems peaceful to Ella. She's so nervous she can barely stand still, but at least she's meant to be on her feet.

Finally, the day is done. Daylight bleeds from the clouded glass of the windows and lingering visitors are expelled from the ward. Ella makes two cups of tea with sugar and leaves them to cool before taking them to bed five.

'Ready?'

He takes a slightly shaky breath.

'Ready.'

She extracts the pills from her pocket, wrapped in the tissue. She props Rhino up using the cranks on the bed and tries to make him comfortable. It wouldn't be impossible for him to take the pills on his own, but his fingers are lightly bandaged, so it makes more sense for Ella to place each pill on his tongue like a communion wafer before he takes a sip of tea. She hasn't been to church for many years, and hasn't believed in the Almighty for longer, but the echo still makes her uncomfortable.

Halfway through he pauses, breathless from the simple effort, and Ella thinks he will stop before they reach the critical dose. But then he sniffs, clears his throat and asks to continue. Finally, the handkerchief is empty. He takes a final gulp of tea, then Ella uses the controls to recline him once more.

The blue cotton curtain surrounding them billows a little as though in a breeze. Neither of them speaks for a moment. Ella leans close to him and whispers.

'Would you like me to stay or go?'

Rhino takes a deep breath, as though stretching his lungs out one last time.

'Just play me something. Then you should go.'

Ella is worried this might draw attention, or be remembered by someone as a suspicious act, or simply be remembered as close to the time he must have slipped away. But she cannot deny him this wish. She goes to the nurses' station and fetches the guitar.

'Any requests?' She feels as though the buttoned collar of her uniform is choking her.

'You just play, Nurse Campbell.'

Ella thinks for a moment, irrationally terrified that she must pick one song out of all the millions of songs in the world.

She starts fingerpicking, soft and low, and it's only when the chords have gone around once that she remembers the tune. She starts to hum 'The Matron', but her mind is elsewhere, remembering the words of Jack Shapiro.

Songs let us call people back, but they also allow us to let them go. There is a reason we sing songs at a funeral. Like pushing a boat out onto a black lake, with the shrouded body inside. Watching as they wind their way down the river Styx and disappear. Songs are that little vessel, bobbing away into the darkness.

When she's finished, Ella can't remember how long she played for. She feels breathless. She looks to the bed where Rhino is silent but still breathing. Ella stands, steps around the curtain, and walks through the ward to get changed out of her uniform.

Out in the car park, everything is quiet. She carries her guitar in one hand, her clothes bag in the other. When she has reached the car, she looks up to the sky. Though it's calm down here it must be windy further up in the atmosphere, because thin-stretched clouds are scudding over the moon and stars. As she watches, a bank of clouds stretching from one horizon speeds toward the moon and obscures it.

Ella puts her things in the boot, climbs into the car and drives away.

6.

The Mother

SOMEONE IS CROUCHING OVER me. I don't open my eyes and, after a minute, the person pads away. I feel dreadful. I'm lying on a hard floor. How long have I been like this? Someone has put a cushion under my head and a blanket over me. Beyond my eyelids it's light, so I've slept through the night. Through the storm

I remember the baby. Before, remembering the baby got me to open my eyes, kept me pushing forward as my body slowed down. But now I can't force myself up.

I hear those padded footsteps coming back toward me. There's a rustling as the person crouches, puts their hand on my shoulder and rolls me onto my back. The pain this causes is enough to make me open my eyes. At first, all I can see is white. I think I'm being dazzled, but no – I'm looking at something white. An outline of a head. A bandaged face.

'Hello, Nurse Campbell.'

I try to speak once, fail, swallow a few times. I think of Robert running the reed of his saxophone over his tongue to wet it. Eventually an old reed would crack, and he had to replace it. Perhaps I've cracked.

'Hello, Rhino.'

'Can I get you a glass of water?'

'Just . . . help me up.'

Gently, he lifts me to sitting. The cabin is a terrible mess, the sofas have slid around, the papers we tidied are strewn everywhere. The cushions I put down for the baby have moved. Camille and Lester are crouched over them.

'Is he all right?'

Camille looks around. 'He's . . . fine. Just tired from crying all night, I think.'

She moves, and I can see the baby in his grubby sleepsuit. His stomach rises and falls slowly. I look around the rest of the room, taking in the mess.

Then I see the guitar.

I'm on my feet before I know what's happening. I hobble to where the guitar is face down in a pool of water that has seeped under the cabin doors. The metal standard lamp which sat next to the sofa has fallen onto the guitar and punched a hole in the back.

Carefully, I pull the lamp out of the guitar and turn it over. The varnish is discoloured pale, like a body that has been underwater. But the strings aren't broken, the neck is intact.

I pick shards out of the hole and try strumming. To my relief, the strings ring out. Its voice has changed a little, but the guitar is still a guitar.

'You still play?' Rhino asks.

'Now and then.'

My mind is elsewhere. There are seven songs. I have to play all of them, though I don't know what will come at the end. I just have to play them. For a moment, I thought I had no instrument. Carefully, I pick up the guitar and carry it to the sofa, then use a cushion cover to dry it. I sit, feeling my body seize up. Rhino perches on the arm of the sofa. I look at him properly for the first time.

'It's good to see you up and about.'

'It's good to be out of that bed.'

'How do you feel?'

'Fine. The pain is gone.'

'Do you want me to take the bandages off?'

He looks down, as though I've commented on the shirt he's wearing. 'Nah. They're part of me now.'

'Do you know what's going on?'

'Yeah, these guys filled me in.'

'I'm sorry to drag you into it.'

He shrugs. 'I'd rather be here than nowhere.'

Camille brings the baby over and places him in my arms. He looks at me with clear blue eyes, which seem to have grown a size since I last looked at him. His arms and legs, which had chubby folds at the wrists and ankles, are almost skinny.

'Right,' I say. My voice sounds different after the storm, like the guitar, but at least I still have a voice. 'Let's tidy up.'

*   *   *

We work all day, and finally the boat is put back together. *Mnemosyne* is recovered but not the same, like a body after illness. I can't work any longer and sit with my head back on the sofa, while Rhino plays games with Rene on the floor. I think she must remind him of his own daughters. Sandy is out on the deck, eyeing the horizon, watching for the next threat. Lester and Camille have disappeared downstairs.

I put the guitar in my lap, trying to remember the next song. Chord shapes come to me without a name. I can't remember if they are sharp or flat, or what key signature they would belong in.

I'm getting worse, I know it. My fingers are strangely nimble, finding frets, finding combinations it took me years to learn. But the rest of me isn't so miraculous. I feel a fog descend on my brain. When I played the first tune, I thought I could lift that fog. That, if I could keep playing, I could rescue myself. But the magic is wearing off. It was only ever a borrowed spell, not mine to keep. My body is full of pains; my heart rattles when I go up the stairs. All I want to do is play the next song, but it won't come. I'm putting the guitar down when I hear a call from Sandy.

'Land! I see land!'

Rene is running out of the cabin before I have a chance to

get up, with Rhino chasing after her, yelling that she shouldn't run on the deck. I heave myself up.

Could this be it? The thought fills me with relief and sadness that I will never discover the final two songs. As I'm hobbling to the cabin doors, Lester and Camille appear from below deck, looking askew.

'Did I hear that right?' Lester asks.

'You two go ahead, I'll catch up.'

They race past me.

I step onto the deck with a backward glance at the baby. He's playing with a chain of teething rings. I join the rest of them at the bow of *Mnemosyne*, out of breath. They're chattering anxiously among themselves. I peer at the horizon but can't make anything out.

'What do you think, Ella?' Sandy asks.

'I can't see, what does it look like?'

'Dark,' Camille says, 'with buildings on it.'

'Buildings?'

'I think so. It's hard to see.'

'We need a plan,' Sandy says.

'A plan for what?'

'To get us over there.'

'Which way are we drifting?' Camille frowns.

'I don't know . . . I think we're moving parallel to it, like this.' Sandy points to our right, not away from land but not toward it either.

We stop and think about this for a minute.

'What about the sail?' Rene asks. 'You put it up once.'

I look to the tangled rigging that covers the deck behind us. 'It's not like before, when it was all trussed up. We just released it. I don't know how to put it up again. Do any of you?'

I look around at their blank faces.

'What about the engine?' Lester asks.

'There's an engine?' says Rhino.

'The engine doesn't work. I tried fixing it, but I don't know how.' Sandy shrugs.

'Well I know a little bit about engines.' Rhino straightens up. 'Let's take a look.'

* * *

We spend hours below deck, hunched over the engine. The water has risen to ankle level again, seeping from under the locked playroom door. It doesn't matter now, if we can get to land. With Rhino to guide us, I start to remember more about engines. Before, I just saw a mass of metal. Now I can see the fuel lines, the piston caps, the carburettor. It's not the same as my old car engine, but all the parts are there in a different arrangement. I use screwdrivers and wrenches and spanners, my hands thick with grease. I pull parts off and tip the water out, bolt them back into place. Rhino talks me through what to do, while Sandy shines a torch. Finally, it's finished. Rhino doesn't know any more.

'We can try again if it doesn't work, but anything after this is guesswork.'

We go to the main cabin, where Camille is dangling a teddy bear over the baby in her lap. A smile curls the corner of her lips. Rene is outside on the deck, throwing bits of splintered guitar overboard, watching as they float away. The light is fading, the sun has just dipped its toes into the horizon.

I walk out onto the deck and a cool breeze rises off the ocean to greet me. The dark line of land is more visible, but it has gotten no closer. We really must be drifting sideways. Everything I want, just out of reach.

'You ready?' Sandy asks.

I nod, 'Let's get this over with.'

I climb the stairs to the wheelhouse. Up here I have an even better view of the sunset blazing to our right. I slump into the chair and search for a moment before I find the ignition. The keys still dangle there with a fuzzy pom-pom. Deep breath.

I turn the key.

Nothing happens.

Nothing happens.

Nothing . . .

There's a judder. It's so unexpected, I jump. The engine shakes itself into life, its pitch dipping a couple of times before smoothing out. I get up and rush down the stairs. Rhino and Sandy are whooping, dancing around on the deck. As I go inside, the lamps in the main cabin flicker on and the micro-wave starts to buzz in the kitchen. There's a rattle as the air-conditioning begins to pump cold air.

'We did it! We did it!'

Camille hugs me. 'So this is it? We drive to land?'

I look at the last sliver of sun, which is disappearing below the horizon. I need to make a decision.

'I think we should wait until morning. It'll be dark soon and there'll be rocks to dodge when we get closer to land.'

'That's a good point.' Lester nods. 'I'm in favour of not sinking ourselves.'

'So what do we do now?' Rene skips circles around me.

Lester grins. 'Tomorrow we might all go up in smoke. Tonight, we have a party.'

*   *   *

As evening deepens, I move less and less. The aches I woke up with have softened slightly. But now I've stopped moving, a new weariness settles over me. We open the last of the food. None of the others eats, but they make me a plate that I eat happily.

Lester and Camille have cigarettes and I don't have the strength to tell them not to smoke around the baby. Sandy finds a bottle of whisky that has been lurking at the back of the cupboard under the sink. The dead may not eat, but they do drink. I accept a dram in a plastic mug. I'm free of responsibilities for a little while.

Night falls, but for the first time since the storm, all the lights are on. My friends talk, recalling memories to one another. There's laughter. With power restored to the kitchen,

Camille brews cups of strong black coffee. Lester tunes the guitar. I feel protective of the instrument but haven't the strength to stop him. Besides, I like hearing Lester play.

Our little cabin glows bright on the dark sea, full of smoke and coffee steam and chatter that I'm only half listening to. My brain tilts with whisky. Something like a last flare rises in me and I raise a hand to Lester.

'My turn.'

He smiles and hands it over. The chatter doesn't stop but is hushed as they wait to see what I'm going to play. I check the tuning, strum a couple of times, and begin.

Weariness falls away like a heavy cloak. I play the song, fingerpicking chords with embellishments I would have been proud of at thirty-seven. I hum the melody and my voice doesn't crack. Haltingly, Lester sings a harmony line. I close my eyes, reeling with the little drink. I sink into the sofa, still playing, until the light and smoke and music wreathe around and obscure me.

The Mother

Jack Shapiro

1981

ELLA SITS ON THE edge of her bed, telephone receiver pressed to her ear, listening to the static of a dead line. She was changing the sheets when the phone rang.

'Hello?'

'Is that Ella Campbell?'

The voice had been Scottish, and some part of Ella had known the news before she was told. They don't call her – she calls them.

'Are you sitting down?'

'I am now.'

'I'm afraid it's your mum.'

Now they've hung up, but Ella can't quite bring herself to put the receiver down. She needs to sit for a moment with this strange, hollow feeling. This feeling of not-feeling. Her mother has been effectively dead for a long time, unremembering her daughter, her surroundings, perhaps even herself. A year ago she took to bed, closed her eyes and steadfastly refused to get up. Ella grieved for her, but it was a strange, drawn-out sort of grief, and it has left her with nothing now to give her mother as a parting gift. She prods at her grief, evoking childhood memories of Bedlay Street, but they echo in the empty space.

Finally, she takes a notebook from the bedside table and dials a number from it. She knows where he is today, though he doesn't always tell her. She gets through to the receptionist at Abbey Road, asks if she can talk to Peter.

'Hang on, I'll see if I can find him.'

Ella waits as she is put on hold and listens to the whirr of the machinery maintaining the connection. At last there is a click.

'Hello? Mrs Fricke?'

'Yes?'

'I'm afraid he's gone – that session finished an hour ago.'

'I see. Well, thank you.'

The line falls dead once more, and Ella slams the receiver down with a grunt. Peter is always like this, but why did he have to be like this today? She hardly ever knows where he is. Half the time he doesn't come home in the evening. Usually she doesn't care, but right now she just needs to tell someone her news. Maybe that way she might feel the truth of it.

She dials another number, from memory.

'Ella?' There's a rustling down the line as Robert makes space to sit next to the phone. She can picture the teetering piles of sheet music, the old copies of *Record Collector*.

'Can I come round?'

'What, now? Sure, I'm free. Shall we meet at Zephirelli's?'

Ella swallows. 'I'd rather come to yours.'

'Oh . . .' Robert sounds puzzled. 'All right then.'

In the last four years, Robert has become her best friend. They meet weekly, usually over coffee but sometimes at a gallery or daytime concert. Robert always knows what's on. He lets her know when Caravaggio is in town or when Mozart is visiting the Albert Hall. Sometimes Ella has convinced herself that it is all this other stuff – the art, music and films – that makes spending time with Robert so different from spending time with Peter. But she is wrong. It's that Robert wants to experience these things with her. To entangle his pleasure with hers. Ella spends time with Peter, but she lives her life with Robert.

Ella knows she loves him. She knows she has loved him since she was eighteen, sitting in that tea shop on Buchanan Street, listening to him talk about music. She's only confused about how long it took her to realize. Perhaps it was because it felt so easy, so obvious, she thought it was an effect he had on everybody. Robert's passion was so infectious, falling in love with him seemed inevitable.

On foot she crosses the river at Richmond Bridge and walks to the station. From the station shop she buys a newspaper and some chocolate biscuits he likes. It's February, and the windows on the train are steamed up. She wipes away a patch of condensation and watches as the leafy greens of her suburb change to browns and greys. She walks from Waterloo, cheeks ablaze in the wind blowing off the river. The streets are quiet; London has not fully woken up. By the time she reaches Robert's she's a little out of breath and waits a moment before pressing the buzzer.

'Come up! I just made coffee.'

Robert's flat is on the second floor, via a tight, winding staircase that reminds Ella of the close she grew up on. She has been to the flat a handful of times in the last few years, but Robert rarely invites her back. Perhaps he is aware that, though Ella is married, he spends no time with Peter. When they meet in public, they have nothing to hide.

At the top, Robert is waiting in the door, warmly dressed in an argyle sweater and clutching a tea towel.

'Come on in, you know the way.' He ushers her past him and closes the door. 'You'll have a cup?'

'Yes, please. One sugar.'

'Just the one?'

'Trying to cut down.'

The flat is as she remembers it. A long hallway first, too narrow for bookcases but nevertheless with piles of magazines and a box of records against the wall. She cannot tell if these are coming or going, being integrated into the flat or expelled from it. First on the left is Robert's bedroom, then straight ahead at the end of the corridor is the living room, and at a right-angle to that are the bathroom and kitchen. She has been in all these rooms except his bedroom, which always has the door closed. She doesn't even know what it looks like.

Ella goes through to the living room. She has always loved it in here. It's on the corner of the building, so two of the four walls have big windows. The other wall is taken up by an enormous, fitted bookcase, crammed with Robert's various collections – books, records, cassette tapes. The enormous bookcase stops a little way off the ground to allow for a long sofa, and Ella sits under it now, feeling herself expand into this place as though it were a warm bath.

Robert returns with the coffee.

'Only had blue milk, hope that's okay,' he says absent-mindedly, rubbing behind his ear. Ella doesn't reply, knowing he's just filling time. He's trying to work out why she's here, or at least why she has invited herself into his flat. She sips the coffee, letting him wonder for a little longer.

'You have so much stuff.' She smiles, looking around the room.

There is a lovely upright piano in one corner, teetering with piles of sheet music and with several used coffee mugs dotting the floor around it.

'I know, I know . . .' Robert huffs a little.

'I didn't mean it as a criticism,' she smiles up at him, 'I like it.'

He smiles and sits down close – but not too close – on the sofa.

'I thought about moving flat a little while ago. Somewhere I didn't have to walk up four flights of stairs every time I get milk. But I couldn't bring myself to do it. This place is so perfect, and I've filled it up with everything . . . A friend of mine calls it my *exobrain.*'

She smiles. 'That's right. Like you had too much going on to fit it all inside your head.'

'I dunno. Maybe.'

They sip their coffee in silence for another moment.

'Now I feel like I'm sitting inside your head.'

Robert smiles a little uncomfortably, unsure what to make of this.

'Ella . . . it's lovely to see you. It's *always* lovely to see you . . . but is everything all right?'

She turns to the window, which looks across the street and through the windows of another flat like this one. A man is ironing shirts in his vest, while someone else, a woman perhaps, moves in the shadows behind him. Ella wonders vaguely what their life is like, what conversations they have, all boxed-up in that little flat. She wonders about all those conversations all over London.

'Mum died this morning.'

She looks at him for a moment, sees the moment he *thinks* he's worked out why she's here.

'I'm sorry, Ella.' Robert puts his coffee down, moves uncertainly closer for a moment, then hugs her.

'It's okay. She's been gone a long while.'

'Still though.'

'Aye . . . still.' She nods into his shoulder, and for the first time since hearing the news, she feels something. It's not a flood of grief, but a small shift, a crack running through her, like one landmass separating from another.

She stands up and walks around the room a little, looking at the pictures on the walls. She sees familiar faces – musicians she's played with, bands she's been in, old friends. Ella is glad they're here, inside Robert's brain, because often she finds she can't remember them any more. She feels as though she's losing the periphery of her life, the way some people lose the edge of their vision. It is contracting down to something small and one-pointed.

Ella turns to where he's still sitting on the sofa, watching her.

'Have you spoken to Peter?'

It's an innocent question, but it's exactly the question she hoped he would ask.

'Me and Peter hardly talk any more.'

Robert's eyes widen in surprise. 'Oh.'

'We live like flatmates. He comes and goes, and half the time if I try to contact him he's not where he said he would be. Sometimes I wonder if he's having an affair . . . then I wonder why that doesn't bother me more.'

She laughs, but Robert looks embarrassed. 'I'm sorry . . . I had no idea.'

She shrugs. 'I don't love him, Robert. I'm not sure if I ever did.'

He thinks for a second, searching for the right question. 'Aren't you angry?'

'Angry?' She weighs up the word. 'Perhaps, a little. But I'm not blameless.'

'Why? What have you done?'

Ella takes a deep breath and looks at the ceiling – 'I let him marry me. I let him think that I was his, and that was wrong.'

'Still, that's hardly—' he begins.

'I love you, Robert.'

It takes a moment to say. In her life, Ella has thought a lot about sound. Sound is just a vibration, the ringing of a cymbal or the blast of a horn. She has listened to so much sound, made sounds for a living for other people to listen to. You could record it of course, but the original sound was dead and gone. It existed only for a moment, vibrated the air in some room or on some street and went no further. Just a tiny ripple that seemed to change nothing. And yet, how often that ripple changed everything.

They are silent. The sound of those three words has already gone. The air has died down like the smooth surface of a pond, and you would never know the sound had been there at all. Robert stands. His arms are at his sides. He rubs his thumb and forefinger together, another action to try and spark thought.

'And I don't expect anything—' she begins again at last, just as Robert closes the space between them with three strides and kisses her. The kiss is brief. He pulls back, alarmed at what he has done.

'I'm sorry, I shouldn't have . . .'

She takes him by his shoulders and pulls him towards her. They kiss.

They kiss, and Ella feels all of London slow to a standstill.

It's as strange as she thought it would be – she is kissing her friend of so many years – and yet not strange at all. She reaches up and runs her hand through his curls.

'I love you too.' Robert shakes his head. 'I should have said it sooner. I shouldn't have wasted so much time.'

She shakes her head. 'Don't be sorry. We have time now.'

When she looks again, he's searching her expression, seeking reassurance. 'Okay . . . yes, okay. We have time.'

Ella takes his hand and leads him to the bedroom.

* * *

After she has seen Robert, Ella decides not to tell Peter straight away. She wants to do this on her terms, not in a rush. She thinks seriously about where she will live, what things she will take with her, what she will leave behind. She arranges a consultation with a solicitor.

Sometimes in the evenings, Ella spends time with Peter. He's not always AWOL, after all. She will make dinner and he will lay the table. She is surprised by how comfortable she feels, doing this. How natural it is to make each other cups of tea, watch a quiz on TV and confer over answers, talk about their friends and relatives. On weekends he will go to his potting shed and bring her seedlings to look at like a proud child. It is so familiar, all of it, that Ella will sometimes turn away with a melancholy convulsion. But when it has passed, she feels no remorse. She knows better now than to linger in this twilight of happiness.

She keeps going to see Robert in the days. Half the time they see a movie or have coffee like they used to. The other half of the time they spend in his flat, stretched out in bed, listening to the bustle of Soho through the window.

The first time they slept together, Robert paused.

'I don't have a condom.'

'No kidding.'

'I mean, we should be careful . . .'

'Robert, I'm fifty-one and you're fifty-three. I don't think we need to worry.'

'Oh, right.' He had smiled at his own stupidity and had drawn her back into an embrace.

They go to movies together, get meals. In some ways it's no different, in other ways everything has changed. The same picture seen from a different angle, and how different it looks. They cook meals together in Robert's little kitchen. One rainy afternoon he teaches her how to make tablet to his mother's recipe. From a book sandwiched between bags of flour he takes out a slip of paper, brittle like a dried leaf. Mrs Mauchlen had written out only the ingredients:

2 lb caster sugar

4 1/2 oz butter

1 tin condensed sweetened milk

1/4 pt milk

1/2 teaspoon vanilla extract if you can get it

Robert remembers the method from memory, placing everything except the vanilla in a pan and heating on a medium heat until it melts. They sit in the kitchen for the next forty minutes, sipping coffee and taking turns to stir the mixture, as the familiar alchemy takes place and the kitchen starts to smell like childhood. Ella has tried several times down the years to make it herself. She followed recipes from library books and recipes written down by friends. She bought a sugar thermometer. It always went wrong, turning brittle or soft like icing.

Robert brings the mixture to the boil, adds vanilla and takes it off the heat, stirring violently until his arm gets sore and Ella takes over. The mixture is setting like cement.

'How long do we do this for?'

'Five minutes.'

'Christ.'

Finally, Robert pours the mixture onto a flat tray and they leave it to cool. She already knows it has worked. After an hour they cut a little square each and eat. Ella is silent for a long moment. She has never read Proust, as Robert has, but knows that he wrote a whole book about the memories evoked by a madeleine cake dipped in tea. This isn't like that – the memories that respond to the taste are not clearly defined or chronological. Rather, Ella feels an almost physical sense of contraction, as though someone is pulling her drawstrings, gathering the fullness of her life close together.

'It's good,' she says, in response to the question in his gaze.

* * *

Hyde Park is sleek and dark with rain, but the sun is shining as they walk down a broad avenue. A month has passed. Even in this limbo state, it has been the best month of Ella's life. She likes to repeat this to herself in quiet moments. It is a long time since she has thought of her best moments as being in the distant past.

Wrapped in winter coats and scarves, Ella thinks she and Robert look older than they are. An old couple, insulated from the cold, enjoying the freedom of retirement. They will buy cream teas in the Orangery and ride the bus for free back to their home in the suburbs, watch soaps and bicker about who left the heating on while they were out. She's fond of the fantasy, though it makes her ache a little.

'Do you think there are many people like us?' Robert asks, staring ahead.

'People having an affair?'

Robert winces a little; he doesn't like this word and likes saying it in public even less.

'I mean, people whose lives are so tangled up. Like two trees that grew too close together, and their roots got all . . .' He does a knotty thing with his fingers.

They walk on. Ella looks at the trees either side of them. She knows it's just a metaphor, and that trees do not thrive when placed right next to one another, but she can't help but feel sad about how spaced apart they all are.

'I don't know. I guess there are lots of people who spend most of their lives together. But we . . .'

'We didn't,' Robert says, matter-of-factly.

'Haven't,' Ella corrects. 'But yeah. We just spiralled around each other for so long. I thought, if we ever finally came together, there'd be an explosion or something. That we'd go up in a fireball.'

Robert grins. 'There's still time for that.' He takes her hand and Ella feels a flush of warmth under all her insulation. The sex is good. She doesn't feel old in bed. They do not behave like she imagines pensioners behave. It is unpretentious; they do not perform for one another. It's a duet, and they know how to duet. They know how to have fun.

They walk a little further, almost to the end of the boulevard, before Robert asks the question.

'When will you leave him?'

Ella knows he tries not to ask too often. She feels the same anxiety. She has arranged an estate agent's valuation when she knows Peter will be out. She owns a smaller portion of the house but will suggest to Peter that it would be nicer to move out and leave the memories behind. She has even looked for places he might buy himself. Despite her preparations, it's too easy to feel that it will never happen. Once before, when Robert asked the question, she answered jokingly – 'I already left.' But today she shares his need for reassurance. She pulls him close by his lapels, rests her forehead against his.

'Soon.'

*   *   *

Ella plans her final moves. She will tell Peter over breakfast. She won't tell him about all her preparations there and then, but she will suggest they meet soon to talk. Then she will get the first train into town, with a bag she has packed. She buys a new toothbrush, deodorant and face cream, stashing them all in the bag which she keeps at the top of their cupboard. After checking his calendar, she decides that Friday will be the best time to tell him.

On Monday Peter is working late, and Ella and Robert go for dinner together. Though they've often sat together in public, this time feels different. They behave like a couple. Robert walks her back to Waterloo and they kiss under the display boards before she goes to get her train.

On Tuesday, Ella returns home with ingredients to make a stew. Without being conspicuous, she's trying to fill the freezer with leftovers. Peter doesn't have anything on until a session in the afternoon, and it has been good to get out of the house. Still, standing in the hall, she calls his name, wanting to know where he is rather than wanting to see him.

He does not reply, so Ella walks through to the kitchen and starts unpacking the vegetables. She takes up a knife to cut into the first onion, but something is bothering her. She looks out of the kitchen door, down the garden to the shed. The door is shut. Ella puts the knife down and goes to look around the house, suddenly gripped by the conviction that Peter has discovered her preparations – tipped off by a call from the estate agents, or by the packed bag at the top of the wardrobe.

When she finds him, in the conservatory, she thinks he must be rooting something out from under the sideboard. He is lying on his front, head turned to one side as though looking into the shadows.

'Peter?'

He doesn't respond. Only when she rolls him over, onto his back, does he make a low, guttural noise, as though trying to speak. One side of his face has gone slack. Ella did not work in a hospital so long without learning what a stroke looks like.

'Wait. Just wait – I'll get help. You're going to be okay.'

*   *   *

Winter has come. The sky is heavy with purple clouds. They seem to sag low to the ground with rain. Ella is sitting in a hospital chair, listening to the groans of the woman next to her, wondering how the hell she got here. This is just a waiting room, of course. They will be transferred for the main event. When the curtains are open, she's confronted by the girl opposite, who can barely be more than seventeen. She glares at Ella with the open hostility of someone who does not understand. Ella doesn't understand either. She is fifty-one years old.

She shouldn't be pregnant.

She has been made to feel that, rather than it all being miraculous, she has embarked on something foolhardy against good wisdom. Her doctor warned of possible complications and asked if she wanted an abortion, then shook his head when she said no, as though she were denying herself a cure for a terminal illness.

Nine months have passed. Summer has gone by and winter is rubbing up against the windowpanes. Nine months since she explained to Robert that she could not leave. *Not yet.* Nine months since she told him that they would still be together, but it would have to wait. She had not realized, as she said it, that she had already missed her period by a week. Even when she noticed, Ella assumed it was the menopause, arrived at last. Nothing else made sense.

Peter visited a little while ago, but he was tired and couldn't sit for long in the plastic chair next to her bed. He spoke haltingly about Christmas and what he wanted to buy for his nephews. She agreed that they were good ideas, talked about getting a Christmas tree from the high street. She asked questions about the size of the tree, a habit she has acquired. Like the exercises Ella devised to improve his dexterity – lifting pennies from a pile on the table and placing them in a jar – conversations are a chance to stretch his language.

There was never any question of her leaving him in a rehab ward. She knows people don't really improve that way, and he would have been helpless at home. It was only fair – Peter saved her once, had the patience to make her well. She cannot deny him the same. He's improved a lot in the last couple of months, but friends are looking after him while Ella is in hospital. Peter will not be much practical use as a father.

When the conversation tired him, he had left. He promised he would call when he got home, though it's unlikely he will remember.

The induction is taking its sweet time to kick in — she's been here for two days and nights already. The drugs don't seem to be doing their job, but they can't give her any more. Early on, it seemed as though it would be quick — she felt the tightening waves of pre-contractions speeding up as she lay there in anticipation. But they had slowed, grown weaker, and now she barely feels them. She asked if they could do a C-section, but this is a last resort.

Two women have come and gone already, to be replaced by the sullen teenager whose name she doesn't know and Mrs Tomassi, an Italian woman who is cordial but not chatty. The teenager is visited by a rotating cast of family and friends, Mrs Tomassi by a man who Ella assumes is her husband. He brings her sandwiches because she never touches the hospital food. When he's not there she reads magazines and a leather-bound book of prayer. The bed next to her is empty.

Ella is using a fork to prod a cemented block of tuna bake when the double doors open. A woman enters with a gym bag slung over her shoulder. She's Chinese perhaps, Ella thinks, somewhere in her late twenties. She looks around the room, smiling, and gives an uncertain wave which neither of the others return. Ella raises a hand, but the woman misses it as a nurse shoves her like an animal coaxed into a pen.

Ella puts her fork down, tuna bake untouched, and zones

out as the nurse goes through the now-familiar routine, the 'induction induction'. She gathers that the woman's name is Patterson. Blood pressure is taken, possessions are stashed under the bed, a run-through of the schedule given.

'You'll want to walk around as much as possible, once the pessary is in. There's a nice cafe up in the main atrium . . .'

Finally, the nurse departs to fetch the poor woman some pasta bake. Mrs Patterson sits on the edge of the bed and for the first time her facade wavers. Ella wants to get up, but she's hooked to something like an earthquake detector which is recording the baby's heartbeat.

'Hey. I'm Ella.'

'My name is Mai.' She smiles. 'I'm here for an induction.'

'So are we,' the teenager pipes up with a sneer in her voice. Mai looks at the floor, blushing a little. Ella shoots the teenager a look. If she seemed aggressive towards Ella, it's nothing to how she's looking at the new woman. Mrs Tomassi has buried herself in her book of prayer.

'You should get settled in,' Ella goes on. 'I've been here for a couple of days already.'

'Really?' Mai's eyes widen. She rubs her sneakers together.

'Oh, but I'm being slow. Probably because I'm so old.'

The teenager makes a gross, phlegmy noise like a snort. Ella ignores her.

'Anyway, I'm sure you won't take that long.'

'I hope so. Baby doesn't want to come out . . .' Mai begins, before the nurse arrives with food and draws all the curtains.

For the next few hours they're enclosed in their little worlds, the blue fabric of the curtains billowing softly when the doors to the room open. Ella has already read the novel she brought with her, and everything in the magazine she found in the hospital shop. Faintly she can hear tinny music escaping from the teenager's Walkman headphones.

At regular intervals now, Mrs Tomassi lets out a low groan, and the frequency increases over the hour until at last they arrive with a wheelchair to take her to a delivery room.

The payphones are down the hallway. Ella has a handful of change left over from buying her magazine. She loads a pound into the slot and dials from memory.

'Hello?' The voice is drawn thin over the line, haloed by crackling static, but Ella feels herself relax automatically.

'Hi Robert, it's me.'

There's a pause. They haven't spoken since Ella told him she was having Peter's baby.

'Is everything all right? Is it Peter?'

'No, Peter's fine. Well, not fine but . . . fine for now. No, it's me, I'm in hospital.'

'The baby?'

'They're inducing me a couple of weeks early, nothing to worry about.'

She explains why they're doing it, tells him how long she's been there already. She expects him to make a joke out of it.

'Are you okay?'

The pips start to sound, and she puts another coin in the slot.

'I'm fine.'

'You're sure?'

She never was good at hiding anything from him. 'Just tired
– can't get any sleep on this ward. Tell me what you're up to,
I'm bored senseless.'

'Oh, let's see . . . I'm just having some eggs on toast. I'm
going later to see a film with Bill Blake. The trumpet player,
you remember him?'

'Vaguely . . .' Ella lies. 'What are you going to see?'

'We found a place that's still showing *Herbie Goes Bananas*.'

'Oh aye. Is it meant to be any good?'

'It's meant to be awful. We're going to throw popcorn.'

Ella smiles. 'You reprobate.'

'Aye well, we've all got to get our kicks.'

The pips start again. 'I'm about to run out of money.'

'You want me to call you back?'

'No, that's okay. I should go have a baby.'

There is a pause where she almost says more.

'All right,' Robert says. 'Call soon, aye?'

'Aye,' she says, but there's a simultaneous click as the line
goes dead.

* * *

By the time she makes it back to the room the teenager has
disappeared, and all the curtains except Mai's have been drawn.
Ella pulls the curtain to shield herself from the door, then sits
on the edge facing Mai. She pours out a cup of water and sips

it, trying not to focus on the sensation that her internal organs are rearranging themselves.

There's a noise from the bed next to her, almost low enough to blend in the machine-hum of the hospital. Mai is humming a note – an unbroken G sharp, until she needs to breathe – then she starts again.

'Are you okay there?'

'Fine . . .' Mai replies, though her throat is constricted. Ella hears her getting up and shuffling to the edge of the bed. She pulls the curtain back a little, and now it feels like a single curtain surrounding both of their beds.

'You're feeling it already?' Ella asks.

'Yes. I told the nurse. She says I need to wait . . .' Mai takes a sharp breath and puts her chin into her chest for a moment before continuing ' . . . to wait before I can have any, what do you call it?'

'Pain relief?' Ella ventures.

'Yes, that's right. My English isn't very good.'

'Seems good to me. What is your first language?'

'Japanese. It is very different.'

'I'll bet.' Ella smiles. 'Is this your first?'

Mai looks down and puts a hand on her belly. 'Yes. He is lazy – just wants to stay inside. Like his father.'

'You think it's a he?'

'I *know* it is. They made me have a scan. I saw him on the screen.'

She draws a rectangle in the air with her fingers.

'You had an ultrasound? I'm impressed.'

'You didn't get one?'

'Yeah, you would have thought that when a fifty-one-year-old pregnant woman shows up, the least you could do is get out your fancy ultrasound machine.'

Mai frowns, but Ella is uncertain which bit of meaning she is puzzling out from Ella's obstacle course of clauses and colloquialisms. She needs to remember to keep it simple.

'You are fifty-one?'

Ella sighs, leaning back with her hands planted on the bed behind her. Something shifts inside her and another contraction starts to swell.

'Yep. Don't ask me how – I've no idea.'

'Your husband, is he fifty-one?'

'Forty-nine.'

'My husband is fifty-five.'

Ella guesses that Mai is still in her twenties but doesn't ask. 'Does he know you're here?'

'He has meetings this afternoon until late.'

The last part of the sentence is spoken in the manner of a direct quote, perhaps from a receptionist or secretary. There is a rumble of thunder and Mai looks to the window.

'There will be a storm.'

'Yeah. Seems appropriate.' Ella settles herself back on her pillow.

'Are you scared?' Mai asks.

Ella takes a deep breath. 'I've been scared the whole time.

If someone tells you they're not scared, I think they're probably lying.'

'Oh.' Mai nods, rubbing her belly. 'Good.'

'Do you think baby will look more like you, or like your husband?' Mai smiles innocently.

Ella isn't sure why she says it. She almost doesn't. Mai isn't a friend. She hasn't known her for more than half an hour. So why does Ella want to tell her a secret that she trusts nobody else with? Mai is about to become one of the most significant people in Ella's life, and she has no idea. It seems unfair to her.

'It's not my husband's.'

She watches the other woman's smile turn to a frown of confusion. She watches as Mai replays the words in her head, checking her question and Ella's response for translation errors.

'Sorry, my English is bad. It's not . . .'

'It's not my husband's baby. It's someone else's.'

Ella breaks away from Mai's querying gaze. She can feel her cheeks flushing red. Why did she say anything? This woman doesn't want to hear her story.

'Oh . . .' Mai takes a deep breath. 'Does he know?'

Ella shakes her head.

'Does . . . does the father know?'

'No. Maybe . . . I'm not sure. I told him the baby was my husband's. He seemed to believe me.'

'Oh.'

Mai sits there, totally still. Ella cannot look at her. What a stupid fucking thing to say to a complete stranger. What a brilliant way to make a bad situation worse. Tears prick her eyes.

Mai gets up wordlessly from the bed, pauses a moment as her stomach uncramps, and closes the distance between them. She folds Ella into her arms like a child. Ella presses her face against the swell of the younger woman's belly. She doesn't feel fifty-one. She feels like a child. She has done something stupid and wants her mother's absolution. It doesn't matter that Mai is not her mother. She rubs her back and makes soft, cooing noises.

After a long moment, she sits down next to her on the bed. 'This's not my first baby.'

'But you said . . .'

'I know. That is what I tell everyone. Nobody knows.' Mai shrugs. 'When I was fifteen . . . I was not married, of course. We used protection, but it did not work.'

'What happened?'

'I had her. A little girl. Then I had to give her away. I wanted to not, but they said I was too young.'

'That's awful.'

Mai shrugs, but her lips press tight together. 'It feels like a long time ago. When I was old enough, I came to England. I wanted to leave it behind.'

At this moment a midwife arrives to take their blood pressure again and give some medicine to Mai. By the time she has gone, Ella has managed to collect herself a little. Mai sits up on the edge of her bed, where she's been hooked up to a measuring machine.

'Would you ever want to go back?' Ella asks. 'To find her?'

Mai smiles a little. 'Maybe, one day. I think about it all the time. I think – what is she doing now? Is she happy? Does she hate school? Does she like a boy?' She shakes her head. 'I just want to know that she is happy. That is all. Then I would not worry so much.'

'Of course.'

Mai looks at her for a moment, then asks:

'Do you love him? The father?'

The question knocks the air out of Ella, so she just nods.

'Okay.' Mai nods in return, as though making up her mind. 'Bad things do not come from love, I think.'

They sit in silence for a moment. Ella wonders if this is how soldiers feel in the trenches, waiting for battle. She wonders if friendships are forged this quickly, with the spectre of fear hovering.

'What's your job?' Mai asks.

'I used to be a musician, but I'm retired. You?'

'I'm an artist. I illustrate books for children. My husband is a publisher.'

'Sounds like you're going to be popular with your baby then. He's going to ask you to draw everything.'

Mai smiles a little. 'I guess so. What instrument do you play?'

'Guitar.'

In the last nine months she picked up the guitar only when

Peter was out at physiotherapy. She pressed it into the curve of her bump and played, feeling the notes reverberate in her belly. She would play nursery rhymes and fingerpicked jazz in a poor impersonation of Django Reinhardt. The baby seemed to like that, kicked its legs like Ella was a big bass drum.

'I wish you had it here,' Mai says, her breath becoming tight. 'You could play something to . . . make us forget.'

She probably means 'distract', Ella thinks, but it seems an apt phrase. Music could have made her forget the present, for a moment, even if only by making her remember the past.

'Do you have paper? You could draw something to take your mind off things.'

Mai forces a smile. 'I have a pad in my bag down there . . . but they told me not to bend down.'

'Stay still, I'll get it . . .'

Ella ignores Mai's protestations, levering herself out of the bed and stepping onto the tacky linoleum. She's less sure on her feet than she was when she got into bed. She crouches down and follows Mai's instructions to find the pad, then a red leather case full of brush pens and colouring pencils. It looks just like Rene's pencil case, she thinks.

Mai opens the pad onto a clean page. Ella glimpses other drawings as she flips through – a pot plant, a cup of coffee, a rabbit soft toy with floppy ears. Each drawing is neat and contained in the centre of its page. Mai takes out a brush pen, pauses to grip the side of the bed with her other hand until a contraction passes. Ella sits on the end of the bed and waits.

'What should I draw?'

'You should draw something for your baby. Something to remember this moment, just before you had him.'

Mai takes a long, shaky breath, then smiles. 'Yes, okay.'

She starts to draw, but Ella can't see what she's doing. She seems to be drawing from memory, and Ella wonders if she understood what she meant. When the line drawing is done, she takes out the colouring pencils.

'Could you get me a little water?' Mai asks.

'Are you thirsty?'

'Not thirsty. These are watercolour pencils.'

She takes a brush from the case, wets it in the plastic glass that Ella has fetched. Ella looks at the drawing. The drawing is her, simplified to a cartoon, but her features obvious even to herself. She's sitting cross-legged playing an oversized acoustic guitar, and little black notes are popping out and floating away on a breeze.

'You like it?' Mai applies the brush to the dry pencil and it liquefies. Ella watches as the powdery blue of her hospital gown turns to shimmering crystal.

'I love it. But I thought you were drawing something for him?' She points at Mai's belly.

Mai nods. 'To remind him of the friendly woman who calmed his mummy down before she gave birth.'

Outside, the clouds break open in earnest, rain turning the powdery world to crystal.

* * *

Mai is taken away first, as a team of people accumulate around Ella. She hears someone mutter it's just their luck, that Ella and Mai would be here at the same time. She's not sure what this means but resents being made to feel like an inconvenience.

Labour is as hard as people say it is. Ella's concern that her body won't be able to go through with the performance is soon forgotten, when the contractions really kick in. Pain limits everything to the present moment; there's no future beyond the next contraction. There's blood and amniotic fluid. Ella could be in a cave, a forest clearing, or under a baobab tree on the savannah. The place doesn't matter, only her body, and her body is driving itself.

Several people move around her but she's barely aware of them. Someone tells her when she should be pushing, urges her to keep going, but Ella isn't sure if it's just a voice in her head. Someone says that the baby is getting tired, but she doesn't know what to make of this information. She can hear heavy rain pattering against the window.

There's a brief moment when everything falls away. She thinks she may pass out. There's a brief glimpse of something . . . of rainfall . . . of water rushing downhill, tributaries gathered into a great river, then broken again into a million, billion branches . . . the whole history of humankind spread out before her as an unbroken river.

'One last push!'

Ella does as she's told. There is a moment of total shock, like missing a step that she thought was there.

'Yes!' someone proclaims.

Yes to the universe. Yes to life. Yes for now.

The baby is placed in her arms. Wisps of pale blonde hair. A squashed nose. A single hand escaping the towel, balling into a fist. Dizzy with relief, Ella bends to kiss the baby on her forehead. Blue eyes open, big blue eyes, and fix on her like twin magnets. Ella is aware of something being calibrated, the shape of the universe bending ever so slightly towards her.

Oh.

The baby sleeps.

* * *

It is later, in the neonatal ward, that she remembers Mai. She's back in a room with Mrs Tomassi and the teenager. This room is coloured differently – pinks and yellows instead of blues – but is remarkably like the old one, as though someone has changed the scenery for Act Two, but they're still on the same stage. It adds to the sense of unreality.

The teenager and her baby are sleeping, thankfully. Mrs Tomassi is awake and fussing over her baby, who mewls occasionally but does not cry.

'What did you have?' she asks Ella.

'A girl.'

'Same here. I wanted a boy, but my husband will be happy.'

Ella is too tired for this conversation but tries to be polite. Her baby is asleep in her arms after a few minutes of desperate nursing. Her arm has gone to sleep but she daren't move.

'Do you have a name?'

'If it had been a boy, he would have been Mario . . .' Mrs Tomassi sighs. 'My husband likes the name Kate.'

'Kate is good. I like Kate.'

'What about yours?'

Ella looks at the scrunched-up face of her daughter.

'Abigail.'

The three syllables slip out of her mouth. A fairytale name, she thinks. A name for heathery highlands and mountain streams. They hadn't discussed names much. Peter agreed to choose when the baby was there to be named. Anything else was chancing fate. Ella knows she should feel bad for not consulting him. But there it is – her name is Abigail.

Mrs Tomassi gives a little nod and a raise of the eyebrows as though to say 'Sure, if that's what you want', and goes back to sorting through her travel bag.

Ella keeps looking to the door. Where is Mai? She feels like they just ran a race, like the cross-country they made them do at school, and she finished first. Now she just wants to see Mai, even if she's limping over the finish line.

* * *

Ella wakes, not remembering falling asleep. There are hushed voices in the room. Someone is occupying the bed in front of her. She hears a baby cry.

'Mai?'

Nobody responds.

Ella checks Abigail, sleeping in the clear plastic cot next to her, swaddled in blankets. She gets out of bed, feeling the pain of gravity rearranging her.

'Hello?' She stops outside the drawn curtains, wishing there was something she could knock to announce herself. The curtain twitches and a bespectacled doctor appears.

'Yes?'

'Is Mai there?' She hears the baby cry once again and looks around the doctor. A baby with jet-black hair is being fed from a bottle by a nurse. There is nobody in the bed. Everyone else is a doctor or a nurse, clustered around the baby boy. Ella feels a familiar certainty curdle in her belly. The doctor puts a hand on her shoulder.

'I'm sorry . . .'

*   *   *

Ella is packing everything away, ready to leave. The teenager and Mrs Tomassi left yesterday, while she was asked to stay the night for monitoring. Abigail is wrapped up and strapped into the car seat that Peter brought. A taxi has been called. They are going home.

'Knock knock.'

A face appears around the curtain. It's the midwife from before. She's holding something.

'I think this belongs to you.'

She hands over Mai's pad, still open at her last drawing.

'This isn't mine.'

'No? That's you, isn't it? I thought you'd drawn yourself.'

'It belonged to Mai. She drew it for her baby. You should make sure it gets to him.'

Ella is about to hand the book back when she has a thought. She takes the brush pen clipped onto the ring binding of the pad and writes her name and address on a spare page in the book. She hands the pad back to the midwife, who can't seem to think of anything to say.

She picks up Abigail.

It's time to face the world again.

7.

The Crone

I T'S THE MIDDLE OF the night. Waking is so soft it barely seems different to sleep. I'm not lying on a hard floor or slumped on a chair with a crick in my neck. I'm on the sofa, tucked under a blanket. I haven't slept in my bed downstairs since the storm. I remember the storm – that was the last time I saw Abigail.

My Abigail.

My baby.

I open my eyes. I'm not alone. Someone has brought the baby's proper cot and placed him next to me. Sitting on a chair next to the cot is Mai. From somewhere she has found a drawing pad and is sketching the sleeping baby by the soft lamplight. The darkness outside seems painted onto the windows.

I sit up and Mai puts down the pen and paper, sits on the

edge of the sofa and puts her arms around me. No words are needed.

'It's good to see you again,' she whispers.

'You too.' I feel as though Mai finally caught up with me in the postnatal ward.

On the opposite sofa, Camille is sleeping, curled like a cat. Rene is on the floor, with the sofa backs making a bed. Rhino is next to her on his back. I can't tell if he's asleep. Out on deck, I can see the glow of Sandy's storm lamp. The room is littered with empty coffee cups and the tumblers we used for the whisky.

'Were you having a party?'

'We were celebrating . . .' I take a minute to remember why. 'We're going to sail to land in the morning.'

'Oh. That's good.'

I nod. I can feel the question under the surface. It wants to be asked. But I don't rush her.

'What was he like? Did you see him?'

'He was small . . .'

I remember wondering how such a small baby had caused so much harm to his mother, then thinking what an unkind thought that was, even in my head.

'Yes?' Mai prompts. Her need to know is like hunger.

'He was small, and he had dark hair like yours . . . quite a lot of it. He cried a lot. Your husband called him Michael.'

'Michael.' Mai nods sadly, sensing this is all she will discover. She must make do with a few details that could fit any number of babies.

'That's how I remember him in the hospital. But I saw him again, later . . .' I try to follow the thread of the memory.

'You saw him?'

'Yes. Well, he found me. Or his father did. He wanted to know who I was, because I'd put my address in your drawing pad.'

'They came to see you.' Mai is breathless.

'We met in a cafe, and I told him about you . . . he asked me if I still played guitar, like the picture . . . he asked if I gave lessons.' I smile at the memory of the large, nervous man. He hadn't been what I expected. He was shy, desperate to make a connection, though I couldn't understand why. He tore his napkin into little shreds while the quiet little boy at his side played on a brand-new Game Boy.

'And what did you say?'

'I said I didn't. But that I could give it a try.'

'You taught him?'

'Every week, Michael came to our house for a lesson . . . He got very good, though he was more interested in building things . . . He liked showing me drawings of the machines he wanted to build . . . He became an engineer.'

Mai is crying softly.

'But he kept coming, right until he went to university. He came every week for a decade, and even after that he would send me a card at Christmas, every year . . .'

The thread runs out. I can't say what became of Michael. I let him go. Mai closes her arms around me.

'Thank you.'

We sit like that for a moment, as *Mnemosyne* tips on the dark sea. Everything is peaceful.

'Would you come with me, downstairs?' I ask.

'What for?'

'I need to unlock a room.'

Mai nods, and helps me up from the sofa. Together we walk through the saloon, where the rest of them are sleeping. Down the stairs I can hear the engine still purring. I turn the hallway light on, and we wade through the waist-deep water to the locked playroom door. I take the key from my dressing gown pocket and fit it into the lock. The edges of the door, though swollen with damp and pressing into the doorframe, bleed water. The water in the hallway is high, but the water seeping from the door comes at least to my shoulder level.

'You might want to brace yourself,' I tell Mai.

She takes my hand. 'I'm ready.'

I turn the key, hear the lock click.

I turn the handle and –

We're thrown back by the wave, slamming into the wall behind. Freezing water covers my face and stings my eyes. For a moment I struggle, thinking that the water is above my head and I will drown. But it's just the wave, rushing out of the playroom. In a few moments the level goes down, equalizing with the water in the hallway until it's chest height. The lights flicker but don't go out. Mai is still holding my hand, and together we press forward, into the room.

By the single light, I can see something ghostly in the water. There's no way I can get to it without crouching down. I let go of Mai's hand, take a deep breath, and submerge myself. It takes a moment for my arms to find their way. I stand, gasping air.

I'm only able to lift the thing in the water because of its buoyancy. I could never raise it above the level of the water, only hold it in my arms.

It's Abigail.

Her long, auburn hair streams out, tangling around her neck. There is a patch of darkness on one side of her head, where she must have injured herself. I wonder if she was still conscious, as she drowned. Her face is pale and bloated, her features so rounded she looks baby-like. All my life, between holding Abigail in my arms for the first time and losing her for the last, are side-by-side. It's like someone ripped out the middle of a book – the book of Abigail's life – so the first and last pages are all that's between the covers. My arms hug her middle, wanting to wrap around her – as a baby or as a woman, I don't care.

I weep. Didn't I weep before? Didn't I realize Abigail was gone forever? I knew. But I preferred the fantasy. She had disembarked while I slept or floated away in a lifeboat. I pretended to myself that Abigail would come back. It's difficult to think clearly; I shouldn't blame myself for fantastical thinking. But I hate myself anyway; as though I'm the one who let her go.

The weeping becomes sobbing. With each convulsion, a

little strength shivers out of me. I have seen a lot of death. I do not rail now, as I would have when young, against the injustice of her passing. This is the way it is. But acceptance has not dulled grief. Rather, grief has grown into the space that my anger left behind. My child – my only child – Robert's child – is dead. She is dead and cannot feel me holding her. The warm body that I cradled in my arms has grown cold. A wracking, shuddering cry passes through me.

My legs cannot bear us. I allow myself to sink down, with Abigail's body still cradled in my arms. I go below the surface with her, holding my breath. Bubbles rise. It is cold down here, and dark. I think I will stay with her, and not rise again. But Mai lays her hand on my shoulder. I ignore her for a moment, but she is insistent.

I let Abigail go.

I cannot see well enough through the water to look at her face one last time. But I watch as the dim shape of her settles. Mai hooks a strong hand under my arm and lifts me. I surface and she holds me in her arms. I weep, but it's gentle now. No sobs. I'm too cold and tired for that. It's not normal tiredness. I wonder if it's true, the old story about elephants walking their last walk to an elephant graveyard. Knowing it's time to die. It feels like another bit of fantastical thinking, but I feel my own clock running down.

The light from the lamp flickers, there's a groan from the engine and the vibrations die.

The lights go out.

* * *

Out on deck, cold winds whip around *Mnemosyne*. The sea is striking sparks off the moon. The darkness spreads out all around us, and I feel dizzy at the thought of falling away from this safe point, this tiny point of not-ocean.

We've inflated the lifeboats. The engine is dead, and the water level has now risen past the foot of the stairs. *Mnemosyne* is low in the water. The lifeboats bob below in the waves, which have gotten closer to the deck. I can see their fluorescent strips. The plan is simple – the dead will go in one boat, because they don't need food or water. I'll go with the baby in the other boat, because he needs space and I need as many supplies as I can get.

I couldn't raise Abigail's body from the lower deck. I pressed a kiss to her forehead through the cold water and let her go. *Mnemosyne* will have to make do for a resting place. There are worse places, I suppose, but I don't like the thought of her down there, all alone.

We work quickly, taking supplies out to the deck. Lester and Sandy clamber up and down the rope ladder, taking food and water to one of the boats. I move with them, much slower and slowing every moment.

'Are you ready?' Sandy puts a hand on my shoulder.

I look at my motley crew. Mai has the baby cradled in her arms. He's still asleep. Lester has produced a pack of Sotheby's and he, Camille and Sandy are smoking.

'Have you got one for me?'

'I thought you'd quit.' Lester grins, reaching into his waist-coat breast pocket.

'When you're eighty-seven there's not much more damage you can do.'

Lester's smile flickers as he hands me the cigarette. He lights it and I draw ghost-smoke into my lungs.

'I never thought we'd end up like this.' I haven't prepared a speech, but I need to say something. I'm not their leader, but I'm the reason they're here.

'I didn't do it on purpose.'

'Happy to be here, personally,' Rhino says, scratching his bandage-wound neck.

'Thank you for keeping me company. I know we'd rather not be leaving the boat behind, but I am glad I am doing it with all of you.'

I take a last drag on the cigarette and flick it into the ocean.

'Let's go.'

We gather around the rope ladder with Lester leading the way. I take a last look at *Mnemosyne*. I've forgotten something. My stomach lurches. I run back across the desk as quick as I can. The cabin doors are open. The guitar is back on the wall where it started. I can't leave it on this sinking ship. I can't send it to a watery grave after all it has done for me. I go and take it off the wall. At that moment, there's a yawning sound from the lower decks.

The boat starts to tilt.

I run, holding the guitar, to the back door. I skid along the deck as fast as my feet will take me. Sandy is halfway down the rope ladder. I throw the guitar down and Lester catches it. I scramble onto the ladder, feeling the coarse rope cut my hands as I start my descent, wobbling back and forth.

I don't mean to jump, but I lose my footing a couple of feet from the bottom and let go, thumping sideways into the second dinghy and winding myself.

Lester is untying the lifeboats and using the plastic oar to push us away from the hull. The lifeboats are tied together. With Rhino and Lester manning the paddles, we start to move into open water.

'Is the baby okay?' Mai asks.

I look to him, wrapped in blankets. He's crying. Not surprising, with the cold air and being thrown about in the little boat. I hadn't realized until now that the size of *Mnemosyne* kept us fairly stable.

'Keep paddling!' Camille yells, scooping water with one hand. The two lifeboats fight through the water and knock against each other. We get a little further away from *Mnemosyne*. There are distant, groaning noises.

'We made it.' Camille hugs Lester sideways, plants a kiss on his cheek.

'I'm scared.' Rene puts her arm around Rhino's neck, but he doesn't stop paddling.

'We'll be okay love, don't worry.'

*   *   *

We've been paddling for some time. Night has passed and the sun is coming up over the ocean. Land is nowhere to be seen.

It's strange, after so long on *Mnemosyne*, seeing her from afar. To see the windows we looked through, the mast with its tangled rigging, the rope ladder we escaped down, dangling near the bow. A little lifetime that we're drifting away from.

When it begins, it happens quickly.

Mnemosyne leans to one side like a sick animal. The bow rises out of the water. We're too far away to hear much, but I can see the water churning with bubbles. Finally, the bow points up to the sky and sinks under the waves. We sit in silence as weak ripples wash under us. With the sun low in the sky, the sea is milky white.

'Well, that's that,' Lester says, at last.

*   *   *

The pale glow in the sky turns to the heat of day. I cover myself as well as I can from the sun and keep the baby under the lip of the lifeboat, moving him when it bobs around. We try paddling in the direction we guess land should be in. But the band of grey doesn't appear on the horizon.

The baby isn't crying, but I wish he would. I feed him the last of the UHT milk and hope it won't make him sick. With Sandy's help I make a canopy out of his sheets and some string, tied to the plastic handles on one end of the lifeboat. It won't stop him getting hot, but at least he won't get sunburn.

Noon comes. I can't do anything except curl up, cover myself in my nightgown. Any patch of sun will brand me like an iron. The plastic of the boat heats up and becomes sticky. With my face pressed against it I can smell nothing else. I drift into sleep and dream lurching, nightmare dreams.

* * *

When I wake the sun has crossed the sky and is beginning its descent. The air is still hot, but I can breathe. I feel baked. How long can I put up with this? How much more can I take? I sit up, light-headed, and vomit over the side of the boat. I hardly have anything to throw up.

I haul myself over to look at the baby. His eyes are open, and he looks at me, but doesn't respond more than that. His little chest pants up and down. I'm about to search for some water to dribble into his mouth when I notice.

We're alone.

The second lifeboat has drifted away. I look around but can't see my friends on the blank horizon. Silence all around. Their voices, brought back so briefly, have stilled once more, this time forever. My whole life was about making some noise to fill the silence, or mask it. Music was an attractive way of doing that, but now, music isn't enough.

I fill my lungs and let out a wordless shriek. I bash my fists against the lifeboat. I scream until the last air in my lungs is used up and my chest is tight as a fist. I want the scream to echo back at me, to echo all the way to land. But the sea swallows it up – my scream sounds like nothing at all.

Alone at last, completely alone. I wonder why we left *Mnemosyne* behind. It would have been quick. Now I'll die in this boat and the baby will die in this boat, and I won't even have the company of my friends.

I find a bottle, half full of hot water, and dribble it as well as I can into the baby's mouth. He drinks it down until the effort of swallowing seems to tire him and he goes back to staring at the cotton canopy. I don't have much in the lifeboat with me, just a few bottles of water, some folded sheets for the baby and the acoustic guitar. I touch the wood and it feels alive with heat. I pick it up and lean back, propping my head against the lifeboat so I'm looking up at the ribbon-like wisps of cloud in the sky.

I remember the final song as easy as that. Did I have to come here to remember it? Couldn't I have remembered it before, when there was something left to lose?

Anyway, I have it now; I may as well play it.

I wonder what Jack Shapiro would have made of his song being played a century after he wrote it, in a lonely lifeboat, many thousands of miles from New York, heard by nobody but an old woman and a baby. No matter – Jack Shapiro is long-dead, the same as his lost Eurydice, whoever she was.

I start to play my final song. The music sounds different here, at the level of the water. There's no cabin to resonate the notes. They just drift out over the water, a few more ripples. That's how I feel – no longer contained. Life is all about containment. As a baby we're wrapped in blankets, placed in a cot, which is in a room, which is in a house. Clothes and houses, cars and buses and boats – all ways of being contained. Your skin, just another barrier, a border between you and the world.

Now it's all breaking down. No house, no roof overhead, no windows or doors. There's only the thinnest bit of material between me and the depths of the ocean, only the thinnest cloth between me and the sun in the sky. I'm bleeding away and I no longer care.

I play the notes as I learned them, all that time ago in my little boxed-in bedroom on Bedlay Street, watching smoke rise from the chimneys serving all the boxed-in bedrooms of Springburn until the morning sky turned grey. I play until the world rises like mist and I'm sure that this, at last, must be death.

THE CRONE

1992

'COME ON, ABIGAIL, LET'S get back to the Tube.'
  'But Mum, can't I have an ice cream?'

Ella pauses for a second, knowing she should say no, but knowing also that she won't spoil the good day they're having. They've looked around the Natural History Museum, where Abigail takes a particular interest in the dinosaur skeletons. Now they're walking down Exhibition Road in the mid-afternoon warmth, with Abigail in her big floppy straw hat, swinging a gift shop bag full of scented pens.

'The next van we see, you can get an ice cream.'

'Yesss. Thanks, Mum.'

Ella knows that she spoils Abigail a little, but she wouldn't if Abigail didn't seem so immune to spoiling. She is so good-natured, so unlikely to throw a tantrum when she doesn't get what she wants, Ella is inclined to give her a treat when she asks for it. They don't have to walk far before a van, painted with crude imitations of Disney characters, presents itself.

Ella has a clear line of sight and the queue is short, so she presses a pound coin into Abigail's hand and tells her to get what she wants. She runs forward, hobbled slightly by her plastic flip-flops with the daisies at the toe, but still running several times faster than Ella could chase her.

Ella often gets mistaken for a grandmother. In fact, she wonders if anybody assumes anything else, before they're corrected. Not that she's unhappy with how she has aged. When she thinks of how old her mother looked in her thirties, Ella is surprised that life has not taken more of a toll. But there's no denying that she is in her sixties, and it seems improbable that the eleven-year-old girl accompanying her is her daughter.

One of the nice things about being an old parent is that she has all the free time in the world to take Abigail places. They see movies together, visit concerts and museums. This summer they went to the Albert Hall together, Abigail's first time. They saw Handel's *Messiah*, and Abigail sat in rapt contemplation of the gorgeous, unfolding music in front of her, gripping Ella's hand the first time the massed ranks of the choir stood up and started to sing.

Ella is walking toward Abigail, who has reached the front of the queue and is relaying her order up to the little window, when something stops her dead. She's not even sure what it is for a moment, because the thing is at the edge of her awareness, somewhere in her peripheral vision. She stops and turns and says hello. She doesn't know why until a man stops and turns.

For a moment she thinks it is Robert. Then she realizes it can't be. This man is older than Robert.

'Ella?'

For a moment she can't say anything. She hasn't heard his voice since that conversation on the hospital payphone.

By the time Ella had seen Peter through his illness for three years, Abigail knew no other father. Ella had been a mother to both of them, while Peter and Abigail had been playmates. She didn't want to change that; she could see the love in her daughter's eyes for the man she thought was her father. Abigail was the most important thing, and Ella couldn't bring herself to risk losing her.

The man in front of her is smaller than the one she remembers, though the clothes are the same. The red hair has faded almost to white. He leans a little on a walking stick. When did that happen?

'Hey, Robert.'

They do not hug, or peck each other on the cheek, or even shake hands. They don't say anything. She never explained to him why she left. Robert never called, never sent a letter. He knew it was her decision to make. What was there to say?

'It's funny . . .' Robert begins, but he never gets to finish what he was saying.

'Mum, the man gave me extra sprinkles for free! Who's this?'

Robert and Ella both look down at Abigail, bearing an already-melting double cone ice cream, with raspberry sauce and sprinkles liberally covering both peaks.

'Abigail, this is my old friend . . .'

'*Very* old friend,' Robert corrects, smiling.

'Very old friend, Robert. We grew up together.'

'You're from Scotland?' Abigail asks. Scotland is a mythical place for her. They went on holiday a couple of times when she was younger, but in her imagination, it has grown into a fairytale land. A country of hills and vales, princes and princesses, sweets that you can't buy in London sweetshops, soor plooms and tablet.

'Yes, I'm from Glasgow like your mum. We lived on the same street.'

'Wow. And you were just walking down this street at the same time as us? That's pretty weird.'

'You're right, it is pretty weird,' Robert nods, smiling down at her. Ella finds herself speechless again, watching Abigail have her first conversation with her father. She wonders if Robert can see the resemblance. Ella sees it every single day.

She isn't sure what else they talk about for the next couple of minutes. They catch up a little, perhaps, and Abigail interjects with a few questions in between licking her ice cream.

'Anyway, I've been meaning to get in touch,' Robert says. 'I'm putting together a band.'

Ella laughs in spite of herself. 'A band? You're going to try and get in the charts?'

'Not a band, really. Just for one gig. At Ronnie Scott's.'

'You've got one gig at Ronnie Scott's?'

'In a couple weeks' time. Thursday the eighteenth. You want to join us?'

Ella can't think what to say. 'I don't play much these days, I'm out of practice . . .'

'Mum is *brilliant* at the guitar!' Abigail enthuses, as though she's Ella's agent.

'I know, I remember.' Robert turns back to Ella. 'It'll just be old tunes, standards. You'll be able to busk it.'

'Give me a call with the set list.'

'Great.'

'All right. See you there.'

'See you there, Ella. Nice to meet you, Abigail.'

* * *

Ella stares at the sheet music, trying to understand. She has the charts spread out on the stand in front of her. She's sitting in the music room with her old jazz electric over one leg. She listens to the faint hum of feedback coming from the practice amp and squints a little harder at the page. Admittedly it's a while since she read sheet music. When Abigail was little, Ella taught her how to sight-read for the first time when she started piano lessons. But that was six years ago, and it's been a long time since Abigail needed help with anything except the more exotic articulation marks.

It has been years then since Ella actively tried to read music, but she didn't expect it to be this difficult. She's had the same problem with reading text recently, so it must be time for new glasses. The optometrist checked her out only at the start of the year and tweaked her prescription, but she must have changed in the interim, because now the notes seem to waver on the staves and the staves themselves seem to multiply as she tries to scan along the line.

Of course she can busk these tunes, as Robert suggested. If she just stops trying to read 'In a Sentimental Mood', she knows 'In a Sentimental Mood' by heart. She knows the tune, knows the chords as they are written in the book, can mentally transpose those chords to any number of key signatures without expending much thought. But she doesn't particularly relish the idea of turning up at Ronnie Scott's after several years of minimal playing to busk in front of jazz connoisseurs.

She struggles for a few more minutes before giving up, playing through the tune as she knows it in her head several different ways, practising a few solos. Then she packs up the guitar and the charts and goes to get her coat.

* * *

She gets to Frith Street by two o'clock and finds a double bassist trying to gain entry by the side door. Inside the club is dark and empty, and you wouldn't know the difference between night and day. The manager, Pete King, lets them in and disappears somewhere behind the bar, telling them to shout if he's needed.

The band are all old friends of Robert. A couple of them come up to Ella and say hello, mentioning that they played together in a band long ago, or that they met at a session decades past. Ella smiles and nods as though she's remembering, but she's busking these memories as much as she's busking the tunes. She's glad at least that there seems to be no one in the band who knew her well. She remembers everything she did with Robert, but her mind seems to have erased all sorts of other relationships and acquaintances.

Robert hugs Ella warmly.

'Glad you could make it.'

'Thanks for having me.'

'Well you know, I could have got one of those young guys to do it, but they don't play the same as we do.'

Ella, who has never thought there was anything particularly special about her way of playing, pulls a face.

'You sure about that?'

'Oh yeah, these kids now, they all play the *scales*.'

Back in her session days, Ella would sneer at players who played the scales. Proper players played the chords, and played around the chords, but they didn't just noodle up and down the scale they happened to be in. The in-joke makes her smile.

'I just hope I'm not too rusty.'

'Don't worry about it,' the double bassist grins at her. 'We're all rusty here. Robert's assembled a death-row lineup.'

They laugh. Ella turns to see Robert. He's not laughing, and his smile doesn't make it all the way to his eyes.

'Right,' he claps his hands together. 'Shall we get started?'

It's a good size band – drums, double bass and piano, with Ella making up the rhythm section, then two trombones, two trumpets and two saxophones, including Robert on his tenor, plus a percussionist who wheels out the house vibraphone and other paraphernalia. They rehearse in the empty club for a couple of hours, taking a break at half four for an early dinner. Robert and Ella go to a cafe and get coffee and a sandwich.

'Just like old times,' Robert says.

'The oldest of times.'

'That tea shop on Buchanan Street. I don't think they had avocado in their sandwiches back then.'

'I don't think we'd even heard of an avocado.'

They catch up with each other's lives, but Ella can't help but feel they're treading around the subject, talking about anything apart from what's important.

She feels an old exhilaration from playing with the band. Her sight-reading hasn't gotten any better in the dim light of the club, but she's had a chance to write where the solos go on each chart, make notes for herself.

'Are you scared?' she asks, reaching over to grab the pepper pot. When she looks at Robert, his eyes have gone wide.

'What?' Robert asks.

'About the gig?' Ella clarifies, not sure what she's said.

'Oh . . .' Robert looks weirdly relieved.

'I know you've not been out of it like me, but do you still get nerves?'

'No, I don't get nervous really.'

'You were always happier on stage than me. I just wanted to play the music.'

Robert smiles ruefully. 'Don't pretend you didn't love the attention. I remember those nights when you'd come back from playing a ballroom, all dressed up. You could have powered the block with the energy you had.'

Ella smiles into her coffee. 'I could never get to sleep on nights like that. Especially in the summer. It felt like all of London was awake, so why was I going to sleep?'

Robert nods. 'I'd just lie awake in bed. I'd put the radio on low to keep me company.'

'I remember!' Ella grins. 'I'd hear it bleeding through the wall and I wanted to go and ask what you were listening to. But I never did . . .'

They look at each other for a moment. Ella takes a bite of her sandwich. Robert clears his throat.

'Long time ago,' he says.

'I guess.' Ella shrugs noncommittally. 'Feels like yesterday. Like we could just go down to The Nucleus and smoke some clove cigarettes and buy a dodgy watch off that guy with the trench coat . . .'

'We called him Errol Flynn because he had that pencil moustache.'

'He tried to ask me on a date once.'

'No!'

They lapse into memories. Ella has become more aware of

this recently, how the centre of gravity in her life has shifted to the past. When they were young, they would talk about the future. Now they are old, and the weight of their lives lies behind them, so they talk of the past. She's glad Robert is here to remember with her. She needs him to prompt her.

'When would you go back to, if you could?' Ella asks, in a lull. She often poses this question to herself. How far back would she have to go, to make things how she wants them to be?

Robert shakes his head. Ella thinks he will say something, but he just sips his coffee and the question goes unanswered.

* * *

They finish up their sandwiches, rejoin the rest of the band at the club by half five, and wait in the tiny dressing room while the crowds filter in. There's bound to be a few tourists in Ronnie Scott's, since it became part of the London attraction circuit, but there are plenty of serious fans too, mostly of an age approaching Ella's.

The lights go up on the stage and Ronnie himself walks out to warm applause.

'Thank you very much, ladies and gentlemen. You've made a happy man very old.'

He runs through his repartee and recommends the chef's special – 'Untouched by human hands – we hire an orangutan.' Finally, he introduces them as the Robert Mauchlen All Stars, featuring Ella Campbell. There's healthy applause from the room, though many of them can hardly have heard of Robert, and Ella is sure none of them have heard of her. She looks sideways at Robert in surprise at hearing her name, but he doesn't return the gaze, smiling straight ahead. They take their seats. Robert clears his throat at the microphone.

'Good evening, ladies and gentlemen. I hope you're all well this evening.'

A few small cheers. Robert wavers.

'Fifty years ago, I started playing jazz . . .' he starts, staring out at the room. They wait for him to finish his anecdote, but it never comes. 'This first number is called "In a Sentimental Mood".'

'One, two, three . . .'

They launch into playing. After practice, Ella feels her fingers have loosened up. Everything comes back to her. The energy of the room seems to contain and intensify their own, and the band is a different band from rehearsal. The rounds of applause after each solo, a convention which Ella has always missed in other musical forms, spur them on.

The set list is eclectic, from Duke Ellington to Carla Bley, 'Coffee Cold' by Galt MacDermot to 'A Call for All Demons' by Sun Ra. Ella might think the set list was all over the place, if it weren't for the fact that she knows Robert, knows his favourite tunes. She can hear him impersonating his favourite players – Zoot Sims, Tubby Hayes, Stan Getz. This concert seems to be an invitation to briefly step inside Robert's brain, to share his way of seeing music for a short while.

By the end of their slot, it feels as though the band has

been playing together for years. Ella has the old sensation of knowing what people are going to do just before they do it, knowing when a drum roll is coming, or that the seesawing of phrases between the piano and the vibraphone is about to come to an end.

Through most of the gig, Robert has remained seated, even for his solos. The last song they play is 'How Deep Is the Ocean'. Ella knows how much he loves this song, especially the John Coltrane recording with Zoot. He stands now, and they play something a little like the record. Robert was always good at doing impersonations, but really, he's all himself.

Ella leans back into the music, she's just there for support on this one, and watches Robert as he plays. The man in front of her is hunched and his shoulders rounded. But really, she thinks, the difference between him and the young man she shared a flat with in Brixton, sitting around the piano with him and Lester and trading parts, is no difference at all.

The gig ends. There is applause. Ella stays for a couple of drinks with the band, and after the manager has come and given them their cheques, she tells Robert she should be going.

'Come on, I'll walk you to the door.'

They head downstairs, and a couple of punters pat Robert on the back and smile affectionately.

'That was fun,' she says. 'I feel twenty again.'

Robert chuckles. 'Really? I feel like I ran a marathon.'

'You'll have to invite me back if you do it again. If I wasn't too terrible.'

He smiles and shakes his head in amusement. 'Ella, you were the best musician on that stage, as always.'

'Get away, you daft old man.' She punches him on the shoulder. 'But invite me again, yeah?'

He nods wordlessly, rubbing behind his ear. He opens his mouth to say something just as a hand claps him on the shoulder.

'Robert! Good to see you, man – let me buy you a drink and we can catch up.'

Robert is caught, mouth still open as though to say something, but Ella just waves goodbye with a smile and turns to walk to the Tube.

* * *

It's a couple of weeks later, and Ella is back in the music room with the jazz electric over her lap, squinting at the sheet music. Her sight-reading seems to be getting a little bit better with practice, but it's still not there. She has an appointment with the optician in a couple of days' time. Until then, she's happy to keep busking the tunes.

She keeps taking out the book full of standards, flipping through until she finds a title that she likes, then will play more or less from memory, humming along with herself. Since the gig she feels she can play and hear the rest of the band around her, hear the things that Robert would be playing in response, so she doesn't need a backing track. She has it all in her head.

The phone rings.

Ella mutes the guitar with her palm, but the last few notes ring around in the spring reverb of the amplifier and ripple in the corners of the room.

The phone rings.

Ella stands, places the guitar on its stand and bends down, vertebrae creaking if not cracking, and switches off the amplifier with a pop.

The phone rings.

Ella walks over to the desk, picks up the cup of tea that she left there half an hour ago which has grown cold.

The phone rings.

She picks up the receiver and puts it to her ear.

'Hello?'

'Hello? Is that Ella?'

She takes a sip of the cold tea. 'Speaking.'

'Ella, it's Bill Blake. The trumpet player?'

She racks her brains. The name is definitely familiar. 'Hey, Bill. We haven't spoken in a while.' This seems like a good bet.

'Yeah, it's been a while. I saw the gig you played at Ronnie Scott's.'

'Oh yeah! I had a great time.' Has he called to talk to her about this?

'I was just wondering if you'd heard . . .'

'Heard what?'

'About Robert.'

Perhaps this is what it feels like for time to stand still. The voice on the end of the line keeps talking, and some other part of her is noting it all down like a receptionist. But she's totally still, and the only thing she can hear is the static around the words, growing in intensity every moment, a hissing pulse washing into her ears like ocean waves.

* * *

I wake in the lifeboat.

The light is soft. Gentle breezes blow over the sea. I know the sun is setting.

'Are you awake?'

I open my eyes to see him sitting by the baby. The light in the sky is pink and gold at the horizon, soft blue above. There's a crescent moon hanging over his shoulder.

'Is the baby okay?'

'He's fine, just sleeping. You want some water?'

'Please.'

I take the bottle and drink a little, more to wet my throat than from any thirst. I don't feel thirsty or hungry, I don't feel any pain. Everything has settled in me, like sediment in an old bottle of wine. He's taken his cardigan off and has his sleeves rolled up to the elbow. The wind ruffles the hair on his forearms.

'We should have spent more time in places like this,' he says. 'We never went on holiday.'

I shrug. 'I like home better.'

'But a bit of sun wouldn't have gone amiss. We spent all our time in auditoriums and basement clubs.'

I run a hand through his hair, letting the curls form rings around my fingers.

'But then we wouldn't have had these beautiful, pale complexions.'

He smiles at me.

'It's strange,' I look to the sunset, 'I feel like I should have loads to tell you . . . but I don't.'

'Like what?'

'Like, I dunno . . . films I've seen . . . new records . . . I feel like I should be able to tell you what I've been up to.'

'What have you been up to?'

I shrug. 'Just existing, I guess.'

'Looks like more than just existing.' Robert gestures at the baby, the lifeboat, the ocean.

'All right, not existing. *Surviving.*'

He laughs, not unkindly. 'Sounds grim.'

'It wasn't so bad, really. But I wish you'd been there.'

He looks from me to the sunset, rubbing behind his ear. 'You don't need to tell me what I missed. I'm just glad I'm here now.'

'Me too.'

He sits closer, puts his arm around my back. I rest my head on his shoulder.

'I keep wondering . . .' I start.

'Mm?'

'I spent all those years practising . . . I knew hundreds of songs, maybe thousands. I knew so many scales. I could change the key of a melody, or keep the melody and change the chords, all in my head. All that practice . . .'

'Yeah?'

'Well, I mean . . . where does all that music go? Does it just fade away?'

'The rest . . . is *silence*,' Robert mugs, in his best Laurence Olivier.

'Which one was that?'

'*Hamlet*.'

'Oh yeah.'

We watch the horizon as the sunset paints the waves red and bronze. The life we're talking about seems like a long, strange dream I've been having.

'No, I don't think it fades away,' Robert says. 'I don't think it really goes anywhere.'

'Really?'

'You remember what I said, when you told me you felt like Rene was still around?'

'In the shipyard?'

'Yeah. I said it was like a record on a turntable. When you're alive, you can only see things from the point of view of the needle. You can only get the next bit of the record by moving forward. But it's just an illusion. The whole record is always there. Everything stays.'

I remember the hours we spent playing in the flat in Brixton.

I feel like the song never stopped. We just stopped playing it, while others took up the tune. Our part of the song has fallen silent, but it's still there. I nod slowly.

'That sounds okay.'

Robert shrugs. 'I could be wrong.'

I kiss him on the cheek. 'Thanks for being here.'

'No worries.' He grins. 'I've got nothing on this evening.'

'Oh yeah? We could catch a movie.'

'Or see what's on at the Palladium.'

'Want to get some food first? I know this Italian place. Does a great tiramisu.'

We sit in silence a while longer.

'I'm sorry I didn't do things differently.'

'Like what?'

I shrug. 'Like telling you when we were still young. Like waiting for a leap year and getting down on one knee. Dragging you to a chapel. If only . . .'

Robert smiles, but he's already shaking his head.

'Nobody gets it right, Ella. Life. I didn't, you didn't, and nobody I knew got it right either. Who knows what our life would have been, if we did things differently?' He takes a deep breath. 'You're the most remarkable person I ever met. I like the record just as it is.'

The sun is below the horizon now, but the light lingers. Soon it will be dark, and the stars will come out.

'He's your grandson,' I say.

'Oh.' Robert looks at the baby.

'Abigail was your daughter, and he's her son.'

'I knew. About Abigail.' Robert nods.

'Really?'

'You didn't think I could tell? Ella, I'm not an eejit.'

'I thought I *might* have fooled you.' I shrug, trying not to cry. If I start I won't stop. 'I didn't want to make it any worse for you.'

Robert shuffles to the front of the boat and peers under the makeshift canopy. The baby is awake. Robert lifts him up to his chest. The baby raises his eyes to look at his grandfather for a moment, then rests his head against his chest.

'Our grandson, eh?' Robert says.

I kiss him.

'Our grandson.' I nod.

'What's his name?'

I'm about to say I don't know. I feel the embarrassment rise in me. But the name is there on my tongue. I never lost it.

I tell Robert the name.

We put the baby down for the night and lie back, side-by-side, holding hands as the colour bleeds from the sky and infinity is uncovered.

*   *   *

It's half six, and Defne is taking the chairs off the tables. The sun is coming up, but she cannot see it yet. She likes this time of day, before the people get up for breakfast, before the sun is beating down on their rank of parasols. Defne thinks that it would be enough of a holiday, to spend a couple of weeks at this time of day, when all the harbour is still, and the air is cool.

Once all the chairs are brought down she fetches a bundle of waxed paper tablecloths from the storeroom and starts clipping them onto the tables. Two cafes down Yusuf, Asya's youngest boy, has emerged to start taking down their chairs. His dark hair sticks up at angles and he's wearing a too-big T-shirt. He waves and she waves back. They do not talk at this time of day.

There are just four sounds – first is the rustling of her tablecloths, second the clack of each chair that Yusuf brings down, third the plashing of waves against the shallow quayside, and fourth the distant sounds of her husband making breakfast.

When she's done with the tablecloths, Berat will bring out a tray with bread, honey and jam, a little cheese and the tea. Berat likes to dilute his tea with water, but Defne prefers it *tavsan kani* – like rabbits' blood. They will eat and drink tea in silence until the other waitresses start to arrive and it's time for Berat to go back to the kitchen.

Defne's just done with the last tablecloth, smoothing out an errant crease, when she spots something out of the corner of her eye. A splotch of fluorescent orange. Bobbing in the sea about thirty feet away is a lifeboat.

She stops and straightens up. There doesn't appear to be anyone in the boat, but she cannot be sure from this distance. They have not had as many migrants here as elsewhere. Defne has seen the pictures of Lesvos on the news and wonders how anyone can cope, with that kind of misery washing up on their front door, day-in-day-out.

They had a small boat wash up a couple of months ago, full of skinny young men, who got lost on the way. The police had been called while Asya rallied the cafe owners into providing a good meal. Some had been reluctant, but Asya wouldn't take no for an answer, and the young men had gone peaceably when the police arrived, bellies full.

Defne calls her husband. Yusuf hears her call and looks where she's looking. Berat appears and walks down to them, drying his hands on a towel.

'What is it?'

She points. 'Look.'

'Should I go?' Yusuf asks.

They look between each other. 'Yes,' Berat says, 'but be careful.'

Yusuf takes his phone out of his pocket and puts it on the side of the quay, then jumps into the water fully clothed. The water at the edge of the harbour is shallow, and he wades out a little way before he has to swim. Berat puts his arm around Defne.

'It'll be fine,' he says, and she realizes she's been knotting her hands.

When Yusuf reaches the lifeboat, he pulls himself up to look over the side. They hear him say something, but not what it is that he says.

'So there is someone . . .'

'I'll get water.' Berat strides back to the kitchen. Yusuf pulls the little boat back, swimming then standing, dragging it behind him with strong strides.

By the time he gets to the quayside, Berat has just appeared with the carafe of water. They look down.

An old woman lies lengthways in the boat. Her skin is pale – she has not escaped from Syria or another warring nation. She must have survived an actual shipwreck. The name of the ship – *Mnemosyne* – is painted on the side of the lifeboat. At her feet is a battered guitar, discoloured in spots by sea spray and sun.

The woman lies to one side, and her head is inclined as though someone is lying next to her. Berat puts the carafe down and jumps into the water. He wades around to the woman and takes her wrist, then puts his head to her forehead. Defne and Yusuf watch him. He shakes his head.

'She's dead.'

There is a cry. From the bow of the little boat, at the woman's feet, the cry of a baby. Berat pulls back the scrap of fabric to reveal the child. He is pale and thin, and his blue eyes seem too big for his face. But his skinny arms are reaching out to him. He lifts the baby out of the boat and up to his wife.

They stand there for a moment, lost for words. The baby hugs his arms around her neck.

Berat goes to call the police, while Yusuf fetches a sheet to cover the body of the old woman, still bobbing in the little boat.

Defne stands, holding the baby, staring out to sea as the sun rises behind them and the cafe owners gather around her. Milk is fetched for the baby, fresh clothes and a clean nappy.

Yusuf returns with a bedsheet. Holding it over his head, he jumps once more into the water and goes to cover the body. This done, he picks up the guitar. There is something scratched into the wood on the back, and he holds it up to look more closely.

'What does it say?' someone calls down.

Yusuf isn't very good at English yet, but he's learning in school. He wants to be a doctor. He recognizes the words, and this phrase is easy enough. The kind of phrase you learn before anything else. He translates for the little crowd.

'His name is Robert.'

Coda

I owe this book to my grandparents, John and Jean Sands, for sharing the stories that inspired it. In many ways their story is more remarkable than the one I have written.

* * *

At a summer season in Ramsgate, 1959, two ice skaters held a party. My grandfather, a Glaswegian saxophonist who would rather have gone to the pub, was convinced by a comedian on the same bill to come along. My grandmother, another one of the ice skaters, sat down next to him and spilt her drink in his lap. Though she has since denied it, her first words of note to him were 'Oh no, not another Scot.'

Nobody could have guessed how much would spin off that moment, myself and this book included.

Here are a few pictures of them.

On their wedding day, December 1959,
at St Philip and St James (Pip and Jim's), Whitton.

Berlin, 1956, touring Germany with the Ice Scala Review.

Astoria Ballroom, Charing Cross Road, 1960,
with the Jack Dorsey Orchestra

With my mum, early 1961.

Acknowledgements

No book is written alone, though we put one name on the cover. Even if the writer retreats to a hermitage, they carry with them the voices of all who spoke to them, all the writers who showed them how it's done.

I didn't retreat to a Siberian cabin to write this book, but I did, appropriately, write much of it on a boat. First thanks then to Charlie Leslie-Cameron, who trusted me to boat-sit the *Himalayan Pup*. The *Pup* was originally a lifeboat on the SS *Himalaya* and sailed around the world many times without ever touching the water. Visited by geese and herons and – once – a passing seal, I was able to write the first draft as the Thames ebbed and flowed.

Thanks to my agent, Laura Macdougall, for her tireless work. Some people fizz with so much energy they must surely be plugged into the cosmic dynamo, and she is one. Thanks also to the brilliant team at United Agents for their support, especially Georgie Le Grice.

Thanks to my editor, Charlotte Ledger. I'm trying to think of something elegant to say, but never mind – this book would be crap without her. If you want to find a better editor, or one who's better company, you'll need some sturdy hiking boots. Thanks also to the team at HarperCollins, those omnicompetent yangs to my bumbling yin.

Thanks to Margaret Baran and all the staff of Whitton Day Nursery, who championed my first book while raising money for a good cause. It bears mentioning that, without their work, this book would have been completed in the 31st century.

Thanks to my early readers, Kate Scott, James Lovegrove and Lynsey Munn. Special thanks to Alex Mauchlen (no relation to Robert). Your advice was invaluable and reshaped this into the book it is today.

This is a book about music, inspired by music. Though there are too many to list, it seems churlish not to mention a few musicians who have brought so much joy and inspiration to me while writing. Thanks to Galt MacDermot, Nick Drake, Nina Simone and Paul Simon. Special thanks to Carol Kaye, who played guitar and bass on more hit records than you've had hot dinners. As a trailblazing female musician, she was a direct inspiration for Ella.

Thanks to Clive Tillin. Though the needle of the present moment has passed over your song, we will always be back then, with a game of Scrabble and a glass of the good red. Go well.

Thanks to my parents, who have always been the only inspiration I need.

Thanks to Alice, the love of my life.

Thanks to Sam, our beautiful son. Without the endless nappy changes and sleepless nights, I would never have thought of this book. Good job you're too young to claim royalties.

Thank you, thank you, thank you.